'Martin Suter's thriller is wry, cryptic and action-packed. If you love crime thrillers, then don't miss this!'
– *Emotion, Hamburg*

'In *Montecristo* the author remains true to his usual elegant style and polished dialogue' – *Spiegel Online*

'A holiday read of the very highest quality. Excellently researched, as usual, and apparently checked for authenticity by those in the know' – *Tages-Anzeiger*, Zurich

'Taking visible pleasure in the plotting and detail, Martin Suter has created a smooth, character-rich play of intrigue which is easily understood despite the complex material, and has well-known names to vouch for its authenticity'
– *Neue Zürcher Zeitung*

'Martin Suter's gaze is fresh and wicked, his ear for dialogue infallible. Quite simply, his works are literary genius'
– *Die Wochenzeitung*

'Martin Suter reaches a huge readership with his novels. He writes exciting, well constructed, almost cinematic, stories; he catches his readers with ingenious, streamlined plots'
– *Der Spiegel*

'Suter is fond of dramatic turns of events with a psychological undertone' – *Matthieu London, Libération*

Novels by Martin Suter

Small World (1997)
The Dark Side of the Moon (2000)
A Perfect Friend (2002)
Lila, Lila (2004)
A Deal with the Devil (2006)
The Last Weynfeldt (2008)
The Chef (2010)
The Time, the Time (2012)
Montecristo (2016)

Allmen crime series:

Allmen and the Dragonflies (2011)
Allmen and the Pink Diamond (2011)
Allmen and the Dahlias (2013)
Allmen and the Vanished Maria (2014)

MONTECRISTO

MARTIN SUTER

TRANSLATION BY JAMIE BULLOCH

NO EXIT PRESS

This edition published in 2017
by No Exit Press,
an imprint of Oldcastle Books Ltd,
PO Box 394, Harpenden,
Herts, AL5 1XJ, UK
noexit.co.uk
@noexitpress

With the support of the Swiss Arts Council Pro Helvetia

swiss arts council
pr⊃helvetia

Copyright © 2015 by Diogenes Verlag AG Zurich
Translation © Jamie Bulloch 2015

ISBN
978-1-84344-822-8 (Print)
978-1-84344-823-5 (Epub)
978-1-84344-824-2 (Kindle)
978-1-84344-825-9 (Pdf)

2 4 6 8 10 9 7 5 3 1

Typeset by Avocet Typeset, Somerton, Somerset TA11 6RT
in Minion Pro
Printed in Great Britain by Clays Ltd, St Ives plc

For Toni

MONTECRISTO

Part One

1

THE TRAIN JOLTED. GLASSES and bottles flew from tables, while the deafening whistle of the engine and the screech of metal on metal accompanied the clattering, shouting and clinking in the buffet car. Until everything fell silent with another jolt.

It was pitch black outside. They were in a tunnel.

The silence was broken by the obligatory joker: 'Are we there yet?'

A few passengers laughed, then everybody started speaking at once and wiping the beer and wine from tables, clothes, handbags and briefcases.

'Emergency brake,' someone stated.

Jonas Brand was sitting in the buffet car of the five-thirty intercity to Basel, surrounded by regulars – commuters who had the same conversations over the same drink every evening, some of them for years. The carriage was thick with the stale odour of alcohol, smoke-impregnated suits, sweat and the almost dissipated notes of men's aftershaves.

His overweight neighbour, who'd managed to rescue

the laptop he'd been gawping at the entire journey, sighed, 'Customer incident.'

Jonas got up to recover the camera rucksack he'd put on the floor beside him, and which had slid some way down the aisle when the train came to an abrupt halt. His camcorder was undamaged, even though as usual he'd failed to pack it away carefully.

He knew what 'customer incident' meant: someone had thrown themselves under the train. Jonas had been on another train a few years back when this happened, and once more he felt a shivering sensation rising from his feet to his neck.

At the rear of the buffet car some passengers were attending to the waiter, who had a cut on his head. Someone was trying to stop the bleeding with a napkin.

Nobody paid heed to the pallid young man who entered the restaurant car, looking around in search of something. He walked past all the tables to the other end of the carriage where Jonas was sitting, almost bumping into the conductress who rushed in and shouted, 'Who pulled the emergency brake?'

Only now did his fellow passengers notice the man. For he answered with a defiant 'Me!'

The conductress gave him a stern look. The man was a good head taller than her. He wore a sleek-cut suit with trousers whose turn-ups sat a finger's width over his pointed shoes.

'Why?'

Now he was standing beside Jonas, who could see how pale and agitated the young man was. 'Somebody fell out,' he stammered.

'Where?' the conductor asked.

'Back there,' the young man replied, pointing to where he'd come from. She led the way and he followed.

Taking his camera and shoulder rig from the rucksack, Jonas followed the two of them.

Stopping by the nearest exit, the man explained how he'd been standing there waiting for the loo to become free. He'd looked out of the window and all of a sudden something had flown past, like a large mannequin, and smashed against the tunnel wall. He'd only seen it for a moment, in the faint light through the train window. But he was sure it was a person; it had a face.

Jonas had the camera on his shoulder and was filming.

'Please stop that,' the conductress said.

Without breaking from filming he showed her his press pass.

'Television,' he explained.

The woman let him continue. She went on her way through a full second-class carriage. The passengers were sitting down, resigned to the delay. Because of the cameraman's presence nobody asked the conductress what had happened.

The next exit was not fully closed. Someone had pulled the emergency release to open the door. The conductor opened it fully and they were met by the smell of damp rock and metal dust.

Jonas filmed the tunnel which was dimly lit by the light from inside the train. Taking a step down, he focused the lens on the rear carriages. In the murky distance he could make out a shape in the narrow gap between the train and the tunnel wall. He couldn't say what it was; he didn't have the right lens.

*

At this point a hard-nosed video journalist would have got out to film the bundle at close range. But Jonas Brand was not hard-nosed. He wasn't even a real video journalist. He'd only landed in this job after a sequence of coincidences. As he liked to see it, it was a stopover on his way to becoming a film director.

But Jonas had been on this journey for quite a while now. Ever since he'd left school, to be precise. After falling out with his parents he'd hung around film sets, jobbing as a runner, cable puller and production driver. He learned about lighting and made it to the position of best boy. With the money he earned he financed a cinematography course at the London Film School and after that worked as a camera assistant. His CV since then included a few feature films, a handful of documentaries and an increasing number of advertisements.

Once he stepped in as cameraman for a sick colleague and filmed a few reports about the World Economic Forum. When the editor on that job switched to a local TV channel he started giving Jonas the occasional commission. Soon Brand was a permanent fixture on the team, and when the broadcaster introduced the role of video journalist as a cost-cutting measure, the man responsible for the words was dropped, while the one responsible for the pictures was retained. And so Jonas Brand inadvertently became a video journalist.

Regarding this job merely as a temporary solution, he hadn't progressed very far. Jonas plodded along without much ambition, content to produce sound work. True, he was soon able to go freelance and became known as a safe pair of hands if the emphasis was on punctuality, reliability and economy. But where creativity was called for, Jonas Brand, now almost forty, would always be second choice.

He was enough of a video journalist, however, to turn on his camera and document this uncomfortable episode.

The cheerful early-evening atmosphere in the restaurant car had subsided and been replaced by a combination of impatience and tedium. Few words were exchanged; everyone was waiting for an announcement.

But when it came, preceded by some ear-piercing feedback, most passengers were startled.

'Due to a customer incident this train will remain stationary for the time being,' the conductress's voice said. 'We apologise for any inconvenience.'

The announcement was immediately followed by sighs of resignation from the seasoned commuters, mixed with anxious questions from the new faces. 'Customer incident?'

'It means someone's gone under the train. We could be here for hours.'

Jonas went from table to table, interviewing the passengers. Some demanded to see his press pass, while two didn't want to be filmed or interviewed. But most of them were pleased for some distraction and happy to respond to his questions.

'It's terrible to think that someone's lying down there squashed.'

'This must be the tenth time it's happened to me in six years of commuting. I get the feeling it's on the increase.'

'I think it's plain rude to kill yourself like that. There are other ways, ones that don't ruin the evenings of a few hundred non-depressives.'

'Jumped off the train? He could have waited till we got out of the tunnel.'

'Or she.'

The waiter, now with a plaster on his forehead, was taking orders again. He was a short, tubby Tamil who the regulars called Padman. He spoke a carefree Swiss German and smiled into Jonas's camera with a magnificent set of teeth. Yes, he explained, this was a regular occurrence. The good life that the Swiss people enjoyed must be unbearable.

The overweight man who'd been sitting next to Jonas had buried himself in his laptop again. He had no objections to being filmed, but didn't want to say anything. Jonas focused on him as he moved down the carriage. The atmosphere was now quite subdued. The few people who were talking spoke softly.

A man in a business suit got up from a table, came towards Jonas, filling the screen before walking past. Jonas heard him ask, 'Have you seen Paolo?'

Jonas panned back to the fat man, who replied without looking up from his laptop, 'Wasn't he sitting with you?'

'His phone rang and he went out to take the call. But he never came back.'

The fat man finally looked up to his acquaintance in the business suit, shrugged and said, 'Maybe he's the customer incident.'

The man shook his head and returned to his table. Jonas was convinced he'd muttered 'Arsehole' under his breath.

*

He was on his way to Basel for a fundraising event, where with much fanfare the great and good of the city made a not particularly large sum of money for a charitable cause which changed each year. He'd forgotten who the beneficiary was this time.

His coverage of the event was a bread-and-butter job commissioned by 'Highlife', a public-service TV lifestyle magazine, and one of his best clients, if not his favourite one.

It was past nine o'clock when Jonas finally arrived at the hotel where the charity ball was being held. He'd been in regular phone contact with the promoter's PR lady, who sounded as if she regarded the incident as a targeted attack on her event, and postponed the auction several times.

Most of the lots had nonetheless been auctioned by the time he found his way into the ballroom. At the climax of the evening, a 'VIM' poster by Niklaus Stoecklin from 1929, which soared to the inflated price of eleven thousand francs, Jonas had to change his battery because of the unscheduled footage he'd taken of the customer incident. He missed the fall of the hammer, for which the buyer posed expressly. Jonas pretended to be filming, giving a casual nod when the press woman asked, 'Did you get that?'

*

It was the beginning of a warm December, full of incongruous-looking Christmas decorations and busy street cafés.

Two and a half months had passed since the incident on the intercity. This had led to a reprimand for Jonas from 'Highlife', his client. The PR agency in charge of the charity ball had complained that the most important moment of the evening, the purchase of the main lot, was missing from his report.

The material from the railway carriage lay unused together with the other fragments that one day Jonas planned to assemble into a major documentary. Entitled 'On the sidelines', it was going to be a black-and-white film presenting the impressions of a video journalist.

All that had been said about the customer incident was that it was a passenger suicide. The privacy laws had drawn a veil over any further details.

*

Jonas was in an excellent mood, and this was down to Marina Ruiz.

He had met Marina all of two hours ago, but had already arranged to see her again. Things never usually happened so quickly for him, but this rendezvous was less of a date and more the next stage of a conspiracy.

Marina was a tall woman from Zürich with straight, shoulder-length hair and oriental features. She worked for the events agency in charge of the film première that Jonas was compiling a report on. The film was being released simultaneously in a number of European cities, and only a few supporting actors were left as the star guests for the Zürich première. One of them, Melinda Trueheart, had been assigned to the care of Marina, who was tasked with accompanying the actress to interviews and shooing away the imaginary fans.

In interview Miss Trueheart proved to be an appallingly affected individual. While Jonas tried to ask relatively serious questions, Marina, who stood behind her, started miming and making fun of her answers. It was so astonishing and so funny that Jonas kept losing his composure. Each time he laughed out loud the starlet turned around to her PR woman for help.

And each time Marina managed to pull an earnest, concerned face at the last moment, which in itself was so amusing that Jonas couldn't help laughing again.

Melinda Trueheart wasn't sure whether the presenter was making fun of her or simply had a comic interviewing style. Gradually she began laughing too, and providing witty answers. By the end her affectation had practically vanished and the result was a surprisingly entertaining piece.

Marina led her ward away. As Jonas was packing up his gear she returned.

'May I invite you to dinner?' he asked.

'I thought you'd never ask,' she replied.

*

The following evening they met in a new Indian restaurant. It didn't appear that word had got around yet, because the place was half empty.

Jonas had suggested the restaurant because he loved Indian food and he hoped his expertise in this area might create something of an impression. But Marina turned out to be a connoisseur too, or at least enough of one to see that the menu was far too long and the dishes deep-frozen and reheated in the microwave.

To begin with they spoke in hushed voices like all the other diners. But Marina had that ability to focus so exclusively on another person that they quickly forgot their surroundings. Jonas told her things he would never normally talk about. She soon learned that he was thirty-eight years old, he'd divorced six years previously, had been a freelance video journalist for eight, and deep down was a filmmaker.

'Filmmaker?' Marina pushed her plate to one side – a stringy mutton buhari – leaned forward on her crossed arms and buried her gaze more deeply into his.

And so he came to tell her about *Montecristo*.

'The story is based on *The Count of Monte Cristo*, but it takes place now. There's this young man who's made millions from a dotcom company he's founded. While on holiday in Thailand a large quantity of heroin is slipped into his luggage. He's caught and sent to prison as a dealer. He's facing the death penalty or life imprisonment. The case causes a stir back home, but when his three business partners, who his lawyer has called as witnesses, surprisingly incriminate him, the public loses interest. The man is sentenced to life imprisonment and vanishes into one of Thailand's notorious prisons. His business partners gain control over the firm and sell it for a fortune.'

Jonas took a sip of his beer.

'Go on,' Marina urged.

'The man…'

'What's his name?'

'Till now I've called him "Montecristo". Do you think that's over-egging it?'

'Can't tell yet. Go on.'

'A few years later Montecristo manages to escape. He's still got plenty of money put aside from before, and now he uses it to exact his revenge. He undergoes a number of cosmetic operations, creates a new identity for himself and travels back home. The rest of the film shows how Montecristo, in the guise of an investor, ruins his three former partners.'

'They're the ones who smuggled the heroin into his luggage, right?'

'Arranged for it to be put there, exactly.'

For the first time since he'd started talking Marina turned her green eyes away from Jonas, looked at her glass and took a sip. After seeing the wine list she'd also plumped for an Indian Kingfisher beer.

She gave Jonas her undivided attention once more. 'You know that with the right cast that could be a blockbuster.'

Jonas gave a grim smile. 'With the right cast, the right screenplay, the right director and right producer.'

Marina nodded thoughtfully. 'How long have you been working on this project?'

Jonas poured out the rest of the beer from their bottles. 'Gross time or net?' he asked.

'Both.'

'I wrote the first sketch of the story in a single night. So about twelve hours net. That was in 2009. So six years gross.'

'And no one's shown any interest?'

'That's what the film business is like. Everyone wants experience, but nobody lets you get any.'

Marina gave a knowing smile. 'And by the time you've got some you're too old.'

'How do you know that?' Jonas asked in astonishment.

'It's what my stepfather always says.'

'Is he in films too?'

'He's a careers adviser.'

*

As Marina's flat was close to the restaurant, they walked back. The Föhn was blowing that night; a hefty wind shook the Christmas decorations of the Turkish, Tamil and Italian shops they passed. Marina had taken his arm and they strolled through the night like a happily married couple on their way home.

She was a tall woman, and the high heels she wore made her a touch taller than Jonas. Right from the start he'd felt very comfortable in her presence, and this feeling now intensified as she walked on his arm, delicately and affectionately, in spite of her height.

She let go of his arm by the entrance to a modern apartment block and fished a key from her handbag. Wearing the same smile that he'd found so funny during his interview with the starlet, she waited for him to say something.

Somewhat embarrassed, he said, 'I assume you don't invite men up for a nightcap on a first date.'

'Oh I do,' she replied. 'But never those I want to see again.'

Taking his head she pulled it towards her and gave him a fleeting kiss on the lips. He put his hands around her waist, but she took them away, unlocked the door and slipped into the entrance hall.

*

Too excited just to take a taxi and go to bed, he set off on foot in the direction of his flat, which was in a different area altogether. He would let inspiration be his guide and then either hail a cab, pop in somewhere for a drink or saunter back the entire way.

The Föhn was still driving its capricious gusts through the unprepossessing streets. Here and there, scattered supporters of a victorious football team bellowed into the night, and smokers stretched their legs outside night clubs.

Jonas had been through several relationships since his divorce, but he'd never been as enchanted as on this unhospitable evening.

Arriving at the main train station, he took the shortcut through the concourse, where there was the usual mixture of movement and inertia. People from the sticks who'd spent the evening in town were hurrying to get their trains back. Commuters who'd been working late met them going in the other direction. And amidst this coming and going, the usual station folk hung around, people who'd come from nowhere and were going nowhere.

There was hardly a soul in the street outside. The wind set in motion the hundred-and-fifty thousand LED lights overhead, but they still paled against the bright Christmas illuminations and advertisements of the shops.

Deep in thought, Jonas passed the watch and jewellery

shops, and the plant troughs and boulders that protected these establishments from being ram-raided.

At the next stop he saw one of the last trams that was heading to his part of town. He got on and leaned against the window at the back of the carriage, even though it was almost empty. Jonas was still full of beans and had no desire to sit.

The handful of passengers were absorbed in themselves. The silence was only broken by the announcements of the successive stops and possible transport connections.

Like a spaceship, Jonas thought, gliding through the nocturnal unreality of the fancy shops and venerable big banks. Two worlds unfamiliar to each other.

The lake dimly reflected the brightness of the streetlights and sporadic night-time traffic. The Föhn rippled the surface of the water, shaking the jetties of the closed boat-hire places and the wrapped-up boats.

A few passengers got off, a few got on, and the journey continued on its way, past the opera house and small station, and into his neighbourhood.

Jonas got out. He wanted to walk the last two stops home. Which would also leave open the option of spontaneously popping into Cesare's.

An option he took. Nodding to a smoker by the door he knew by sight, he went in. The volume of the music suggested the place was busier than it actually was. A few drinkers were chatting at the bar and a few tables were still occupied. Here two people in a serious discussion, there a couple who hadn't yet decided on his place or hers.

Jonas went to one of the bar tables. An Italian waiter asked him what he'd like to drink. He stuck with beer.

A young woman came over. She was holding a glass with

more greenery than liquid, and having trouble maintaining her balance in her stilettos. 'I know you,' she said, putting her drink down next to his beer.

People would occasionally recognise him because he sometimes edited himself into an interview to make it appear more natural, but also to get a bit of screen presence. It facilitated access to the semi-important people and could be helpful in these sorts of situations.

This was not one of those evenings, however.

The woman was pretty in a rather conventional sort of way. She wore more make-up than was necessary and had clearly reapplied her lipstick in advance of this encounter. 'You're from Highlife, aren't you?' she asserted.

He shook his head and took a large gulp of beer to show her that he wasn't planning on staying long.

'But I've seen you on Highlife. You're a reporter.'

'You may have done; I do the odd bit of work for them,' he replied, looking around for the waiter.

She looked him in the eye and said, 'In a hurry?'

'Sort of.'

The woman nodded ironically. 'Just in urgent need of one last beer. I know what it's like.'

The waiter came and put his heavy purse on the table. 'All on the same bill?'

'We haven't known each other long enough for that,' Jonas said.

'I've got plenty of time,' she pouted.

Brand looked in his wallet for six francs, but all he could find was a little change and a two-hundred. 'Sorry, I haven't anything smaller.'

'That's OK. It makes it quicker to count up when I clock off,' the waiter said, giving him his change.

The woman with the empty glass watched the notes changing hands. 'Some have time, others money.'

Jonas couldn't help laughing. Pointing to her glass he said, 'And another one of whatever that was.'

'A mojito,' she said. 'But you've got to have a drink with me.'

He waited until the waiter returned with her mojito, toasted her with his last sip of beer and wished her goodnight.

'Shame,' she said, before looking around for someone else.

*

It was no more than ten minutes to his flat. The wind storm had become so violent that Jonas carefully avoided the pavements close to house fronts. The Föhn clattered and creaked in balconies, roared through bare trees lining the streets and hammered unfastened shutters.

Number 73 Rofflerstrasse was a four-storey brick building from the 1930s. The entrance was behind a narrow, neglected front garden, and flanked by four ugly, standard aluminium post boxes on either side, which had been added later. Jonas collected his post and went up the three steps to the front door.

Acquiring his flat had been one of those instances when his presence on screen had come in handy. At the viewing a queue of interested parties had lined the steps, as affordable period flats with high ceilings were a rarity in this part of town. The elderly lady from the property management company had recognised him. Although she hadn't actually said anything, Jonas had developed an inkling for whether someone recognised him from television.

At any rate, he was preferred to all the couples and families, even though on the questionnaire he'd made no secret of the fact that he was divorced and still single.

To liven up the three rooms and generous hallway, he'd furnished and decorated them with everything he'd been able to lay his hands on. Jonas became a regular customer of the city's second-hand shops, flea markets and junk dealers.

Brand was a collector without an overarching plan. He bought Asiatica, militaria, porcelain, folk art, textiles, posters, trinkets, photographs, kidney tables, tubular furniture, crystal chandeliers – simply anything he liked the look of or found striking.

This unsystematic collecting fury gave his flat a rather museum-like cosiness, which didn't suit him particularly well as his style was basically unfussy and straightforward. But sometimes he had the feeling that he was starting to adapt to his surroundings.

He hung his coat on the round stand that looked as if it had come straight out of a 1950s school staffroom, went into the sitting room and embarked on his lighting ceremony. The room didn't have a central ceiling light, but was full of desk and wall lamps, standard lamps, spots and floor lights. A neon sign for a club called 'Chérie' and an illuminated Michelin man served as further light sources.

Jonas switched everything on, made himself a green tea and lit a sandalwood incense stick.

On one of his forays he'd come across a small collection of bizarre incense-stick holders. Nymphs at the end of elongated ponds, which caught the ashes; leisurely looking skeletons, whose eye sockets accommodated the incense sticks; or dragons into whose jaws the sticks were inserted like spears. He'd acquired the entire collection for a very good price, and as a bonus the stallholder had given him a handful of boxes with different perfumes of incense. Which made him doubt that he'd got such a bargain after all. But he did acquire a taste for incense.

He sat in a leather armchair which he'd covered with a kanga to hide the damaged patches. This printed garment showed a green palm tree and four coconuts on a yellow background with the writing: *Naogopa simba na meno yake siogopi mtu kwa maneno yake.* Which was Swahili for 'I fear a lion with its strong teeth, but not a man with his words.'

Jonas grabbed the remote control, turned on the stereo and gave a start. The guitar intro to Bob Dylan's 'Man in the Long Black Coat' tore through the silence at full volume.

The volume setting was from one of those sentimental evenings which sometimes came upon him and degenerated into a session with too much alcohol and too loud music. Infrequent and always occurring without prior warning, they were characteristic of the loneliness of the single man. If he were being honest, he even quite enjoyed them.

Jonas turned down the volume, stood up and put on something that better suited his mood. He wasn't sad, or at most only a touch sad that she hadn't invited him up.

Marina had elicited things from him that he had scarcely told anyone else. He very seldom spoke about himself, and whenever he did he always felt bad later, like after an evening with excessive alcohol and hazy recollections.

But this time there was no bad aftertaste. He'd been at ease from the outset and it had felt perfectly normal to talk about himself.

It was as if he'd known Marina for years. He'd never felt anything like this before and, now alone in his flat, he was still buoyed by their encounter.

Going into the kitchen he made himself another tea. As he listened to the kettle getting louder his gaze fell on the notebook that belonged to Frau Knezevic, his Croatian cleaning lady. It lay on top of the espresso machine, precisely where Jonas couldn't miss it. This meant that the money he left inside the book was now all gone. Or even that she'd had to pay for things out of her own pocket. Not much, surely, for he suspected that she always did a little shopping at the right time just to give him a bad conscience.

He took his tea and the notebook into the sitting room. It bulged with all the receipts and lists it contained. Brand would check her calculations each time, even though he'd never yet discovered a mistake. He didn't want Frau Knezevic to think that he wasn't concerned about a few francs here or there. Even though that wouldn't be entirely wrong.

Money wasn't especially important to Jonas. Not because he had a lot of it, but because for him it was no more than a means to enjoying a more or less comfortable life and taking the odd holiday. He didn't regard his car as a status symbol either. It was only of interest to Jonas as a means of getting himself and his gear from A to B, and thus he'd never made an effort to keep his diesel VW Passat, almost ten years old now, looking pristine.

Brand's indifference to money might cause him to lose track of his finances, risking a call from Herr Weber, the long-serving and amicable account manager at his bank, because he'd gone overdrawn.

Every September when his tax declaration was due, he also strained the nerves of the bookkeeper at his company, Brand Productions, because he was sloppy about making a strict distinction between business and private accounting, and mixed up or mismatched his receipts.

But he was always precise when it came to Frau Knezevic, taking great care to add up every item.

He owed her eight francs. He placed a pedantic tick by the balance sum, scrunched up the receipts and threw them in the bin. He would always refill Frau Knezevic's empty coffers with two hundred francs. Opening his wallet all he could find was the hundred plus the change the waiter at Cesare's had given him, so he had to go to the safe.

Brand's safe was in his bedroom, beside a wall full of butterflies mounted under glass. It was a statue from Vietnam, a seated woman in a green-lacquered dress with bronze trim and a matching turban. He'd bought it from an antiques dealer in Saigon who'd told him it was a mother goddess from an ancient Vietnamese folk religion.

Part of the stole could be detached at the back of the statue, revealing beneath a lid varnished in exactly the same lacquer as the rest of the dress. If you pressed the edge in the right place the opposite edge would slide up enough for you to take hold of it and remove the lid. Behind this was a hollow opening measuring about nine centimetres by nine. This was where the woman's soul had once lived, the antiques dealer had told him. When she swapped her existence as a goddess for that of a figurine the soul had taken flight. The empty space now provided enough space for a few banknotes.

Currently there was just one hundred in there. Taking it, Jonas returned to the sitting room and placed it beside the other one inside the notebook, on the front of which Frau Knezevic had written 'Cash' in her rather childish hand.

There they lay, the two banknotes. On the right, the portrait of Alberto Giacometti, who always appeared to Jonas as if he had a blocked nose and had to breathe through his slightly opened mouth; on the left, his most famous sculpture, *L'homme qui marche* (The Walking Man), who looked to Jonas as if he'd just swung his right leg over the barrier of digits that comprised the banknote's serial number. The last seven digits would have made a pleasing telephone number: 200 44 88.

Startled by a loud crash, Jonas ran into the kitchen. The Föhn had blasted open the upper part of the kitchen window, whose catch hadn't been properly fastened. Jonas closed it and calmly went back into the sitting room.

The gust of wind had blown the notes from the table. The one with the serial number ending in 200 44 88 was right beside the armchair he'd been sitting in.

He found the other one under the flower stand beside the window, in which a fern was fighting for survival. Picking up the errant banknote, he examined it and noticed the last seven digits: 200 44 88.

What a strange coincidence, he thought, comparing the two notes. He wasn't mistaken. The last seven digits were identical. And not only that – the first three characters were the same too! Both hundred notes had the serial number 07E2004488.

What could that mean? Only one thing, according to Brand's layman's amateur knowledge of banknotes: one of the two had to be fake.

He took them to his studio, as he called his study. Unlike the rest of the flat it was decorated very soberly. White office furniture and matching shelves with carefully labelled archive boxes. The heart of the studio was the editing area: a large, tidy desk with two flat screens, a keyboard and a mouse. In front of the desk stood a shiny chrome executive chair with leather upholstery, which he'd bought a couple of years ago after suffering a prolapsed disc, and was occasionally embarrassed about when visitors came round.

He took out a magnifying glass from the top drawer of the mobile filing cabinet, switched on the desk lamp, pointed it at the banknotes and examined them. Which one was fake?

Jonas couldn't see any difference, but then again he didn't know what he was looking for. One of the hundreds felt newer and crisper; it was the note he'd taken from the statue. All that remained of his last visit to the cash machine.

The other note had already passed through many hands and was slightly limp. This was the one the waiter in Cesare's had given him. Was this the fake banknote? And if so, had the waiter known?

Brand put the notes into his wallet. He'd go to the bank first thing tomorrow morning and find out which one was fake and which one genuine.

He went to bed and fell asleep, while the wind made merry mischief outside.

beginning of his business relationship with Herr Weber.

At the time Herr Weber was in his late thirties and hadn't yet given up hope of making it far up the career ladder. He was a short, thin man with a hairline set low on his forehead, making him look faintly apelike. During the first few years Herr Weber behaved like a banker, trotting out the same clichés and attempting to fob investments and services onto Jonas, which he referred to as 'products' as if they were tangible.

When, years later, his business card still read 'Private Account Manager / Cashier', he must have realised that he was at the end of his career progression, and he started siding with his customers. Turning his nose up at the bank's internal bureaucracy, he would never talk about his superiors without a hint of irony.

He reminded Jonas of his corporal in military training school, who bullied the recruits until the day he found out he wouldn't be recommended for a commission, after which he fraternised with the young trainees. But unlike Herr Weber, who even in his most ambitious phases Jonas had never seriously been at the mercy of, he hadn't forgiven the corporal. To the present day.

Herr Weber, whose hairline was still in close proximity to the bridge of his nose, carefully scrutinised the banknotes and explained to Jonas the eighteen security features: the shimmering, transparent magic number, the translucent crosses, the watermark portrait, the line structures that change colour, the fading copperplate digits, the dancing number on the shining foil, the perforated number indicating the note's value, the two micro texts illegible to the naked eye, the chameleon number that changes colour according to the light, the digits only visible in UV light, the letter 'G' that glints when you move the note, the 'tilt' number that can only be read from a very oblique angle, the tactile symbol for blind people, the metallic security strip and the two serial numbers.

All were present and all in order.

'As far as I'm concerned they're both genuine,' Herr Weber said finally.

'So how's it possible that they've both got the same serial number?'

'It isn't possible. Have you got a moment? I'd like to consult a colleague.'

Jonas watched Herr Weber go up to a colleague's desk in the office behind the counters, where the two men pored over the banknotes. They were joined by a woman who'd been serving at a neighbouring counter, and soon a little group of bank employees had gathered to marvel at the phenomenon.

Jonas was feeling a little impatient by the time Herr Weber finally came back. 'Strange. All of us think that both notes are genuine. Do you mind if I make a photocopy?'

'I thought that was illegal.'

'It wouldn't be the first time that something illegal's been done in this place,' Herr Weber admitted with his ironic smile. He vanished with the notes.

When he returned and gave the money back to Jonas, he advised him, 'Make sure you look after these – they're collector's items.'

Jonas took out some cash for Frau Knezevic and his day-to-day expenses, then left.

Back in the flat he tucked the two collector's items into the back of the mysterious Vietnamese deity.

*

The following evening they met up again. Jonas had waited until ten o'clock before calling her. She must have stored his number in her contact list because she answered, 'How did you sleep, Jonas?'

'All alone,' he replied. Then, without beating about the bush, they arranged to have dinner together.

This time he listened, gazing spellbound into her eyes. They were oriental eyes, almond-shaped with a double crease below the lids, but the colour was a European green. Her straight, shoulder-length hair, with the fringe cut just above the eyebrows, had a brown sheen. She had prominent cheekbones and full lips, which were redder than yesterday.

'Most people think I'm the daughter of a Swiss bloke who couldn't find a wife here so bagged himself one in Thailand.'

'But?'

'But I'm the daughter of a Filipino dad who bagged a Swiss woman here.' She laughed as if having offered up a joke she'd told many times before. 'My father was awarded a fellowship to study agronomy in Switzerland. When he finished he went back to the Philippines with my mother. I was born there.'

'Do you speak Filipino?'

'Oh, only a few words. My parents separated when I was six. My mum came back to Switzerland with me and married again.'

'A Spaniard?'

'Because of the Ruiz, you mean? No, the name comes from my real father. Many Filipinos have Spanish names. My stepfather is Swiss.'

Marina told him about her life as if she were applying for a position in his. She answered his questions too, even those that he didn't pose.

'Why haven't you asked me if there's someone in my life?'

'Well, you didn't ask me that either.'

'What would your answer have been?'

'Occasionally. How about you?'

'Occasionally. And years ago something more serious.'

Jonas smiled. 'Same with me. I've even been married.'

'With me it was just a close shave.'

With that the subject was ticked off.

Later, Jonas asked, 'How on earth did you end up in event management?'

'Maybe in a similar way to you and lifestyle journalism.'

'So it's a temporary thing?'

She laughed. 'No, I mean by chance. I temped for an event agency during student holidays.'

'And you found you liked it?'

'Better than law.'

'Did you want to become a lawyer?'

'My mother wanted me to.'

'What about now? Do you still like event management?'

Marina stroked the hair from her face and pondered. 'It's OK. There's variety to the work; I do many different things. If you like communicating with people and don't mind the irregular hours, then it's not a bad job. The pay's decent too. And you get to meet a lot of people – sometimes even interesting ones.'

She gave the same conspiratorial laugh she had from behind the back of Melinda Trueheart. And just as that laugh had led to an immediate dinner date, so this one sped up the course of things too.

'So what now?' Jonas asked.

'Your place,' Marina replied.

*

It was only ten o'clock in the evening when Jonas unlocked his front door – they were in a real hurry.

It started with a lengthy kiss in the hallway and, when they finally broke off from the embrace to remove their coats, Marina asked, 'Have you got anything to drink?'

Jonas went into the kitchen and found a bottle of Nero d'Avola that he'd recently been given by an ex-Mr Switzerland after interviewing him at the opening of his new boutique. He filled two glasses and took them into the hall. But Marina wasn't there any more.

She wasn't in his studio or sitting room either. Eventually he found her in the bedroom, lying on the duvet with her arms and legs stretched out like a dog that wants to be tickled. She was naked. Her small breasts rose barely higher than her smooth pubic mound.

He put the wine glasses down on a bedside table and undressed beneath her provocative gaze.

Later, when he was sitting up at the head of the bed, and she sipped the heavy wine with her head nestled into his right shoulder, she made a vague movement with her glass in the direction of the butterfly collection, which he'd bought on a lucky day as a job lot from a second-hand shop, and said, 'All those butterflies.'

'There are more – in my tummy,' he replied.

She laughed. 'Is that what you tell all the girls after the first time?'

He pulled her closer and kissed her forehead, but didn't reply. She wouldn't have believed him if he'd told the truth. Which was that the comment had only just occurred to him.

*

'Which one is the half room?' Jonas asked the following evening at Marina's flat.

'Where the dining table is. The sitting room is a whole one, the dining room a half room. Hence sitting–dining room.'

He was standing with Marina by the counter that divided the kitchen from the sitting–dining room, watching her chop coriander with a large knife. On the cooker, chicken was simmering in a sauce of soy, vinegar, garlic, bay and chilli. 'Adobo: national dish of the Philippines,' she'd said when he asked her what smelled so fantastic.

'You're cooking me a memory from your childhood?'

'No, I don't remember it. I only learned how to make it as an adult. Someone said to me. "You can't look like that and not know how to cook adobo".'

Having finished chopping the coriander, she gathered it into a neat pile with the knife on the white chopping broad. Then she went to the sink to wash her hands.

'Stop!' Jonas called out. He went over and took her left hand, which had been holding the herbs in place. It was long and slender, and her nails painted red. Bringing it to his nose, he sniffed and closed his eyes. 'How can something so beautiful smell so wonderful too?'

Marina laughed. 'What does it taste like?'

He put one of her fingers into his mouth and sucked.

'You know what?' she said. 'Adobo tastes better the longer you leave it to cook.'

*

When Jonas arrived home the following day, his front door was unlocked, which could only mean that Frau Knezevic was there. It wasn't her day, but sometimes she switched her rota. She'd always leave a note the day before, however. And she hadn't this time.

There was an unfamiliar smell in the flat. His first thought was that Frau Knezevic had used a new detergent. But the odour was too cosmetic. Perhaps she had a new fragrance?

Brand had once read that women have a much more heightened sense of smell than men and that this stays with them until they're old. If that were true then he must have a woman's nose. He often picked up on scents that women didn't notice.

Jonas went into the kitchen. Some doors to the old-fashioned, lime-green sideboard were open and a number of drawers had been pulled out.

Frau Knezevics's notebook was on the floor, with the receipts and calculations scattered about the place. He picked up the book. No sign of the two hundred francs that he'd put in it two days ago.

'Frau Knezevic?' he called out.

No answer.

He walked along the corridor to the sitting room. Everything was in a mess here, too. Books on the floor, trinkets knocked over. His leather armchair had been overturned, the green-and-yellow kanga lay beside it on the floor.

'Frau Knezevic?' he called again. And all of a sudden the image came to his mind of his cleaning lady tied up in the bathroom, bedroom or his studio.

The bathroom presented the same picture as the kitchen and sitting room. The mirrored cabinet had been opened and some of its contents were in the sink.

In his studio the archive boxes were on the floor by the shelves, most of their contents strewn all over the floor. The drawers of the filing cabinet had been pulled out as far as they went and their contents rifled through. The cupboard in which he kept all his filming gear was open, but everything was still there.

In the bedroom they'd turned the mattress over, a few of the butterfly frames were on top of the duvet on the floor, while more drawers as well as the wardrobe had been opened. He had to climb over a heap of trousers and jackets with pockets hanging out to get to the Vietnamese mother goddess, who'd been knocked over. Two of her outstretched fingers with their red-lacquered nails had snapped off.

Jonas removed the piece of the wooden stole, pressed the side of the lid and opened it.

The burglars had not found his hiding place; the money was still there. Including the notes with the duplicate serial numbers.

*

The policeman who sat opposite him at the kitchen table appeared to hold the burglary against Jonas. 'Like I said: no traces of any break-in,' he repeated waspishly. 'Are you sure you locked up properly?'

It was not the first time Jonas had given his answer either: 'I've twice had to call out the locksmith and he's managed to get in without leaving any traces too.'

'Why have you needed the locksmith?'

'Forgot my keys.'

'Are you often forgetful?'

'What's that got to do with this burglary?'

'Could it be that you'd forgotten to lock up?'

'Can we move on, please?' Jonas asked, now feeling irritated.

'That's something you'll have to leave to the police,' the officer informed him.

Jonas said nothing.

'Right, what's missing apart from the money?'

'Don't know. I imagine I'll only work that out when I tidy up.'

'So, nothing of any particular value that you'd immediately notice if it were missing?'

'No, doesn't look like it.'

'Do you keep money anywhere else apart from in your cleaning lady's notebook?'

Jonas hesitated for a moment then said, for the record, 'Yes. In a book.'

'Is it still there?'

'I haven't checked.'

'Forgotten?' the policeman asked sarcastically. He stood up. 'Come on, show me.'

Jonas showed him into the sitting room, where two of the officer's colleagues were standing chatting. When their superior entered with Jonas their conversation stopped and they continued taking photographs and looking for trace evidence.

'Which book?' the policeman asked.

Jonas looked around, finally bending over a guide to Bangkok which was open, facing down on the floor.

Picking it up, the officer thumbed through the pages and shook it. Nothing fell out.

'How much was in there?'

'About fifteen hundred,' Jonas replied. God knows how long he'd been paying insurance premiums for nothing.

They went back into the kitchen. 'Clearly they were only after money. Foreign criminals. Albanians, Romanians, Moroccans – we know them all.'

They sat down again at the table and the policeman returned to his report.

'About fifteen hundred cash in the guidebook, plus two hundred in the household book.'

'Four hundred.'

'You said two hundred.'

'I made a mistake. It was four hundred.'

The officer corrected the figure and muttered, 'Doesn't really matter; I don't imagine the insurance company will pay out anyway.'

'Why not?'

'No signs of a break-in. I have to write that. They'll assume that the flat was open.'

'It was locked,' Jonas protested.

'Yes, yes,' the policeman mumbled.

*

Jonas sensed someone was meddling with him, feeling in his trouser and coat pockets. He tried to resist, but someone was holding his hands in an iron grip.

Then everything blurred, and when he came out of his dream he could hear footsteps hurrying away.

He refused to open his eyes. He didn't want to return to reality, so he stayed lying there.

Footsteps approached, short, rapid women's footsteps with clacking high heels.

He kept his eyes shut. Then: Marina's perfume, her hand on his brow, her voice uttering his name gently but emphatically. 'Jonas? Jonas? Wake up! Jonas? Jonas?'

He remembered what had happened. A good sign. Years ago when he'd taken a fall skiing as a young man, he was unable to recall how he'd tumbled. It turned out that he'd had concussion.

This time he did remember. Hearing footsteps behind him, he'd deliberately refrained from turning around, to avoid seeming paranoid. The footsteps came closer and closer. They belonged to two people. Still he didn't turn round. Only when they caught up with him did he step aside to let them past on the narrow pavement.

In his mind he could still see the arm of one of them come crashing down, he felt the blow to his skull and the pain that shot through him.

Then: the hands searching his body, the footsteps of the attackers as they ran away, Marina's heels coming closer. Perfume, caress, Marina's voice.

He stood up and felt his head. There was a bump where the stabbing pain was coming from.

'What happened?'

'Two blokes followed me and then clobbered me.' Now he felt his coat. His wallet, mobile and purse had all gone.

'Shit!' he shouted.

'Is everything gone?'

'Everything.'

'And I thought I lived in a safe area.'

It was only now that Jonas realised they were practically outside Marina's house. They'd arranged to meet at hers because his place was pure chaos. They'd planned to have an aperitif and then go out for dinner. He'd bought a bunch of roses, which he now picked up off the floor. When he bent down he felt dizzy and had to hold onto Marina.

'Should I call an ambulance?'

'Police would be better.'

Jonas walked the few paces to the entrance of Marina's house and sat on the bottom step.

Now he noticed that his watch was missing too. His father's golden Certina, which he'd been given for thirty years of loyal service to his firm. Two years before they laid him off during restructuring. And four years before he committed suicide. Fifty-six and still out of work.

Marina had stayed where she was and rung the police. Against the light of the car headlamps her tall, slim figure looked very thin. Like Alberto Giacometti's bronze sculpture on the hundred-franc note.

Jonas felt weak and humiliated. He'd been violated twice in close succession. First his private possessions, then his body.

He tried to hold back the tears welling inside him, to spare himself at least this further humiliation in front of Marina, who was now approaching him.

But when she got there he burst into tears. She sat beside him silently and laid an arm around his shoulders.

*

The police car took no more than a few minutes to arrive. It had switched on its blue light but the siren was silent.

Two wheels mounted the pavement before the car came to a halt, its blue light still flashing. A pair of officers got out, a woman and a man, and came over to them, their arms slightly splayed out, like two Western heroes before the shootout.

'Did you call?' the policewoman asked, as if telephoning the police constituted an offence.

'I did,' Marina said.

'Do you have any ID?'

'Not on me. But I live up there,' she replied.

'What about you?'

Jonas was still fighting back the tears. Marina came to his aid. 'He's had everything stolen. He was attacked.'

'Where?' the policeman asked.

'Just over there.'

'Could you show me the place?'

Marina let go of Jonas, stood up and took the police officers to where she'd found Jonas. There was nothing to see apart from a rose petal on the tarmac.

'That's from the bunch he'd brought for me.'

The policewoman took a torch from her belt. In the bright light they could make out an impression on the petal. The tread of a sole.

'Yesterday he gets burgled and now this!'

The policewoman returned to her car and radioed the station.

*

On the breakfast bar in Marina's flat were two champagne glasses, an ice bucket with a half bottle of Veuve Cliquot and a glass containing a few breadsticks, which looked like a bundle of Mikado biscuits.

Marina invited the officers to sit at the dining table and tried to help Jonas into a chair opposite them. But he declined and sat without her assistance. 'I'm all right,' he muttered, before saying to the police officers, 'Please excuse me; it's just all been a bit much. The break-in yesterday and now this.'

'Do you think the two are related?' the policewoman asked?

The question took Jonas by surprise. 'What makes you say that?'

'Well, it's possible.'

'That they're related?'

'No, that you might think they are.'

Jonas mulled this over, before finally shaking his head. 'No, I don't think so.'

But throughout the entire interview he couldn't get it out of his head.

Were the two related?

*

It was almost two in the morning when they returned from casualty. Marina had insisted that he get himself checked out.

And so Jonas had reluctantly let her drive him to hospital in her Mini once the police had finally left. They'd spent two hours in the waiting room; more urgent and bloodier cases had repeatedly taken priority.

After his name was eventually called they spent two further hours behind a curtain, Brand on a couch and Marina in a visitor's chair.

They didn't talk, because on the other side of the curtain a man kept griping to himself and uttering, 'Fucking arsehole, you'd better fucking watch out, you fucking arsehole!'

When an exhausted, young junior doctor finally pushed the curtain aside, Jonas was already asleep.

The doctor woke him, tested his reactions, checked his pupils, quizzed him about symptoms such as dizziness or nausea, asked whether he recalled any details from before or after the attack, examined his bump and ordered him to get in touch if he experienced any symptoms such as nausea and sickness, light-headedness and dizziness, impaired vision, headaches, insomnia, or heightened sensitivity to light and noise.

He prescribed Jonas something for headaches, looked at his watch, suppressed a yawn and discharged him.

Now they were back in Marina's flat. Jonas had suggested, without much insistence, that she should drive him home, but Marina wouldn't countenance the idea.

The ice in the champagne bucket had melted and the label was floating beside the bottle in the lukewarm water.

Jonas let Marina put him to bed like a child and fell asleep instantly.

*

He woke with a sense of disquiet and it took him a moment to fathom where this was coming from. When, a few seconds later, he'd collected his thoughts, he wanted to steal straight back into sleep.

But he had to report the loss of his credit cards, his mobile and his documents; he had to sign off work with his clients for two days; and he had to deal with the mountain of paperwork that came in the wake of an incident like that.

In addition, he'd arranged with Frau Knezevic that she should come and clean his apartment at ten o'clock.

He got up and looked in the mirror at the plaster covering his bump. Maybe it hadn't been such a good idea to shave off his thinning hair, which would have concealed it at least partially.

On the table were a note from Marina and a set of her keys:

'Didn't want to wake you. When you read this go back to bed, and when you've had enough sleep give me a call to tell me how your head is. If you have to leave the flat for any reason, please lock up. And take the keys with you. See you later, Marina.'

Beneath this she'd jotted down her number, which he'd lost with his mobile.

Jonas didn't go to bed; he sat down and made the necessary telephone calls. When he hung up after the final one he caught sight of the blue digits on the oven clock: 11:16.

Frau Knezevic!

Her number had disappeared with his mobile, too. He called his home telephone, hoping that she'd pick up for once.

She didn't answer until the third attempt. 'Yes?' her suspicious voice said.

'I'm really sorry, but I overslept. I was attacked yesterday evening.'

The word didn't exist in her German vocabulary. 'What is "attacked"?'

'Two men hit me on the head and stole everything,' Jonas explained. 'Money, mobile, IDs, credit cards.'

'Must be Serbs,' Frau Knezevic said.

＊

He had to ring the bell because Frau Knezevic's key was in the lock on the inside. It took a while before he heard her voice through the door: 'Who is it?'

'It's me, Jonas!' he called back.

She opened the door a crack, peeked through and let him in.

Frau Knezevic was a small, plump woman around forty. Her short blonde hair needed the roots doing. She was wearing a blue apron with the University Hospital logo, even though she'd never worked there. When she saw the plaster on his bald head she twisted her face into a pained expression.

'Does hurt?' she asked.

'It's OK.'

The flat smelled clean. It was chilly, because windows were open in every room, the bathroom and kitchen had been cleaned, the bedroom put back in order and all the furniture restored to its rightful place. His clothes were hanging in the wardrobe; his underwear and shirts had been put away too. The contents of the drawers were still on the floor, but now in neat piles.

'I not know where it all goes,' Frau Knezevic said.

Frau Knezevic got to work on the sitting room while Jonas stayed in his bedroom.

The Vietnamese deity wore an inscrutable smile on her broad, almost white face, enlivened with a touch of rouge, as if she knew more than Jonas would like. A little paint had flaked off the corner of her left eye, lending a shiftiness to her gaze.

Turning her around, Jonas opened the secret compartment, took out the two hundreds and went into his studio.

Here everything was exactly as he'd left it. Most of the archive boxes were on the floor, their contents scattered everywhere. Brand switched on his Mac, lifted the lid of his scanner and placed the two banknotes on the glass. Then he sat in front of the screen and opened his scanning software.

The noise of the image sensor moving into position made him jump. He no longer felt safe within his own four walls.

After he'd scanned both sides of the notes he returned them to their hiding-place. Then he called Marina.

She answered in a hushed voice. 'Where can I call you back? I'm in a shoot.'

He gave her his landline number and hung up.

Then he made a start on tidying away the things that Frau Knezevic didn't know belonged where.

The ring of the telephone was further proof of just how jumpy the events of the last couple of days had made him. It was Marina.

'How do you feel?'

'OK.'

'None of the symptoms the doctor mentioned? No dizziness or giddiness?'

'No. I just feel a bit listless and worn out.'

'You should have stayed in bed.'

'But I can't just leave everything in such a mess.'

'I've got to work this evening; it's a release party and it'll be late. But you've got a key if you don't want to stay at yours.' She sounded more considerate than enticing.

'Thanks. I'll see how long I need here.'

At the grocery round the corner Frau Knezevic had bought bread, meatloaf and apples, and set the kitchen table for lunch. They ate in silence until Frau Knezevic said out of the blue, 'Were not Serbs.'

'How do you know that?'

'Would have taken computer. And camera. And stereo. Everything.'

'The police say it must have been Albanians, Romanians or Moroccans.'

Frau Knezevic pondered this briefly, then shook her head firmly. 'No. Would have taken everything too.'

*

Frau Knezevic had gone two hours ago, leaving Jonas hard at work putting the scattered notes, tapes and memory cards of his reports back into their wallet folders and then these back into the right archive boxes.

On the side of the boxes were stickers listing the contents, numbered consecutively. Each number referred to a wallet folder that contained the data storage devices, plus all notes and documents relating to a particular report.

Sorting through the material took him back deep into his past, to the beginning of his time as a video journalist and to reportages that he'd long forgotten.

One of his first independent pieces of work was a feature on long-distance lorry drivers. Jonas had spent days and nights hanging around the lorry parks of motorway services with his first camcorder, in search of drivers who spoke one of the languages he was conversant in, and who had no objections to being filmed and interviewed. The memories that remained from that time were smelly drivers' cabins with unmade bunks, oriental ready meals heated up on gas cookers, country music and cold rain. He remembered, too, the response of the editor he'd offered the film to: 'What's this supposed to be? A film essay? And why's it in black-and-white? We've got colour telly here.'

It was one of the first dampeners on his artistic aspirations – and it wouldn't be the last.

Jonas looked through the stills from the reportage, which were in a transparent sleeve. Although they only dated from ten years ago they looked old. The drivers' haircuts, their clothing, the cars in the background and the way the photographs had been copied – in high contrast on glossy paper – all appeared a bit drab and passé.

He tucked everything back in the wallet file and put this in the right archive box. He marked the corresponding number on the contents list of the box with a yellow highlighter, as a note that he wanted to transfer the tape to DVD. When he finally had a spare moment.

Many of the files he'd put back in order contained, besides the raw material for a report and his edited film, a second version cut by the respective editors because they found it better. Most had been annotated by comments in Jonas's handwriting, such as 'worse', 'much worse' or simply 'crap'.

It had taken Jonas a while to get used to the fact that he was merely a supplier to an editor and to seeing his reports billed as someone else's work. This is why he'd focused all his artistic ambitions on *Montecristo* and treated his job as a video journalist purely as a money-earner.

But now that the burglary had forced him to engage with his work from the past few years, a doubt nagged at him whether this had been the right decision. Maybe from time to time he ought to raise the bar after all.

Dusk had set in and rain pattered gently against the window. Getting up from the floor, Jonas stretched his limbs, stiff through hours of crouching and kneeling. He went to the window and looked down at Rofflerstrasse. A few windows were lit in the house opposite, also built of brick and dating back to the 1930s. On two windows, one directly above the other, drawings and other children's artworks had been stuck. Jonas could see the mothers busy in their kitchens. He knew the families by sight, but it had taken him a long time to distinguish the one from the other. The children were roughly the same age, the women had been pregnant at the same time and he sometimes saw the fathers barbecuing together in the front garden.

There were moments when he felt sorry for them. But recently there had been more moments when his pity had been directed at himself.

He returned to his tidying. The floor was now almost empty and the archive boxes were in their places on the shelf. He bent down over a memory card, which was dated September of this year and labelled 'Customer Incident'. The unedited material from the train journey to Basel. Back at the time Brand had asked a few broadcasters whether they might be interested and, as expected, each one had come back with the same answer: 'Can you do a rough edit? Then we'll let you know.'

As so often before, he hadn't had time for a rough edit. Or no desire to spend a lot of time for nothing. There wasn't sufficient material for a proper reportage. It was just an impression, a brief aperçu taken out of context. To have a chance of selling it to a broadcaster he needed more background material on the passengers and the victim. In other words, probably hours of extra unpaid work.

He put the data storage device and the corresponding notes into their file. But instead of stowing the file away in its archive box, he placed it beside his monitor in the editing area. Maybe this was an opportunity to raise the bar.

All of a sudden Jonas was struck by a paralysing tiredness. Was this one of the symptoms the doctor at casualty had mentioned? With heavy legs he plodded into the bedroom, took off his shoes and lay fully dressed on the freshly made bed.

But he couldn't get to sleep. He was prevented from doing so by unusual noises and the knowledge that someone had rifled through his things and violated his private space. He felt like a stranger in his own home.

After an hour he gave up, got dressed, packed a small bag with necessities, ordered a taxi and went to Marina's.

*

When he arrived she wasn't at home. He sat on her white sofa and waited.

Her flat was the opposite of his. No trinkets and bare walls. The only decoration was a bookcase with four shelves full of books arranged by size.

In truth, his flat would look like this too if he hadn't decided to fill the large space with more than just his presence. And maybe that decision had just been a reaction to his ex, who'd accused him of being a minimalist. On an emotional level too.

That was a lie. Jonas was a sensitive, emotional and often sentimental person. He'd only affected the minimalism to rein his feelings in.

His gaze roamed the sitting–dining room, which looked like the waiting room in an expensive beauty clinic. How did that relate to Marina? Was she just as ordered and neat on the inside? Or did the flat disguise a seething mass of emotions, passions and moods?

There was one thing he knew for sure: Marina was the most sensual woman he'd met in his life. Which rather suggested the latter possibility.

The tiredness that had afflicted him at home and yet hadn't allowed him to go to sleep returned. What he really wanted to do was to climb straight into her bed, but they didn't know each other well enough for that. Giving someone your house keys was one thing; finding them in your bed was quite another.

Removing his shoes, he lay down on the sofa and nodded off almost instantaneously.

*

Once upon a time Max Gantmann had been the man who explained economic affairs to the television audience. But even prior to the outbreak of the financial crisis he had been banished from the screen on the highest orders. The official explanation given was restructuring, but actually it was for aesthetic reasons. Television viewers simply couldn't be expected to put up with Gantmann's physical appearance any longer.

The editorial office had turned a blind eye for ages, both in recognition of the man's brilliance and out of consideration for the reason behind his self-neglect: the death of his wife. She had been killed in a car accident, leaving him bewildered and helpless.

Since then he'd been working in the background. He wrote analyses and commentaries for his more dapper colleagues and was the port of call for all financial and economic questions. He worked at the end of a long corridor full of doors with witty stickers. There was nothing on his door; it was the only tidy thing about his office.

Jonas had met Max when he'd worked as a cameraman at

the World Economic Forum, not long after the death of the commentator's wife. Max had missed an interview with Tony Blair because he'd been blind drunk the night before. Jonas had covered for him, corroborating his excuse that early that morning their car had got stuck in the snow. Max had never forgotten him for this.

Jonas had to knock three times before a gruff voice called out, 'Come in!' He took a deep breath and entered.

Max's office was fogged with cigarette smoke and the place was as chaotic as the home of a compulsive hoarder. Everywhere stood piles of manuscripts, books, newspapers, prospectuses, fast food packaging and rubbish. A narrow path through all this mess led to a visitor's chair – which also served as shelf space – and thence to a large desk with two screens, behind which sat Max Gantmann.

'I'd completely forgotten you were coming,' he said.

'Otherwise you'd have tidied up?'

Jonas weaved his way over, Max held out a sweaty, fleshy paw and the two men shook hands.

He was very tall and very fat. The white of his long, thick hair, tied into a ponytail at the back of his neck, had yellowed and afforded a stark contrast to his bloated, crimson face. He was wearing, as he had permanently since the tragedy, a black three-piece suit dotted with ash and food, and a white shirt but no tie. Max made an unconvincing effort to get out of his chair, obeying at once when Jonas said, 'Don't get up.'

'Have a seat, if you can find one,' Max invited him, without taking the cigarette out of his mouth.

Jonas looked around, before shifting a pile of papers from the edge of the desk, placing it on the floor and perching on the space that he'd freed up.

'Still working in the "popular" sector?'

After that World Economic Forum, Gantmann had regarded Brand as his protégé and he'd taken exception to Jonas's going freelance and accepting commissions for lifestyle and celebrity programmes. 'Popular journalism,' he'd said, 'is just a fancy way of referring to gutter journalism! It aims to appeal to the basest human instincts. You're deliberately operating below your potential. Do you know what that is? Cynicism! A journalist's worst character defect. Popular! – ugh! The only people who exalt this as a genre are those who were once far better and who've ended up there.'

'They're just bread-and-butter jobs,' Brand had pleaded in his defence. 'I'll only do them until I can make a living doing those jobs which match my potential, as you call it.'

But there was no let-up in commissions from Highlife in his freelance years. On the contrary, the name Jonas Brand had become a regular fixture in the opening and closing credits of celebrity and lifestyle shows. Something which hadn't escaped the attention of Max Gantmann, of course.

'What can I do for you?' he asked, cigarette still in mouth and eyes screwed up against the smoke.

Jonas pulled an envelope from his inner jacket pocket, took out the two hundred-franc notes and held them under Max's nose.

'Do you owe me this? I'd forgotten.'

'Take a close look. Do you notice anything?'

Gantmann pushed the glasses he wore on his head like a diadem down onto his nose and examined the banknotes. Jonas watched his faintly trembling, nicotine-stained fingers with their unkempt nails turn over the notes back and forth, and side to side. Jonas gave him a clue: 'The serial numbers.'

Max compared them. Looking up at Jonas in surprise, he took the cigarette from his mouth and stubbed it out in the overflowing ashtray. 'That's impossible.'

'I wanted to hear it from you – that it's impossible to have two identical serial numbers.'

Gantmann started checking the security features.

'They're both genuine. I got confirmation from GCBS.'

Max slowly shook his head. 'So what did they say?'

'They told me to look after them carefully as they're collector's pieces.'

Max laughed grimly. 'They sure are. I'd look after them too. *Very* carefully. And I'd look after myself carefully as well.'

'What do you mean?'

'I imagine that there are people out there who would be most displeased if this became public knowledge.'

Brand shifted his gaze to the window. The glass was covered with notes, scraps of paper and newspaper cuttings. In between Jonas could make out industrial buildings, garages, sports grounds, roads and apartment blocks. 'Two days ago my flat was burgled and turned upside down. Yesterday I was attacked and robbed.' He lowered his head and pointed to the bump. 'Do you think…?'

'Absolutely,' Max replied. 'Does the name Coromag mean anything to you?'

Jonas had heard of it before, in connection with an arts prize. He'd reported on the award ceremony once. 'A printing works isn't it?'

'Not just any old printing works. A security printer. They print banknotes for lots of countries, including Switzerland.'

Max lit another cigarette and typed something into his computer. Then he swivelled the monitor so that Jonas could look. He saw a chart. In the top left of the screen it said COROMAG, and a graph showed a line that zigzagged from the top left to bottom right, before flattening out just before the end of the graph.

'What you see here,' Max explained, 'is the picture of a firm that can't afford to make any mistakes. Not a single one. And certainly not one like that.' He picked up the notes from the desk and passed them back. When Jonas took them, Max blew on his fingers as if he'd just burned himself.

'Spend them as fast as you can,' he advised Jonas. 'This isn't a matter for celebrity television.'

3

ADAM DILLIER WAS HAVING his best day in months. He'd been the first in the office, as always, passing the security controls of the night shift with a spring in his step, and entering the still-empty reception area. Leaving behind his scent in the lift, which today consisted of a little too much eau de toilette, he made straight for the coffee machine. As ever, the security men on the night shift had kindly made a couple of coffees before he arrived, to prevent Dillier's first one from tasting too stale.

He hadn't always been an early riser; it was the course of Coromag's business that had turned him into one. He would go to sleep like a baby and wake an hour later with the feeling that he'd slept through the night. After that he dozed in short bursts, between which he turned over Coromag's problems in his mind, of which there were plenty. They had diminished slightly ever since the second last-minute rescue of the firm, but afterwards the rather particular nature of the salvage process had been the cause of sleepless nights. And when this had been sorted out, too, he'd become so used to his sleep deprivation that he continued to get up between four and five o'clock, took an early-morning jog around the neighbourhood and showed up at work between six and seven.

For a long time, the position of CEO at Coromag had looked like the salvation of his career. Before that he'd been chairman of a large, important industrial firm, where he'd come unstuck as the result of a failed attempt at diversification. He'd agreed on an official version with the board of directors – who were also keen to keep the matter quiet – which aroused no suspicions, not even amongst headhunters, and so he'd landed the job of CEO at the company which, besides securities, travel documents and banknotes for a number of countries, also printed the Swiss currency. What the firm lacked in size and impact on the stock exchange, it made up for with respectability and tradition. These two qualities had allowed him to overlook the few skeletons that lingered in Coromag's cupboard.

Dillier was not a turnaround manager, and he was out of his depth facing Coromag's problems. It was something he'd never admit, but it tormented him as he tossed and turned beneath the sheets at night.

He knew perfectly well that if he failed at Coromag, there would be no second 'agreed version of events' to save him with yet another leading position in Swiss business. This is why from day one he'd been determined to go as far as necessary to prevent such a failure. He could never have dreamed, however, that he would go quite as far as he actually did.

But now everything seemed to have finally turned out for the best. At the last finance meeting he'd been able to surprise the analysts with figures that had finally halted the slump, and even showed a slight upwards trend.

And now this request from Highlife. He only knew the lifestyle programme from those rare occasions when he watched television with his wife, but he'd noticed that business leaders of his rank or higher were increasingly featuring on the show. And he knew from his PR adviser that a certain media presence in a public milieu, if not overdone, was also beneficial to the firm's market value.

Jonas Brand, who was familiar to his wife as a reporter for Highlife, was planning a series on the private lives of business leaders and had suggested a meeting this morning to conduct a short preliminary interview and discuss the format of the programme. After a brief, feigned hesitation, Dillier had agreed. Maybe this would finally be the watershed.

Dillier had suggested scheduling their meeting for eight thirty. Early enough to show the television man how disciplined the work ethic was here, and late enough to ensure that even the last workers would have clocked on. It was now just before seven o'clock. At half-past seven his personal assistant would arrive with fresh croissants for their visitor, and they'd address a few pending matters until he arrived.

Until then he wanted to go through once more the statements that he'd prepared with his PR man.

*

The television man was taller than he'd imagined, but his clothes pretty much lived up to Dillier's expectations: jeans, leather jacket, roll neck jumper. The three-day beard and three-day stubble on his shaved head went well with his distinctive face. He could have been in his late thirties, perhaps a little older; Dillier was not good at guessing men's ages.

He received Jonas in his office. They sat on the leather suite; the PA served coffee and croissants. Dillier caught himself speaking a little too verbosely and laughing too loudly, two signs that he was a touch nervous. He said, 'Let's get cracking. So, what's the format?'

'It's quite simple: work–life. I show managers in their work environment and private sphere, then compare and contrast the two.'

'Not too private, I hope.' Again Dillier laughed too loudly.

'As private as you like.'

'When's it scheduled to be broadcast?'

'I can't say at the moment; that's a decision for the editorial office. They want to see an example first. The feature on you is the pilot, so to speak.'

Dillier wasn't sure what to make of that. The bad news was that the project hadn't yet received the broadcaster's blessing. The good news was that the series would begin with him as its first subject. 'So I'm giving up my time without any guarantee that the programme will make it to the screen?' This was supposed to sound cheerful, but he didn't manage to pull it off.

'Guarantee? I'm afraid there are no guarantees in our business. But the idea is a new one, and editorial teams are always on the lookout for new ideas. I'm confident this is going to work.'

'So am I then. How do you want to proceed?'

'I thought we'd start with a little discussion about your line of work, and I can edit in the key bits later.'

'And where would you like to do it?'

'Here would be best, exactly where you're sitting. I'll just quickly set up the camera and some light.'

'How long will that take?'

'A few minutes.'

'I'll leave you to it. In our business, every minute counts.'

Dillier went into the anteroom, sat on his PA's chair and read the statements again.

When he returned to his office there was a camera on a tripod and an LED lamp beside it. A microphone had been placed on the coffee table. He sat in the designated armchair and Brand focused the camera.

'Camera's running,' Jonas announced, sitting opposite him. 'Herr Dillier, you have a licence to print money,' he began.

Dillier laughed and corrected him: 'Actually, Coromag has the licence; I'm just its CEO.' Maybe that was a bit pedantic, he thought. Then again, people surely expect a degree of precision from the man who's responsible for manufacturing the nation's money.

The journalist asked him a few general questions, which he was able to answer with the help of his prepared statements. Dillier's nervousness subsided, his replies became more thorough and sharper too, he thought. He felt relaxed and, to be honest, felt he was putting on a good performance.

A few minutes into their conversation Brand handed him a hundred-franc note. 'I'd like to move onto something more specific now. Could you tell our viewers about the security features of your products? I need to adjust the set-up here slightly and film with the camera on my shoulder so I can pan and zoom.'

Brand unscrewed the camera, mounted it on a shoulder rig, sat opposite Dillier again and focused on him. 'Camera running.'

Now Dillier was in his element. He talked about the magic number, the transparent cross, the watermark portrait, the watermark digit, the line structures, and he sensed the lens panning from his hands to his face and back again.

When he got to the serial number the journalist interrupted him: 'Is it possible for two notes to have the same number?'

Dillier sat up and noticed that the camera was aiming

straight at his face. He shook his head with a forgiving smile. 'Absolutely out of the question. The serial numbers are printed on the finished sheets of paper, then the notes are cut and checked electronically. All errors are identified in this process. Every faulty note is automatically weeded out and shredded. And of course precise records are kept on this, which are held by the Swiss National Bank, our client.'

And then came the moment which turned Dillier's best day in months into the worst: from the coffee table Jonas took another hundred-franc note, which Dillier hadn't noticed before, and passed it to him.

'So how do you explain this to our viewers then?'

Dillier took the note and knew that he was expected to compare the numbers. To win time he compared all four numbers in great detail, although he was well aware that the worst case scenario had just arisen.

He looked up and the camera panned from the notes in his hand back to his face.

Dillier smiled. 'Just give me a moment, would you? I need to take a closer look.'

He started checking the security features of the second note. Then he stood up, fetched a magnifying glass from his desk and compared the features of the first note with those of the second, then those of the second with those of the first. He went about this elaborate procedure despite knowing for certain that all he'd find was confirmation of the terrible truth that the statistically impossible had just occurred.

Only now did Dillier realise that the journalist had kept the camera running the whole time. He looked up, held his palm up before the lens like a policeman stopping a car and said, perhaps somewhat too brusquely, 'Turn that off for a while.'

Brand obeyed and took the camera off his shoulder.

'Thanks,' Dillier said as a conciliatory gesture. He was about to resume checking the security features, but then looked up and asked, 'Where did you get these notes from?'

'One was given to me as change in a restaurant, the other from a cash machine.'

'So these are your own money?' Dillier had assumed that someone had slipped him them. The chance that they'd come directly into the hands of a journalist was statistically even more improbable.

The journalist said, 'It suggests that there are a lot of these, don't you think?'

Dillier didn't react. He tried to bring some order to the thoughts that were spinning around his head.

Brand waited.

Finally, Dillier found his voice again. 'When I said it was absolutely out of the question that two banknotes could have the same number, perhaps I exaggerated a little. Given certain, statistically insignificant conditions, it could theoretically occur. From the point of view of security it's totally irrelevant; the serial number is only one of eighteen security features.'

'In which conditions could it occur?' the journalist asked.

Dillier hesitated only briefly. He'd found his defence strategy and felt the ground beneath his feet again. 'Let's just say we're talking about a highly unlikely coincidence of what are themselves highly unlikely events, which for security reasons I can't go into detail about. I'm sure you understand.'

'What about the electronic security check?'

'It's part of this chain of – once in a lifetime coincidences.' He was pleased with this formulation and Brand, too, appeared satisfied with the explanation.

Dillier looked at his watch. 'Shall we move on?'

The journalist asked a few more questions that he filmed with the camera on his shoulder and rapidly brought the interview to a close. Dillier suspected that Brand was mainly interested in the two banknotes which were still on the coffee table.

When Jonas made to pick them up, Dillier covered them with his hand. 'I was going to suggest that I exchange these notes for you. They'd be very useful for the internal investigation into our,' he said, gesturing inverted commas with his fingers, '… mishap.'

'Actually, I was going to keep them as good luck charms.'

'Yes you can, you can, just as soon as our enquiry is concluded you can have them back.'

But the journalist held his ground. 'I've got a suggestion. You make a photocopy and I'll keep the originals,' he said.

Dillier had not yet given up. 'My people in quality control would obviously prefer to work with the originals.'

'Sorry,' Brand said, 'but I'm a little superstitious. I must insist on keeping them.'

Dillier sighed. 'Then I'll photocopy them while you pack up.'

He took the notes and went along the corridor to the copying room, where he removed his wallet from his breast pocket and saw that it contained only two-hundreds and twenties. On the way back he'd cadge a couple of hundred notes off his PA, switch them for the journalist's ones and hope he wouldn't notice. If he did, Dillier would plead overriding national interests.

But before the copier had spat out the last sheet, Brand entered the room.

Dillier gave him the notes. 'I trust that you'll be treating this matter strictly off the record,' he urged.

Brand mumbled something incomprehensible and put the notes away. He didn't want to create the impression that he knew just how important the matter was.

No sooner had Jonas gone than Adam Dillier barricaded

himself in his office and spent the rest of the morning trying to contact someone who was uncontactable.

*

After Jonas had got through security at the entrance to Coromag and was on his way into town, he was fairly certain that Dillier had nothing to do with the break-in or mugging. His acting skills would never have allowed him to feign the surprise he'd exhibited on seeing the identical notes side by side. But it had definitely made him nervous. Jonas was sure that Dillier would have swapped the notes if he hadn't appeared in the copying room in time.

So what now? The idea for the interview hadn't been properly thought through; it had come to him spontaneously after his discussion with Max Gantmann. He wanted to show his mentor that he was capable of more than 'popular' journalism, and that lifestyle TV was a highly practical way of getting in with people you'd never be likely to get close to otherwise.

In the can he now had the scene where the CEO loses his composure upon being confronted with the two identical serial numbers. But where to go from here? How was he going to turn this into serious reportage? If anyone could help him, it would be Max. But he couldn't ask Max without reinforcing the latter's hunch that perhaps 'popular' wasn't beneath Jonas's potential after all.

His only option was to have a shot at finishing the piece and then show Max the final result. If it turned out well he'd find a slot for it on a business programme. If not, Max would never set eyes on it.

It was not yet eleven, but the line of cars he was in was moving no quicker than walking pace. Jonas was worried that he wouldn't get to the bank before Herr Weber took his lunch break.

But when he arrived at the GCBS customer car park and went into the bank, his account manager was still there, and free.

'I had a break-in at my flat; I think it's time I rented a safety deposit box,' he said.

'Very sensible,' Herr Weber said, fetching the necessary forms. 'The smallest costs five hundred francs.' When he saw the surprise on Brand's face he added, 'Per year.'

He helped fill out the forms. Jonas had to sign a declaration that he was not depositing explosives, firearms or drugs. And that it was his own responsibility to insure the contents. Herr Weber accompanied him to the lift and they descended two floors.

Jonas was surprised by how spartan the rooms looked down below. Instead of florid carpets and dimmed crystal lamps he found concrete floors and neon lighting. It felt like the air-raid shelter of an apartment block, except for the reinforced door to the deposit box room, which opened automatically.

Herr Weber took him to the smallest lockers, inserted a key into number 463 and invited Brand to put his key in the second lock. The door opened and Herr Weber took out a metal box which fitted exactly in the locker. He passed it to Jonas and took him into a little room with a table, two chairs and three engravings of Zürich on the walls.

'I'll leave you to it. Just ring the bell when you're finished.'

Herr Weber left the small room.

Jonas put on the floor the briefcase he'd brought from the car to make it look as if he had a number of valuables to lock away. Then he took the two hundreds from his wallet, placed them in the metal container and waited for five minutes.

Herr Weber appeared soon after Jonas rang.

'What if the bank goes belly-up?' Jonas asked as a joke.

'It doesn't affect your valuables; they're your property.'

'How about the money in my account? That's my property, too, isn't it?'

'Theoretically,' Herr Weber replied ambiguously.

Jonas carried the metal box back to the deposit room, accompanied solemnly by Herr Weber. When they'd completed the locking ceremony and were heading back along the corridor to the lift, they saw two men coming in the other direction. One was a colleague of Herr Weber. The other was an elderly, elegant gentleman, who put on a pair of sunglasses when he saw them in the distance and now looked like a Greek shipping magnate. As they passed each other only the bank employee returned their greeting.

*

'Here's to the hundred-franc notes!'

Jonas, who'd nodded off, opened his eyes. Marina was standing beside the bed, holding two glasses of champagne and staring down at him. She was wearing what she'd had on when she got out of bed: a black, high-necked silk blouse that went down to her waist and a pair of black pumps. Nothing else.

She waited patiently until he managed to tear his eyes off her and take the glass.

'This is the bottle we weren't able to drink the other night,' she said, using each foot in turn to slip the shoe off the other. Climbing tantalisingly slowly over Jonas, she sat beside him. He loved the combination of her reserve and wantonness.

She sat with her legs tucked up and her hand poised by the glass that she was balancing on a knee. 'That Dillier's one of our clients,' she remarked.

Jonas was lying on his side, resting his head on his right hand and holding his glass in his left. 'Do you do his arts prize event?'

She nodded. 'This year it's supposed to be a bigger event again. In the last two years I've heard they've just kept the thing ticking over. The difficulty was: how to turn an event into a non-event without the analysts noticing?'

'How?'

She shrugged. 'The analysts *did* notice and the share price fell further.'

'Companies listed on the stock market have to take great care. Even the smallest thing can have a knock-on effect on the share price.'

'Do you understand a lot about business?'

'No.'

Both of them took a sip.

'But this banknote thing, that's a business story, isn't it?'

'If only journalists would stick to reporting things they have some understanding of…'

Marina laughed and they clinked glasses: 'To the charlatans of this world!'

Once they'd finished their glasses she kissed him on the mouth. When their lips parted briefly, he just had time to say, 'Now without the blouse on, perhaps?'

*

Jonas was scarcely back in his flat the following morning when he was struck by that uncanny feeling again. He still thought the flat smelled different, the creaking of the parquet floor beneath his shoes sounded like someone else's footsteps, and he hesitated a moment before opening the door to his studio.

Everything looked normal, and yet he sensed that something

had been changed. Jonas went into every room, and in every room he had the feeling he was in a stranger's flat. He caught himself whistling like a child in the dark.

His answer machine was flashing, announcing four messages. Two from the Highlife editorial office, one from his insurance company and the last from Max Gantmann.

He called Max back first, who wasted no time on pleasantries. 'Are you doing something on the banknote affair?' he asked.

'Maybe,' Jonas replied.

'If you're not, give me the material. But if you are then think of me. I can find a slot for it, assuming that it's any good, of course.'

'Thank you. If it is any good then I will certainly take that into consideration.' Jonas, too, could be sarcastic.

After a pause Max said, 'If you want to check Dillier's explanation of a chain of several improbable coincidences, I've got an address for you. Write this down.'

Jonas jotted: Oskar Trebler, Numismaco, Bechergasse 14, 8001 Zürich, phone 044 374 12 81.

'Trebler is *the* authority on banknotes. Don't do anything on paper money without having spoken to him first.'

Jonas thanked Max for the tip and said goodbye. Then he called back the Highlife editorial office, where he was put straight through to the executive editor. 'How come I know nothing about your work–life project?' was her opening question.

'Dillier's been in touch with you then?'

Ignoring his question, she said, 'I don't like being used for leverage without knowing anything about it.'

'I was going to wait until the pilot was ready so that you could make a decision.'

'You could have told me that too.'

'I'm sorry.' After a pause, he asked, 'What did you tell him?'

'I confirmed we were running with the project. But next time I'm going to leave you high and dry.'

'Thanks.'

She didn't say anything.

'Are you still there?'

'Well, when am I going to see something?'

'Do you like the idea?'

'Depends on what you do with it.'

'I'll be in touch.'

He hung up and called the number his insurance company had left on the answerphone. A man whose name he didn't get answered. He didn't sound as cheerful as his usual agent, for whom there was not a single problem that couldn't be solved by insurance, death included. He introduced himself as a claims inspector, and his voice sounded as joyless as Jonas supposed it must if you spent your whole day dealing with nothing but damage. He informed Jonas that there was a problem with his claim.

'What problem?'

'According to the police report there are doubts as to whether the flat was locked.'

When Jonas finally got through to an appropriate police officer, the latter told him that he could only speak about the case face-to-face. He would have to make his way to the police station.

*

William Just stood smoking on the balcony of the Dragon House. He kept a slight distance between himself and the sandstone parapet because he had no head for heights, something which was a well-kept secret.

The Dragon House was a grand building dating from the mid-nineteenth century. The façade was adorned with two weathered dragons that held the builder's family crest. Below them the River Limmat flowed sluggishly, reflecting the grey December sky from which rain would soon be falling. An old woman was concentrating hard on feeding the ducks and swans equitably, and two mothers were chatting away as they pushed their prams along the embankment. Apart from them there weren't many signs of life on the promenade on this chilly morning.

Just shuddered. He plunged the glowing butt of his cigarette into the sand of the large ashtray and went back inside.

The fourth floor of the Dragon House was a mixture between an apartment and an office. This was where the bank put up important guests who didn't particularly want to stay in a hotel, and there were also large and small, elegantly furnished conference rooms for informal meetings.

The ground floor housed the branch of a regional bank that belonged to the GCBS conglomerate. You could access the fourth floor either via the bank or directly from the street.

Just entered the 'gentlemen's room', as Herr Schwarz called it. For as long as anyone could remember, this elderly man had been looking after the Dragon House as a sort of caretaker, secretary and butler. It was a panelled room with mahogany furniture and leather armchairs. The walls were hung with landscapes from GCBS's collection by Ferdinand Hodler, Giovanni Giacometti, Frank Buscher, Cuno Amiet and Otto Fröhlicher.

Flames were crackling away in a fireplace, which was also panelled. William Just opened the jacket of his basalt-grey suit, buried his hands in his trouser pockets and stood in front of the fire.

He was of medium height and a little over sixty years old. His blond-grey hair, still thick, was in a crew cut, and to look youthful he wore contact lenses rather than glasses. His angular face had softened; he'd put on a little weight in the past three years. But he still went mountain hiking to overcome his fear of heights, and continued to be one of the leading members of the bank's skiing squad.

He'd been the CEO for five years now. He knew the business back to front because, apart from a few breaks, he'd spent his whole career at GCBS.

Herr Schwarz knocked at the door. The visitor had arrived.

Adam Dillier was half a head taller but Just managed to make him look shorter. He greeted him with supercilious warmth and pointed to a leather armchair, into which his guest sank deeply. He sat on an upholstered chair which he'd taken from beside a small Biedermeier bureau.

'Around this time of day I like to drink a cup or two of Lung Chiang. Will you join me?' He waited for the answer as if seriously expecting that Dillier might decline. When Adam said, 'Lovely, thanks,' Just nodded to Herr Schwarz, who promptly left the room.

'If it stays this dry we're going to have a rather green Christmas in the Engadin Valley,' Dillier remarked.

'We always spend it in the Berner Oberland.'

'The Föhn's the problem there.'

'You can ski all year round at Les Diablerets – it's at three thousand metres.'

Herr Schwarz came in with a tray, placed two wafer-thin porcelain cups on the coffee table and poured the tea. The two men stayed silent until he had left the room.

'You're pissed off with me, aren't you?' Just said with feigned contrition.

'Not exactly pissed off. But I would like to know how that could happen.'

'Me too.' Just picked up the cup with his right hand, holding the saucer in his left, and blew on the tea.

Dillier had a slight advantage. 'The deal was: only in an absolute emergency. To the best of my knowledge there hasn't been one.'

'It was averted,' Just corrected him. 'By involving authorities who were obliged to turn a blind eye to prevent the worst case scenario, we were able to discard the reserves you very kindly provided us. But you are absolutely correct. There seems to have been a breakdown during the elimination of series two.'

'What sort of breakdown?'

'Human failure.'

The truth was dawning on Dillier. 'I assumed that only one hundred per cent reliable people were involved.'

'Shredding mountains of real money that no one's ever going to miss – it's a huge temptation.'

'Do you know who it was?'

'My experts do.'

'How much did he take?'

'Just over a thousand hundred notes as far as I know.' With great care, Just took a little sip of Lung Chiang.

Dillier was horrified. 'You mean more than a thousand duplicate notes are in circulation?'

'No, we still have almost half of them.'

'Still – more than five hundred!'

'Wasn't it your statisticians who calculated the probability of two notes with the same number ending up with the same person? I seem to recall rather a large amount of zeros after the decimal point.'

'You know how it is with statistics. If the situation does occur we're at one hundred per cent.' He hadn't touched his tea, while Just was emptying his own cup.

The CEO of the largest bank in the country continued undeterred: 'The possibility of it happening a second time is several million times less likely.' He put his cup back down on the coffee table. 'And the probability of anyone noticing? Forget it.'

'You ought to have informed me all the same.' Now Dillier reached for his cup. He had to lift himself a fair way out of the armchair to get hold of it.

'You're right. I'm sorry. We didn't think it necessary to burden you with it. We were trying to protect you.'

'Well done.' Dillier turned it over in his mind as he sipped his tea. 'How about the chap who pinched the banknotes? Surely he's still a risk.'

Just poured himself more tea. 'Not according to my experts.'

'And what about the journalist with the duplicate notes? He seems to be a persistent type.'

Just blew on his teacup once more, holding the saucer beneath. 'My experts are onto it. But they need your help. What do you think of the Lung Chiang?'

*

Marina stirred the onions in the black, cast-iron pot. Using two dishcloths she'd improvised an apron because Jonas didn't have one. His view was that you should cook in a way which didn't need an apron.

Jonas had invited her over for a curry to make up for the

dinner at the new Indian restaurant on their first date. She'd accepted on the condition that he let her cook with him. She wanted to learn the basic curry recipe he'd told her about.

He'd finely chopped two large onions and heated four tablespoons of olive oil, one of his personal deviations from the original recipe: extra virgin olive oil instead of coconut oil or ghee.

'Indian recipes always underestimate the time it takes to sauté the onions until they're dark brown. You have to keep stirring on a medium heat for between twenty-five minutes and half an hour so that they brown without burning. During this time you can't do anything else.'

Jonas liked to cook but rarely had the opportunity. It was no fun cooking just for himself, and inviting people over to dinner didn't really fit the life of a single man. He had occasionally cooked with one of his flings, but he soon learned that cooking together required a greater intimacy than sleeping together.

That's why he'd invited her over to his place. To eat and cook. And also because he no longer felt at home alone in the flat.

He'd put to one side a saucer with three-quarters of a teaspoon of ground coriander, and another with a quarter teaspoon of cumin, half a teaspoon of turmeric, a quarter teaspoon of garam masala and a whole teaspoon of paprika. He was now chopping up garlic and ginger, which Marina was to add to the pan and sauté at the very end when the onions were dark brown.

Both of them were silently absorbed in their work, a homely couple.

'I was at the police station for over two hours today.'

'And?'

'Nothing.'

She glanced at him over her shoulder.

'They let me wait for one hour and fifty minutes, just to tell me that there are no new leads and probably won't be any in the future either. No witnesses to the mugging and no traces of a break-in for the burglary.'

Marina stirred the onions, Jonas started peeling the tomatoes which he'd poured boiling water over.

'And I had to listen to it all in that horridly flippant police tone. Do you know what the guy said to me? Without any traces of a break-in we have to widen the list of suspects to include anybody who is capable of opening an unlocked door?'

Marina shook her head. 'In fact the list is narrowed down to those who are capable of opening a door without leaving any traces. Professionals in other words.'

'That's what I said too.'

'And what did he reply?'

'He said he had to go; other cases to deal with. I told him I hoped they were solvable ones. Not involving professionals.'

Marina laughed. 'Don't think you should have said that. Now, look – brown enough yet?'

Jonas glanced at the pan. 'A few more minutes.'

He diced the peeled tomatoes with a sharp knife and swept them from the chopping board into a small china dish. Then he chopped some fresh coriander. The aroma of the fried onions mingled with that of the fresh coriander.

'What about the banknote thing?'

'Well, that's working on two levels. Highlife is interested in my notional work–life project; can you imagine? That means I'll do some more filming at the printing works and a little with Dillier at home: his private life.'

'What's the second level?'

'That's where it gets exciting. I'm interviewing a numismatist, *the* expert on the printing of banknotes. One of the things I'm going to ask him is whether Dillier's explanation for the duplicate serial numbers is believable.'

'What if he says no?'

'Then Coromag has a problem.'

'And maybe you do too. Just be careful!'

'I will.' He looked at the pan with the onions and added the ginger and garlic. 'We'll stir that around for a minute.' Glancing at the clock he got the ground coriander ready. 'The idea for the numismatist came from Max Gantmann.'

'Is he still alive?'

'Very much so. They just don't allow him in front of the camera any more. For aesthetic reasons.'

'He should move to radio.'

Jonas added the ground coriander to the onions and Marina stirred vigorously to stop the powder from sticking.

'Do you think the break-in and mugging have anything to do with the banknotes?'

'Max isn't ruling it out.'

'But what do you think?'

The minute was up. Jonas tipped the saucer with cumin, turmeric, garam masala and paprika into the pan. 'Maybe they do,' he conceded.

'But you're going to continue with it anyway.'

Jonas poured a tin of coconut milk into the pan. 'I'd just like to do something proper again.'

'Investigative rather than celebrity and lifestyle journalism.'

Jonas peered at Marina, but saw no hint of mockery in her expression. 'That sort of thing, yes.'

'Don't you think it's dangerous?'

'A little, perhaps. But let's face it: we *are* in Switzerland. Journalists don't get bumped off here.'

She placed an arm around his shoulder and gave him a kiss.

'So? What next?'

'With the curry?'

'That too.'

'Let it cook for ten minutes then we'll add the tomatoes, and five minutes after that the lamb. Then you let it simmer on a low flame.'

'For how long?'

'Long enough.' They kissed again.

*

A black Golf entered the underground car park beneath a GCBS office building on the edge of the city and parked in the visitor's space. The driver was a man of medium height in a dark suit. He looked like a bank employee, his only striking feature being his red hair which he'd spiked up with gel.

Taking a briefcase from the driver's seat he got out and walked purposefully towards the lift. Rather than entering it, he continued through to parking sector C, where the employees' cars were.

He approached a beige Mazda 5, a slightly old model, took a small tool from his pocket and opened the driver's door after a few attempts.

He bent down towards the lever to open the bonnet and pulled it. Closing the door he moved round to the bonnet and crouched down. He was no longer visible from the entrance.

Setting his briefcase on the ground, he opened it and took out a small box about three by four centimetres. Stuck to one side was some tape, the sort used for laying carpets. He removed the protective film and put the box on the ground, sticky side up. Then he took a small bottle of nail polish remover from the case and poured some onto a cotton-wool pad.

Only now did he fully unlatch the bonnet and lift it high enough so he could get to the airbag sensor beneath the latch.

With the cotton-wool pad he cleaned the curved metal plate protecting the sensor, waited for a moment until the liquid had evaporated and stuck the box to it.

The red-haired man put the nail-polish remover and cotton-wool pad back into his briefcase and closed the bonnet.

Standing up, he locked the car, returned to his Golf, got in, prepared an e-cigarette and waited.

*

There were no windows in Pedro Birrer's office because it was on the first basement floor, which also housed the archives, the materials store, some of the air-raid shelter rooms and the safes.

Birrer had been employed by the bank for more than twenty years as a gopher. He was responsible for the internal and external post, he ran errands – official ones for the departments and private ones for those in the higher echelons of the company – helped out with issuing supplies, was the contact for the cleaning company and was available for special tasks. It was a position of trust, if not a prestigious one. And after twenty years he'd abused that trust, the idiot.

He'd been brought in to help with a task requiring the very highest degree of trustworthiness and loyalty, as the Chief Security Officer had put it. The matter was so confidential that neither Birrer's direct superior nor the two rungs above him in the hierarchy had been informed of it.

The task was to shred large quantities of so-called duplicate notes, real banknotes whose only fault was that their serial number was not unique.

It was a monotonous job in large armour-clad storerooms at various sites in Switzerland. The only person to talk to was an uncommunicative soul from Ticino who spoke nothing but Italian, was on the verge of retirement and had a similar job to his in the bank's Ticino headquarters.

All day long they silently shredded immaculate one-hundred, two-hundred and one-thousand franc notes, and in the evenings the two of them would return together to the three-star hotel in whichever town they happened to be in, eat separately and go their own way. The man from Ticino back to his room, he to a bar or, being a confirmed bachelor, to a night club if there was one.

At some point he started putting the odd note into his pocket rather than the shredder. Nobody noticed a thing. The man from Ticino didn't pay attention to Birrer and the security guards were not privy to what was going on and had no orders to frisk the two gophers.

In this way he'd manage to assemble more than one hundred thousand francs almost without noticing. But finding the whole thing creepy, he stopped pocketing money and started spending some of the notes that nobody was missing. Eleven thousand eight hundred francs in total, mostly hundreds that he slipped into the tangas of table dancers.

And then the unthinkable happened: one of these hundreds ended up with someone who not only had a banknote with the same serial number but noticed it, too. This led to his second-ever meeting with the Chief Security Officer.

After their conversation Birrer was reminded why he'd remained loyal to the bank for so long. Although he was given such a severe dressing-down that he, as they said at the bank, 'could walk upright through the gap beneath the door', he kept his job. Obviously Birrer had to give back the notes still in his possession plus as much of the eleven thousand eight hundred francs that was in his savings account, and pledge to pay off the rest in time. But he kept his job.

He'd have liked to see the firm which wouldn't have sacked an employee on the spot after such a breach of trust!

Since then Birrer knew that the Chief Security Officer was a gentleman for whom he'd do anything. More than just this private errand he'd been asked to run today – he was to go and collect the skis that the CSO had forgotten in his holiday house in Davos and which he now needed for a pre-Christmas skiing weekend in Gstaad.

In current traffic he could manage Zürich to Davos and back in five hours. He didn't have any plans for the weekend and if he set off right now he'd arrive around six, fetch the skis from the woman who looked after the house and go for a bite to eat somewhere cosy. He had in mind a bowl of the local barley soup and a plate of cured meats. But no gherkins or pickled onions, as the liquid made the meat go all limp.

Naturally, a glass of Veltliner to wash it down wouldn't be bad, but he didn't want to push his luck. He'd buy a bottle over the counter and enjoy it at home, to wind down.

By ten o'clock at the latest.

*

Just after Sargans large snowflakes started to fall. The cars in front of him slowed down and he fell back to put a few more cars between himself and the beige Mazda.

The driver of the Mazda – he didn't know the name, didn't want to, one of his business maxims – had driven the whole way with the infuriatingly anal habit of sticking just below the speed limit, which kept causing other drivers to make either very long or illegally fast overtaking manoeuvres, thus removing the two or three cars cover between them.

An electronic cigarette emitted its artificial smoke, while Maria Callas's ethereal voice resonated from the speakers. When renting the Golf he'd made sure that he could connect his smartphone to the stereo. Without his opera collection he could barely live, let alone work.

The job was relatively simple. But it was so well paid that he'd opted to use a new method. It was fairly elaborate but highly refined. And one of his specialities: accidents.

None of the cars between him and the Mazda was indicating right, which meant he found himself directly behind it again on the exit. He could only hope that the driver hadn't already noticed him. When he reduced his speed, someone came right up behind him and started flashing their lights. The red-haired man didn't react and was overtaken at the first opportunity by two cars honking their horns.

They drove along the River Landquart towards Davos. The snow was falling more heavily and visibility became so bad that he couldn't see the Mazda any longer even when for once it wasn't concealed by a bend. He put his foot down slightly although the snow was settling and the road getting slippery.

When they got to the village of Serneus he suddenly saw brake lights up ahead. It was the Mazda stopping at a roundabout to let in a car coming from the other direction, which then turned into the village.

Coming to a stop barely two metres behind the Mazda, he could make out the driver's silhouette. He was moving his head to a slow rhythm; probably listening to music as well.

The red-haired man clenched the steering wheel and shut his eyes. He didn't want to know; he found it too personal.

The whole thing had only taken a few seconds. The Mazda

drove on, took the second exit at the roundabout onto the cantonal road and accelerated.

Now the red-haired man stayed close on his tail. In the short tunnel before the bridge the Mazda sped up again.

He'd chosen the location carefully. It was ideal for his purposes: a cable-stayed bridge more than half a kilometre long with an elegant sweep boasting a radius of five hundred metres.

Opening the glove box, the red-haired man took out a small remote control unit.

The Mazda now tried to shake him off. They passed the first column with its new steel cables, where after a straight entrance the bridge started on its broad curve.

*

Pedro Birrer was delighted to see the unexpected snow. Finally his purchase of this four by four MPV was justified. With the snow settling on the cantonal road he was one of those who could continue to drive at the designated speed limit.

He'd put on the '30 Love Songs' CD by Engelbert Humperdinck, his favourite singer. The perfect musical accompaniment to the snowstorm.

He was close to Serneus; only another twenty minutes or so to Davos. He put a Marlboro in his mouth and pressed in the cigarette lighter. Birrer was a moderate but incorrigible smoker. He'd never attempted to give up. Five to ten cigarettes per day, apart from when he stayed out late, which happened occasionally at weekends.

The lighter popped out with a gentle click. He lit his cigarette and put his foot on the brake because he'd reached the roundabout with the Serneus turn-off.

Birrer had to stop and let another car through. In his rear-view mirror he saw a black Golf. He had the feeling that he'd seen it behind him earlier. No surprise, really; in this weather his four-wheel drive was far superior to a Golf.

He drove on and the Golf stayed close behind him. He was asking to be shown.

In better visibility he'd be able to see the houses of Klosters village in the valley by now.

Turning onto the bypass, he drove into the short tunnel that led on to the elegant Sunniberg Bridge. The Golf was still right behind him, which made Birrer slightly exceed the speed limit.

The straight section after the tunnel was the last opportunity to overtake. He put his foot down even further.

Just before the bridge curved to the right and Birrer had to turn the steering wheel, there was an explosion. He was hit by something that pressed him into his seat and blocked his vision.

'Airbag' was his last thought before he felt the terrifying impact. And the rollover. And the long drop.

*

Numismaco was in the centre of the old town, in a little house whose sandstone doorframe had the year 1739 chiselled into it. There was a small shop with a window displaying a few dozen coins arranged with military precision on velvet trays. Framed banknotes hung on the back wall of the window, also covered in velvet.

Jonas put down his bags. He'd come with his full equipment: four lights, a soft box and a tripod in addition to his shoulder rig.

On the shop door it said, 'Please ring and enter'. Jonas pressed the button and the door buzzed soon afterwards.

Behind the counter stood an elderly lady adjusting her hair.

Maybe she'd been having a nap in the armchair at the back.

She took him up two steep, narrow steps to a small room with a low wooden-beamed ceiling. Half the room was taken up by a massive walnut writing desk. 'Herr Trebler asked me to tell you he's running a little late. In the meantime you can get yourself ready.'

Jonas set up the lighting, sound and camera as best he could in such cramped surroundings. Then he stood by the window.

Beneath him was a back yard with a wooden shed and a pergola swathed with the leafless stems of an old vine. A man in a blue smock was standing in front of it, varnishing something wooden, perhaps part of a piece of furniture.

The door opened and Trebler entered the room. He was younger than Jonas had imagined and his deep, rather brittle-sounding voice on the telephone had intimated, not yet forty, around Jonas's age. He wore jeans and a blue, round-neck cashmere jumper, from which the top of a striped shirt collar poked out. The only thing that fitted Jonas's idea of a numismatist was the rimless glasses.

'Please excuse me. Business isn't so great that I could tell a customer I was too busy to see him.' Trebler offered Jonas the visitor's chair and sat at the desk. 'I must say, I'm very excited about these banknotes with the same serial number.'

On the way to the shop Jonas had collected them from the bank safe. But he didn't bring them out yet. 'You'll see that they're both genuine and bear the same number. First, I'm going to ask you on camera how something like that could happen and then I'll hand you the notes.'

'OK, let's begin. I really don't have much time. I can say that to you; you're not a customer.'

Jonas attached a microphone to the numismatist's jumper, dabbed the shiny patches on his forehead and nose with a make-up sponge, turned on the lights and switched on the camera. 'Ready?'

Trebler nodded.

'The camera's running... Herr Trebler, how can it happen that two one-hundred franc notes have the same serial number?'

Trebler cleared his throat and replied, 'It can't actually just happen. It has to be intentional.'

There was a pause. Trebler was clearly waiting for Jonas to dig deeper. But he couldn't think of anything more original to say than: 'Could you explain that in greater detail?'

'The numbering of the notes happens right at the end on the finished sheets. These are then cut and the notes run through a processing machine which carries out electronic checks for errors. Incorrect or missing security features, irregularities in colour, creases etc. And of course it checks the serial numbers too. All previously used numbers are stored on the system and so a duplication would be identified immediately. The good notes are shrinkwrapped; the faulty ones sorted out and shredded. Any shredded notes are recorded on the National Bank's database.'

'As far as you're concerned, therefore, it's impossible for two Swiss banknotes to carry the same serial number?'

Trebler hesitated. 'Not impossible. But extremely unlikely. And if it were to happen, then in my opinion it would have to be a deliberate act on the part of the printing firm, with the control mechanisms switched off. I'm talking about genuine banknotes here; obviously it's possible with counterfeit ones.'

Jonas felt in his breast pocket and handed the two notes to the numismatist. 'So what have you got to say about these? Wait. I'd like to film this part from my shoulder – it gives me more flexibility.'

He removed the camera from the tripod and mounted it on

his shoulder rig. 'Camera running.' He repeated his previous question: 'So what have you got to say about these?'

He panned from Trebler's face to his hands holding the banknotes. In close-up he filmed the hands examining and comparing the hundreds. Zooming out again, he filmed Trebler switching on a light box to backlight the banknotes.

Then he got up and went to a small gadget on a sideboard next to the desk. 'Here it seems to be the second scenario.'

He switched on the device and placed the first note on the feed. It was drawn in with a faint buzz, then spat out again. Trebler set the second note on the tray. The banknote scanner sucked it in, stopped and beeped. A red light went on. The numismatist took out the note and held it in front of the camera.

'One of the best forgeries I've ever seen. But look, you can see that the dancing number isn't dancing, while the chameleon number doesn't change colour.'

Jonas turned off the camera and removed it from his shoulder. 'That can't be right. My bank, GCBS, checked the notes and confirmed that both of them were genuine.'

'As I said it's a brilliant forgery.'

'The CEO of Coromag, Adam Dillier, checked them too and said they were genuine.'

'Did he use a scanner?'

'No. It all seemed quite clear.'

'It isn't. You've seen with your own eyes – the machine flagged it up.'

Jonas wasn't giving up. 'Anybody who uses computers knows how reliable electronic equipment is.'

'I only need the scanner as a back-up. I already knew I had a counterfeit note in my hand.'

'Shit!' Jonas hissed under his breath.

Trebler looked at him sympathetically. 'I'm sorry to have ruined your story. But maybe you can still turn it into something. After all, you discovered a superb forgery. And the coincidence of getting hold of two notes with the same serial number – well it's a miracle, statistically at least.'

*

Seething with anger, Jonas drove straight to his bank. He had to wait ages for Herr Weber, who was busy with another customer.

When it was finally his turn, his fury had subsided somewhat. The 'How do you explain that one of these two notes you declared to be genuine turns out to be counterfeit?' didn't come out as caustically as he'd intended.

Herr Weber took the two notes and checked the security features before muttering, 'Just bear with me for a moment,' and shuffling off into the large office space behind the counters.

Jonas saw him show the notes to a colleague, who shook his head and pointed to a particular spot. Then the two men walked past a filing cabinet to a small machine, which Jonas recognised as a banknote scanner. He was almost certain that they hadn't used it the first time they'd checked the notes.

Herr Weber came back. 'Sorry, but this one here is in fact a forgery. You should go to the police.'

'How come you didn't notice the first time?' Jonas huffed.

Herr Weber gave an embarrassed smile. 'I expect it wasn't my day.'

*

'So it's below you to do lifestyle journalism?'

'Below my potential.' Jonas opened another can of beer and

held it to his lips. A few empty ones lay on the kitchen table, all of them crushed in anger. 'I'm producing stuff I'd never choose to consume myself. That's cynical.'

The word that Max Gantmann had used was still preying on his mind.

'But other people do, like parachute makers.'

'But the reason I don't consume the stuff I make is that I feel intellectually superior to it.'

Marina laughed.

'OK, OK, I get it. Maybe the parachute maker does too.' He sounded agitated.

'Do you get aggressive when you've had too much to drink?'

Jonas was embarrassed into silence. Then he attempted a somewhat strained smile. 'I'm sorry, I was expecting so much from this. And now the whole thing's simply collapsed.'

She pushed her hand beneath the table and placed it on his clenched fist. It felt soft and cool.

It was well past midnight. Marina had been at an event. Their original plan was to sleep at their own places, but when she rang him to say goodnight she'd noticed he sounded glum, and so asked, 'Or would you like me to come over?'

'Please,' he'd answered.

After she'd arrived an hour ago, he'd told her all about his misfortune and tried to explain why it bothered him so much.

Now it was her turn to use the word that was bugging him: 'Children's authors write below their level of intellect. Don't you think that's cynical too?'

Jonas thought about it. 'No, you can't compare the two. People like me provide fodder for the basest instincts: voyeurism, gossip-mongering, sensationalism, schadenfreude, envy and so on.'

'And that's cynical?'

'It is if you do it while laughing up your sleeve.'

'Is that what you do?'

'We all do it. You can't work on that sort of stuff and be serious about it. You have to keep your distance. It would be unbearable otherwise.'

'What about those journalists who are on the same level as their audience?'

'Well, they can't do it.'

'Why not?'

'They're too stupid.'

Marina laughed. 'Now that's *really* cynical.'

'You see?'

'How long have you been doing this?'

'Video journalism?'

'Working below your potential?'

'Eight years.'

Marina got up, placed her palms on his temples and kissed him on the lips. 'Then it's high time that something changed.'

'What?'

'Either continue doing what you're doing but with fun and conviction. Or do something else.'

Part Two

1

'I'M SURE IT WAS a person. It had a face.' The tall young man was pale and flustered. He looked down at the conductress, who turned to the camera and told him curtly, 'Please stop that.'

The camera jigged about, then Jonas's hand appeared in the picture, holding something up to the conductress. She nodded and turned away. The camera followed her through a full carriage.

An elderly lady looked at the conductress inquisitively, swiftly turning away when she noticed the camera. Two teenagers were staring at an iPad and didn't look up when Jonas passed them. A businessman with a laptop asked, 'Is this going to take long?' A young lady in a green skiing jacket was on the phone. Four middle-aged men had large cans of beer between their knees and were plonking cards down onto the small collapsible table. A man in a dark suit with red hair spiked up with gel was dozing. A woman was shielding her eyes from the light of the carriage with both hands and staring into the darkness of the tunnel.

The conductress passed through the automatic sliding door into the vestibule, where the train door was ajar. She opened it fully and descended the two steps, followed by the camera. The picture went dark and then became brighter when the sensor adjusted to the different levels of light in the tunnel. The camera zoomed in as far as the lens would allow on a bundle, although it was impossible to say for certain what it was.

Cut. He stopped the video.

Jonas had taken out the material he'd filmed three months earlier in the intercity train and was viewing it. Marina was right: it was high time he changed something in his life. That he stopped seeing his career as just an interim solution until he could realise his great project. He finally had to admit to himself that he'd abandoned faith in *Montecristo* long ago, and instead focus his ambition on what he was doing.

He planned to have a transitional period during which he continued covering lifestyle and celebrity stories for Highlife, but focusing on intelligent, quality reportage. And rather than be discouraged by setbacks such as the banknote affair, he'd just move on to the next topic. Which for him was the 'customer incident' project.

He started the video again and began selecting the most interesting statements from the passengers in the restaurant car.

An older man with a red face and blond hair, his tie at half-mast: 'This must be the tenth time it's happened to me in six years of commuting. I get the feeling it's on the increase.'

The man opposite him, ring of grey hair, pale, featureless face and thick hearing-aid glasses: 'I think it's plain rude to kill yourself like that. There are other ways, ones that don't ruin the evenings of a few hundred non-depressives.'

A heavily made-up woman in her late thirties, black jacket,

white shawl-collar blouse: 'It's terrible to think that someone's lying there squashed.'

The Tamil waiter with plaster freshly applied to his forehead: 'The Swiss enjoy such a good life; it must be unbearable.'

An overweight man – Jonas recognised that he'd sat next to him on the journey – glancing up from his laptop: 'Film if you like but I'm not giving a statement.'

The camera panned down the carriage. The atmosphere was muted, with just the murmur of hushed voices.

A tall, slim man in a business suit got up from his table, came towards the camera, filling the screen, and walked past. The camera followed him. He stopped beside the fat man and asked something.

Jonas wound back and increased the volume. Now it was intelligible: 'Have you seen Paolo?'

The fat man: 'Wasn't he sitting with you?'

'His phone rang and he went out to take the call. But he never came back.'

Jonas also had to play the fat man's answer back twice: 'Maybe he's the customer incident.'

Jonas made a note to provide subtitles in both cases. Also for the final word that the man looking for Paolo uttered as he returned to his seat, shaking his head: 'Arsehole.'

Jonas moved the clip to the folder containing the others he intended to use.

Had Paolo really been the customer incident?

Opening his browser, Jonas searched the death announcements between 20 and 30 September for Basel and the surrounding area. He came across a short notice published on 23 September: 'On 19 September Paolo Contini left us unexpectedly. In deepest sorrow, Barbara Contini-Hubacher, Mia and Reto.'

That very evening Jonas decided to take a trip on the 17.30 intercity to Basel.

*

If the 16.08 from Chur was on time, there were six minutes to wait on platform eleven before travelling on to Basel on the 17.34. The regulars from the buffet car arrived extra early to be amongst the first to push their way past the passengers getting off and make a dash for their seats.

But if the train was delayed, as now, the throng on that section of the platform where the buffet car stopped was so large that they risked losing their regular places. To occasional passengers like Jonas Brand.

He stood nervously with his camera rucksack and kitbag on the cold platform, keeping in his sights the overweight man he was going to stick to as soon as the train stopped.

The announcements came over the tannoy in that same sing-song tone he recalled from his childhood, which had never failed to stir feelings of wanderlust.

He recognised some of the individuals who'd appeared in the footage he'd taken. There was the woman with too much make-up, who'd been troubled by the idea that someone lay squashed under the train. And the tall thin man who'd asked the fat one where Paolo was. The two men were ignoring each other.

The arrival of the delayed intercity was announced, leading to a commotion on the platform. The waiting passengers picked their luggage off the ground, put away their free newspapers or stubbed out cigarettes,

Jonas stayed close to the overweight man; he'd know how to secure a seat.

The train slowed and the buffet car got closer, coming to a stop almost precisely where the man was expecting it. At the very last moment he took a few steps in the other direction, placing himself not by the door of the buffet car but by that of the adjacent carriage. It opened and passengers started alighting. After waiting for three people to get off, the fat man said loudly and clearly, 'Sorry, I've forgotten something!' before forcing his way on. Jonas followed him, passing irate passengers who grumbled, 'Oi!' and 'Let people off first!'

The man stood at the door connecting to the buffet car and waited until the last passengers had exited before storming in and sitting down at the first two-person table. A rear-facing seat.

'Is this seat free?' Jonas asked, stowing his bags on the luggage rack without waiting for an answer.

In less than a minute every seat in the buffet car was full. Mostly with regular customers, those who'd got in first having reserved places for the stragglers.

The train pulled away and by the time they'd reached Schlieren most were already nursing their drink, which the waiter – Padman was on duty again – had brought them without asking.

In front of the fat man was a laptop, beside that a bottle of Féchy. Jonas waited for him to look up from the screen, but in vain. Even when the conductor came past, he simply held out his season ticket without averting his gaze from the computer. And so, after showing his own ticket, Jonas asked, 'Would you mind if I interrupt you?'

The man scowled as he looked up. 'I would rather,' he muttered.

'My name's Jonas Brand. I'm a video journalist. I don't imagine you'd remember, but three months ago the two of us sat at this very table when there was an accident.'

'You were the chap with the camera.'

'Exactly.' He offered his hand. 'Jonas Brand.'

The man took it reluctantly. 'Kägi,' he muttered.

'I'm doing a reportage about the incident. You might be able to help me.'

'In what way?'

'By answering a few questions.'

'How long will it take? I've got work to do.'

'Just a few minutes.'

'But no filming.'

'I'm a video journalist.'

The fat man gave a shrug of regret and returned to his laptop.

'OK, we'll do it without the camera. But can I record it?'

'No, written notes only.'

Jonas took a notebook and biro from his breast pocket. 'When the train was in the tunnel, you asked an acquaintance of yours whether he'd seen a man called Paolo. You replied that maybe he'd been the customer incident. Were you being serious?'

'No, but I was right.'

'Paolo Contini? Around that time a death announcement was published in Basel with that name.'

'Precisely. It's thanks to him we were delayed.'

'How did you know him?'

'He was a work colleague.'

'May I ask what job you do?'

'Banker,' he said with defiance.

'Does anyone know why he took his own life?'

'Maybe someone does. Not me.'

Jonas noted down these unproductive answers with exaggerated effort. 'Do you know how old he was?'

'Around forty, I guess.'

'He had two children.'

'You know more than I do, then.'

'It was in the death announcement.'

'I don't read death announcements.'

'But surely you chat to work colleagues when things like this happen?'

'We used to chat, when they still had the old trading floor. Nowadays no one has time to talk. Is that all?'

Jonas snapped shut his notebook. 'Thanks very much.'

'If you want to know any more you'd be better off talking to that chap over there,' he said, indicating the tall, thin man who was sitting a few tables away. 'He knew Paolo well. I think they were friends.'

'Thanks for the tip. What's his name?'

'Heinzmann. Jack Heinzmann.'

*

Jack Heinzmann was far more forthcoming than his overweight colleague, Kägi. Jonas went up to his table, introduced himself and explained what it was all about. Heinzmann suggested they meet at his place an hour after the train got in and gave Jonas the address.

Now they were sitting by the fire in his penthouse. Heinzmann had changed for the camera and opened a bottle of wine. 'Are you married?' he asked as they clinked glasses.

'Divorced.'

'Me too. Any children?'

'No, thank God.'

'I do. Thank God. I have them every weekend.'

Jonas had put the camera on his shoulder rig and installed the small LED light. He wanted to film the report in the same style as the material he'd taken on the train: simple and improvised.

'What do you want to know?' Heinzmann asked.

'I happened to be in the buffet car when Paolo Contini jumped from the train in the tunnel, and I started filming after the emergency brake. I'd really like to accompany the footage with commentaries from you and other passengers. About how you felt at the time and afterwards when it became apparent that someone had died. What you thought of Herr Contini. I'd like to speak to his widow too. I'm looking to produce the story of a suicide and the portrait of a victim.'

Heinzmann nodded thoughtfully. 'Maybe you'll get to the bottom of why he did it.'

'Did he not leave a suicide note?'

'Nothing. And there's no reason why he should have taken his own life. In fact there were heaps of reasons not to. Paolo was the star of the trading floor. He was happily married and had two children he was besotted with – five and seven. No one in his situation kills themselves.'

'But sometimes traders lose massive sums through speculation.'

'Paolo didn't.'

'How can you be so sure?'

'I'd know. The whole bank would know – no, the whole industry. Certainly after his death at least. No, no; there's no reason at all.'

'He was sitting at your table in the buffet car. And then? Tell us what happened.'

'Then his mobile rang, he excused himself and went outside to take the call.'

'And never came back.'

'Exactly. And shortly after that the train came to an emergency stop in the tunnel.'

'Was he in any way different on this journey, downcast, preoccupied? In retrospect can you think of any clues suggesting that he was about to take his own life?'

'Nothing.'

'Could it have been an accident?'

'What sort of accident? That he mistakenly fell out of the door? When the train's moving you have to pull the emergency bolt to open it.'

'A crime, then?'

'You mean someone opened the door and shoved him out?'

'That sort of thing.'

'Paolo was very popular; he didn't have any enemies.'

'So you're saying it *was* suicide?'

'It seems as if we're going to have to come to terms with the idea.'

'What does his widow say?'

'Wouldn't you rather ask her yourself?'

'Do you think she'd be prepared to give an interview?'

'I'll call her if you like.'

Jonas stopped filming and took the camera off his shoulder. 'Great. When?'

'Now.'

*

Barbara Contini looked as if she was in her mid-thirties. She had straight black hair, sad brown eyes and jolly freckles. She'd agreed to an interview straightaway, and an hour later welcomed the two men into her small terraced house on the outskirts of the city. From the way in which she greeted Jack Heinzmann, Jonas concluded that the two of them knew each other well.

She spoke quietly because the children were asleep, and took them into a small living room full of designer furniture and children's toys. 'After my husband's death,' she said, 'we moved here from our large house.'

A picture window gave onto a back garden illuminated by a few spotlights, where there was a slide and sandpit.

'Where should I sit?' Barbara Contini asked.

Jonas plumped for a black leather armchair, which he moved so that the garden was in the background. When the lighting, sound and camera had been set up he asked, 'Is there anything you'd prefer I didn't ask?'

She thought about it. 'You can ask anything you like. I can always decide whether I answer it or not.'

'Frau Contini, do you believe that your husband committed suicide?'

'No.'

'Why not?'

'Because he was happy.'

'So how did he fall off the train?'

'Someone pushed him.'

'Why?'

'I don't know.'

'Do you believe that someone undid the emergency bolt, opened the door and pushed him out?'

'I think that someone undid the emergency bolt, opened the door, called him and asked to meet him in the vestibule. And when he got there that person pushed him out.'

'So it was someone he knew?'

'Or someone who knew someone he knew.'

'Do you have any inkling who that might be?'

'Number withheld. That was his last call.' She wanted to continue talking but her voice failed and she covered her eyes with her hand. When she'd regained her composure she said, 'His mobile was still intact.'

'Shall we stop for a bit?'

'It's OK.'

'What do the police say?'

'Suicide.'

'Did they follow up your theory?'

'No.'

'Why not?'

'I've been asking myself that question. I've been asking it for three months now, but can't come up with any answer.'

'And the police?'

'Suicide, suicide, suicide.'

'And you say your husband's behaviour was totally normal that day.'

'Not totally normal. He was happy; he hadn't been on such good form for ages. If he'd been totally normal I'd have had fewer doubts.'

'Sorry, I don't understand.'

'Beforehand he was stressed. Worried. He was often like that; it's normal in his job. Isn't it, Jack?'

Jonas panned over to Heinzmann. 'Working on the trading floor is stressful. We have to take risks. Often we come home in the evening and don't know till the next morning whether the last thing we did the previous day turned out well.'

'But in the week before his death he was relaxed.' Jonas panned back to the widow. 'As if a burden had been lifted from his shoulders.'

'Do you have any idea what sort of burden?'

'We never talked about his job. I don't understand anything about financial markets. But I could always sense when work was weighing down on him.'

'And this wasn't the case.'

'Quite the opposite. Like I said, he was happy.'

Jonas switched off the camera and thanked her.

'I hope it leads to something,' Frau Contini said.

He must have looked slightly baffled, for she added, 'I mean I hope it encourages the police not to close the case. Or to open it again if they have already closed it.'

'To be honest, that wasn't the aim of my reportage. I just wanted to present the background of this tragedy I happened to be a witness to.'

'But now it's taken a different turn, hasn't it?'

'A very different one,' Jonas replied.

*

He was sitting in a virtually empty regional train to Olten, on the phone to Marina. They had stopped at a signal just before Liestal. Outside it was sleeting heavily. Three drunk army recruits staggered through the carriage, leaving a fug of beer and tobacco in their wake.

'It can happen,' she said. 'Occasionally people just kill themselves out of the blue, without any warning or signs.'

'I'm more familiar with the opposite: people who keep threatening suicide but never do it.'

She giggled. 'I was stuck with one of those once upon a time.'

'You can tell me about it when you tell me the story of your life.'

'On the day when we're both off at the same time. If that ever happens with our jobs.'

The train pulled away. He looked at his watch. 'I can be with you in three-quarters of an hour.'

'We'll have time to talk, then.'

He laughed. 'And afterwards?'

'There isn't any afterwards.'

He laughed once more. 'Is this telephone sex?'

'Telephone foreplay.'

The train stopped at Liestal. A man got on. A few melting snowflakes glistened on his wet hair, and the shoulders of his woollen coat were also damp in places and dotted white. He looked around the sparsely occupied carriage, took off his coat and sat in the row of two beside Jonas.

'Are you still there? What happened to the foreplay?'

Jonas lowered his voice. 'I can't continue; I've got company.'

'Doesn't bother me.'

'Well, it does me.'

*

'Please take a seat,' the elderly man at reception said, picking up the phone.

Jonas was in the building that housed GCBS's trading floor. He had an appointment with its boss, Hans Bühler.

Setting his gear down on a couple of chairs, he stood beside it.

Five minutes later a woman of around forty in a business suit came up to him, smiling, introduced herself as 'Hofstettler' and showed him into a small meeting room.

Jonas peered around the windowless room.

'Are we going to be filming in here?'

'We shan't be filming,' Hofstettler replied.

'But I had a different arrangement with Herr Bühler,' Jonas protested.

'Herr Bühler sends his apologies. If you'd gone via me you'd have saved yourself the trouble. I'm the company's media spokesperson.'

'What's the problem?'

Like Brand, Hofstettler was still standing beside the meeting table, showing no signs of offering him a seat. 'First, it's company policy not to talk to the media about employees who've passed away, as a mark of respect. Secondly, the television companies know nothing about this project.'

'I'm a freelance journalist; I offer editors my finished pieces.'

'I know you're a freelancer. For Highlife in particular.'

'For Highlife amongst *others*,' Jonas corrected.

But all he could do was pick up his gear again and beat a retreat.

*

That same afternoon he had a meeting with the Basel district police in Liestal, on whose territory Paolo Contini had met his death. Jonas had contacted the press office and told them he was compiling a report on the subject of 'railway suicides'. A friendly sounding man had immediately given him an appointment.

He went by car. The weather had turned warmer and drier, and he had no desire to fight over a seat again on the way back with all his gear.

Jonas parked in the visitors' area in front of the police building and signed in at reception.

He didn't meet the person he was scheduled to see here either. After he'd waited almost a quarter of an hour in a small room, a wiry, tanned, plain-clothed officer came in and handed Jonas his card. 'Sergeant Jacob Schneebeli, S.D. officer'

'What does "S.D." stand for?' Jonas asked.

'Special duties.'

Sergeant Schneebeli's special duty evidently consisted of fobbing off Jonas Brand. Although Jonas made out that he was interested in train suicides in general, the policeman didn't appear surprised when he brought up the Contini case.

'Listen, Herr Brand. Out of respect for victims and their families, the Basel district police always urges the media to exercise restraint in their reporting of such cases. So I'm not going to discuss with you on camera a name which you can only have learned via an indiscretion.'

The lifestyle journalist in Jonas would have usually backed down at this point, but the investigative journalist steeled himself and asked, 'Is it certain that we're dealing with a suicide here?'

The sergeant briefly clenched his jaw muscles. 'Well, more certain than your break-in was a break-in and your mugging actually a mugging.'

Jonas was lost for words. Before he found them again the special duties sergeant asked, 'Any further questions?'

*

On the short way back from the entrance of police headquarters to the visitors' parking spaces he already noticed that it had turned colder, and when he reached the A22 the thermometer on his dashboard read minus two degrees. A grey sky was accelerating the dusk. Shortly before the Oberfrick turnoff it began to snow. A light-grey film soon appeared on the tarmac and the cars in front left behind dark tracks.

Reducing his speed, Jonas cursed himself for not having taken the train.

The sergeant had been in touch with the Zürich police to make inquiries about him, and been informed about the break-in and mugging. They also told him that there was doubt over the statements Jonas had given.

Was it normal for police to make inquiries about interviewers in advance? Was it even legal? Were police authorities in different cantons allowed to exchange information about someone if they were a victim, not a criminal? Or did they even doubt *that*?

Jonas put a CD into the car stereo: Leonard Cohen, 'Old Ideas'. The perfect music to accompany his mood and this lonely drive on a snowy motorway.

The tail lights of the cars in front were blurred by the veil of falling snow. The speed of the convoy had now fallen to below eighty km/h. Even at their fastest setting, the windscreen wipers were fighting a losing battle.

All of a sudden the brake lights of a few cars further ahead stained the shroud of snow red. The cars behind reacted. Brake!

The Passat swerved twice and came to a halt just behind the car in front. Jonas braced his neck back against the head rest and waited for the impact from the car following him. But the driver behind managed to avoid a collision too. In the rear-view mirror Jonas watched him swerve out of the way at the last moment, finishing up beside the Passat, his nose level with Jonas's back seats.

Now he heard the persistent hooting of two cars, and in the snow he could see the reflection of hazard lights ahead. He'd become involved in a pile-up.

The first doors started to open, a few drivers carefully got out and trudged forwards.

His heart thumping, Jonas stayed where he was, clenching the wheel and staring into the chaos in front of him, which now rapidly filled with life.

The two hooters were still blaring away at their different pitches, but now Jonas could hear people shouting too.

It took a while before he realised he could go out with his

camera. He walked along the pile-up until he came to the front, where he saw a Range Rover with a seriously damaged horsebox. A man in riding boots and a crying woman were trying to open the jammed door of the trailer. 'It's alright, Dally,' the woman sobbed, 'we're coming. It's alright.'

Behind this stood a delivery van with a dented cab. An ashen-faced man was sitting on the hard shoulder. He was bleeding from a cut above the eye, saying over and over again, 'The horsebox brake lights weren't working; the police will find that out. They weren't working. I couldn't see that they were braking.'

Next came a Golf that was a write-off. An agitated group of people was crowded round it, attempting to free someone from the car.

Jonas aimed his camera on the scene. Suddenly he noticed he felt sick. Dismounting the camera from his shoulder, he headed back to the car. But he had to throw up by the side of the road before getting there.

Maybe he ought to stick with lifestyle journalism after all.

*

The place where Max Gantmann spent the second largest amount of time was the Schönacker, a local pub just a few steps from his flat. It was where he ate his three meals of the day, and spent the evenings and weekends playing cards with the landlord and a handful of regulars.

The Schönacker was renowned for the generosity of its portions. Here you could get schnitzels that spilled over the rim of the plate, sausages so long they had to be served on oval dishes and pork chops served with such ample volumes of vegetables that these needed a plate all to themselves.

Another of the Schönacker's features was its smoking lounge. Although, by being only a third of the size of the entire premises, it didn't fall foul of the law, the landlord, a militant smoker, had installed a small self-service buffet in the two-thirds where smoking was not permitted, to satisfy the minimum legal requirements. The smoking lounge was the actual restaurant with fifteen tables, smoke and gargantuan portions.

Jonas met Max there for lunch and told him about Paolo Contini. And about how he'd been rebuffed by both the bank and police.

Max listened to the story without exhibiting much interest, his attention focused on a large, fatty Waadtland sausage and potato salad.

When Jonas had finished Max asked, 'What about the banknote story? Why did you drop it?'

'It fizzled out into nothing.'

Max pushed his empty plate to one side and lit a cigarette. 'How so?'

'Trebler, the numismatist, discovered that one of the notes was a forgery.'

'But you said that the bank as well as Dillier confirmed that they were both genuine.'

'They were wrong. Trebler says it's a good forgery, but a forgery all the same. He had a money scanner, but he'd had his doubts even beforehand.'

Gantmann shook his head. 'Strange. The bank and Dillier must have machines to check notes too.'

'But they didn't use them, or at least I didn't see them using them.'

'They didn't use them because they were quite certain that the two notes were genuine. And Dillier is the expert. Surely he would have made use of every opportunity to prove that one of the two was counterfeit. If he'd had even the slightest doubt he wouldn't have admitted to you that they were both genuine.'

The waiter brought Max another beer and cleared away his empty plate. He took a sip and, without wiping the froth from his lips, said, 'No, Jonas. No, they've been taking you for a ride.'

'What, Trebler?'

Max mulled this over. 'No, I don't think so. Trebler's a man of integrity. He's got a reputation to lose. He can't pass off a genuine note as a forgery, certainly not on camera.'

Max pondered again. 'Where did you keep the notes?'

'In a highly secure place.'

'Where?'

'In my safety deposit box at the bank.'

Max snorted into his beer. 'Not, by any chance, the bank where you asked them to check the notes?'

'Yes, GCBS. Do you think…? But you need two keys – they've got one, I've got the other.'

'My God, how naïve can you be? You show them the two notes; they confirm that both are genuine. Then someone breaks into your flat, rummaging through everything. Then you're attacked in the street and robbed. And then you go and put the banknotes in a deposit box which they've got a key to!'

'Only one.'

'So what if the owner of the deposit box dies? Do you think they blast the lock open? Obviously they've got a duplicate of your key.'

'Are you saying they switched the note?'

'It wouldn't surprise me.'

'But why should they? After all, the duplicate numbering isn't the bank's problem.'

'That's what you'd think.' Max removed the cigarette from

his mouth for the time it took him to take a large gulp of beer. '*But*... when you had the break-in and you were mugged, the printing firm didn't yet know about the two notes. The bank did, however.'

The waiter brought a portion of apple cake with crème fraîche and put it in front of Gantmann. Placing his half-smoked cigarette in the ashtray, he started eating at once. 'The bank wants to prevent the matter from going public.'

'Why?'

'That's what I don't know yet. But one thing I do know.' He shovelled a piece of cake into his mouth; a blob of crème fraîche stuck to his top lip. 'They succeeded.'

Jonas sighed. 'But they won't with the dead trader story.'

'That story's too "popular" for my tastes.'

'It wasn't before I spoke to the guy's colleague and widow. It was a reportage about the reasons for a suicide to which I happened to be a witness.'

'But it becomes so sensationalist. You have "Suicide or murder?" in bold letters.'

'Sometimes stories write themselves.'

'Those who tell them shouldn't allow that to happen.' Max gestured to the waiter to bring two more beers,

'Mine's almost full,' Jonas protested.

'It'll have gone flat. By all means do the suicide story, but I'd dispense with the murder-or-suicide question if I were you. The buffet car full of commuters, which suddenly comes to a stop in the tunnel because one of the commuters has jumped off the train, is terrifying enough. I would take the footage from the tunnel, the reactions of the passengers and their statements before they knew that the dead person was someone they sat in the buffet car with twice a day. And now I'd ask those same people how they reacted when they did find out, and what they... what's his name, Conti?'

'Contini?'

'What they thought of Contini. I'd leave out the reason for the suicide.'

Jonas was unconvinced. 'Why won't the police say anything about it?'

'Their refusal to release information on suicides to the media on ethical grounds seems perfectly plausible to me.'

'How about the break-in and mugging?'

'That's what the police are like. They made informal enquiries to find out what their colleagues know about you.'

'Are they allowed to do that?'

'That's another story. Don't lose your focus.'

'What about the bank?'

'Same thing. They're being discreet for ethical reasons. Their PR department has made some routine internal enquiries about you and come up with the duplicate serial numbers. Which brings us back to the really big story here.'

The two beers arrived and Max waved away Jonas's half-empty flat glass. Both of them took a sip.

'If it wasn't a murder,' Jonas said, 'then there's still the question of why he committed suicide. His widow says he was nervous and gloomy for weeks on end. Then, in the week before he died he was suddenly happy and relaxed. As if a huge burden had been lifted from his shoulders. Maybe it's got something to do with his job. Maybe he lost money speculating.'

'So what would the reason be for the sudden change of mood a week before his death?'

'Maybe because he'd made up his mind to kill himself.'

This question made Max pause for thought. He took another gulp of his beer, rested his heavy head on his hand and finally said, 'Perhaps you could pursue this line after all.'

2

ALTHOUGH THERE WAS NO snow on the ground, that Friday afternoon had a distinct Christmas feel to it. A grey blanket of cloud lay thickly over the city, sucking up so much light that the festive illuminations on Bahnhofstrasse were already sparkling way before dusk.

The passers-by laden with presents thronged along cold pavements and into cosy shops with a mixture of anticipation and last-minute panic.

Jonas, who had totally ignored Christmas since his divorce, had been infected by the festive hustle and bustle, and was out to buy a present for Marina. It had to be something small that he could hide in his coat pocket when they met up later. Marina, who knew nothing of Jonas's Christmas abstinence, was also present-buying, and they'd arranged to meet at six in Tail-Cock, a fancy new bar in the old town,

Jonas was useless at buying presents. He'd always asked his ex-wife what she wanted, and whenever she'd put the same question to him he'd rarely been able to come up with an answer.

121

Perfume was a small gift, but he didn't know which one she wore, and it was too risky to pick one at random. A silk scarf would also fold into a neat small packet, but he felt this intervention in her personal style was too hazardous as well.

Which is why he ended up in a shop selling antique jewellery.

The security man on the door looked him up and down suspiciously as if he intended to give him a body search there and then. The sales staff ignored him as they were all busy with customers.

Jonas went from cabinet to cabinet, studying the glittering items on offer. He stopped beside a simple coral necklace made up of around forty deep-red, pea-sized pearls, with a clasp made from an oval piece of coral about three times the size, set in gold.

'Can I help you?' a voice behind him asked.

Pointing to the necklace, Brand asked, 'How much is that?' Like a farmer up in town for the day, he thought.

'It's wonderful, isn't it?' The sales assistant opened the cabinet, picked up the necklace and slid it into his hand. It felt heavy and cool. A small price tag was stuck behind the lock. It said '900.00'. No – '9,000.00'.

The sales assistant could see that it was too expensive for him. 'What sort of budget do you have?' she asked.

'I don't know, but that's beyond it.'

Her smile was sympathetic. 'But it's got to be coral?'

He was going to say, 'Not necessarily,' but instead plumped for, 'Yes, if possible,' so as to avoid looking completely clueless.

The sales assistant took him to the counter and brought out a satin-lined tray from a drawer. It was divided into compartments containing bracelets, one of which was coral. It was smaller than the necklace and lighter in colour. The clasp was a miniature version of the one on the necklace.

She pushed up the heavy golden bracelet she was wearing and put the coral one around her wrist, which was slender like Marina's. 'Thirty corals,' she informed him. And when he failed to ask the question, she gave him the answer unsolicited: 'One thousand eight hundred.'

'Why so much cheaper?'

'Size, colour. And the other one is Mediterranean coral. You don't find it any more; it's extinct. This here is from Asia.'

Only in comparison to the price of the necklace could Jonas find 1,800 francs a small sum. In comparison to what he'd intended to spend, however, it was still a fortune. But he was not stingy and it was approaching six o'clock.

So he whipped out his credit card and watched the manicured hands of the shop assistant make up a charming little Christmas package.

The narrow alley that was home to Tail-Cock was full of people. A Salvation Army Choir was causing congestion. Jonas decided to take a detour via the side street he'd just come down. Turning around, he went back.

He passed a man he'd seen somewhere before. He had red, spiked up hair.

*

They were not the only ones to have hit upon the idea of meeting in Tail-Cock after Christmas shopping; the bar was rammed. It smelled of cold coats and perfumes. Jonas stayed at the entrance with all the rest of the people waiting for a seat to become free, and scoured the bar for Marina.

Carefree laughter rose time and again from the general hubbub. And occasionally, when the clamour subsided momentarily, leaving an eerie silence, Jonas could hear Nat

King Cole crooning Christmas songs in the background.

For some strange reason he thought about the man with the spiky red hair again. He remembered where he'd seen him before: in the footage he'd taken on the intercity. Weird coincidence.

He caught sight of Marina. She'd been hidden behind a few people who were now moving towards a table that looked as if it would soon be free.

She sat at the bar, deep in thought, beside her a second stool covered in bags and her coat. The reddish light softened her oriental features even further.

A man approached her, pointed to the laden barstool and asked a question. Marina replied, shaking her head.

'Excuse me,' Jonas said, pushing his way through the crowd towards Marina. Taking her in his arms he gave her a kiss.

This must be how it felt when I used to be happy, he thought.

*

The coral bracelet suited Marina, especially now it was all she was wearing.

They were lying in bed in an oversized chalet. Through the window they could just about make out other chalets through the curtain of rain on a grey afternoon.

They were in Gstaad, where the agency had assigned Marina to look after Theophania Tau, who was appearing at a ball on the Sunday evening. The event was being sponsored by a jeweller who was one of the agency's important clients.

'Are you going to come with me, or do you only do serious pieces now?' she'd asked him.

Jonas had said yes and even persuaded the Highlife editorial office to pay his expenses, as they hadn't got wind of the fact that Theophania was coming to Gstaad.

They'd left on Saturday with the plan of spending a nice day in the mountains, maybe taking a cable car up to the top and having a walk followed by a hearty lunch on the sun terrace of a mountain restaurant.

But as they drove, dark clouds gathered and it started raining in the Simmental. They managed to make a nice day of it nonetheless, only without the cable car, walk or sun terrace.

Theophania was due to land at the tiny airport in Saanen the following day at one p.m. At ten o'clock, however, the news came through that take-off in London had been delayed due to poor weather.

They'd stayed in bed, waiting for the weather to improve. But it steadily worsened, the rain became heavier and a Föhn storm had blown up, closing the airport. At three o'clock disaster struck for the sponsor: Theophania cancelled.

Jonas informed Highlife and promised instead to take some footage in the Gstaad Palace, where the ball was being held, and obtain some reaction to the superstar's cancellation.

*

For someone of his standing, William Just was dressed rather casually: cords, cashmere houndstooth sports jacket, striped shirt and silk cravat in an open collar.

He was sitting in one of the deep armchairs in a corner of the Palace lobby. The waiter had brought him a port.

At the neighbouring table sat two Russian families. They'd drawn up extra chairs, were drinking champagne and talking at the tops of their voices.

Just didn't mind; he was about to have a little chat which

was not for anyone else's ears, a chat with someone he could be seen together with, but by no means had to: Konrad Stimmler, President of the Swiss Banking Supervisory Authority, SBSA. It was not a complete coincidence that Stimmler, too, was spending the holidays in the Saanenland and they'd arranged to meet here for an informal aperitif.

Just had arrived slightly early. For tactical reasons – it allowed him to select the place and his chair, and he became the host rather than visitor.

A bar-room pianist was playing cocktail music with slightly too much electronic accompaniment. Just had placed himself where he couldn't be seen from the entrance, and thus he couldn't see who came into the lobby either. But he'd told the head waiter that he was expecting a guest.

From the outset it had been Just's view that one mustn't give a man of Stimmler's professional and intellectual competence the authority to stick his oar into bank affairs. But there were advantages, too, with the choice of Stimmler. Just knew him from when they'd worked together at the bank many years ago. They'd both embarked on their careers there and providence had quickly decreed that Just should become his boss, soon progressing so far ahead of Stimmler that the two no longer even saw each other.

But when Stimmler sought to re-establish contact after his appointment to the SBSA, Just could detect that the man retained some of the deep respect from the old days, and responded with friendly condescension.

He'd kept up this patronising attitude even after it became impossible to stop the SBSA getting wind of the matter and Stimmler had him over a barrel. Although the SBSA president had enjoyed having the great William Just at his mercy, his behaviour became almost more obsequious than before. He missed the opportunity to exploit his power over Just, and soon the two of them were back in the same boat.

The head waiter took Stimmler to the table. Just hauled himself out of his chair and feigned exaggerated delight at seeing him again.

The waiter helped Stimmler out of his bulky, dark-brown sheepskin jacket. Underneath he was wearing an ice-blue, ski suit, which was clearly brand new. Another reason why Just didn't want to be seen with Stimmler.

'Straight from the piste, eh?' he smiled. Stimmler gave an embarrassed grin in return.

The SBSA president ordered a beer, but not a cold one, and once more the CEO of GCBS felt vindicated in his judgement that the man had no style or class.

Just launched into some small talk and, before he was able to broach the real subject of their conversation, he noticed a tall, shaven-headed man with a video camera on his shoulder, making his way slowly between the tables, filming the bar and the guests.

Recognising the man at once from the television clips his special team had shown him, Just grabbed his glass and tried to hold it so that his hand covered his chin, mouth and nose. 'Don't turn round,' he whispered. 'Jonas Brand is back there filming us.'

'You mean the man with the serial numbers?' Stimmler gasped. He turned round and stared straight into the video journalist's lens. He, too, quickly lifted his glass to cover the bottom half of his face.

For a moment it looked as if the boss of the Bank Supervisory Authority and the boss of the big bank were raising a toast to the television camera.

*

On the screen in his editing area he was playing the scene from the Gstaad Palace bar, frame by frame. He identified the man in the jacket straightway: William Just, the CEO of GCBS with the double-digit million bonus.

He also recognised the man in the ski suit, but he had to Google him to work out who it was: the president of the SBSA, the regulatory body that kept a sharp eye on the banks. Maybe he could make a little allusion to this in the Highlife piece.

The rest of the footage wasn't exactly spectacular either: a variety of comments about Theophania's cancellation. One from the hotel management, one from the boss of the jewellery shop, one from the lead guitarist of her band and some from guests as they arrived. The best response was that of a young couple from fashionable society, who turned on their heels as soon as they heard she'd cancelled.

Jonas compiled a three-minute report, mixed with images of the rain-swept and storm-lashed airstrip, of horse-drawn carriages with guests in capes and of the gables of chalets decorated with chains of lights. He included an amusing comment from a carriage driver. Jonas asked him if it was obligatory to decorate chalets with lights and he replied, 'If everyone does it, then it is a bit obligatory.'

The report concluded with some atmospheric footage from the Palace lobby, including the scene where Just and Stimmler looked as if they were toasting the camera. Accompanied by Brand's witty commentary: 'It was so relaxed that even the CEO of GCBS and the boss of its highest supervisory authority got on famously.'

He'd ended up with a nice little piece that would fit perfectly in a Highlife Christmas special.

Then his thoughts turned again to Contini, the dead trader.

Could there be something to the theory that a great weight had suddenly been lifted from his shoulders because he'd identified suicide as a way out of his crisis? It must have been one hell of a crisis if a young, successful husband and father saw death as the only way out. So maybe he *had* speculated and lost. Lost heavily. But Heinzmann had said that if that were the case the whole bank and the entire industry would have known about it.

He dialled Max's number. After many rings he picked up and said, 'I'm busy, Jonas.'

'This won't take long. If a trader gambles away huge amounts of money, is there any reason for the bank to keep it quiet?'

Max didn't need to think for long. 'Depends on how much and what shape the bank is in. If the loss is massive and the bank's sickly, then yes. Why?'

'Contini. A gigantic loss through speculation could have been a motive. But there's no indication anything like that happened. Maybe the bank hushed it up because its very survival was at stake. And if it hushed the loss up,' Jonas said, the thought coming to him as he spoke, 'this could be an explanation for Contini's relief too.'

Max considered this for a moment. 'Which eliminates the motive for suicide.'

'Precisely.'

The two of them fell silent. Then Jonas asked, 'How could a bank pull that off – hushing up a loss that could have brought it to ruin?'

Once more Max needed a pause for thought. Then he said. 'It would be quite a feat, I must say.'

*

Jack Heinzmann and Jonas Brand were at a round standing table, eating the city's most famous bratwurst.

Jonas had reached Heinzmann on his mobile and requested a meeting as soon as possible. The trader had agreed and suggested this place.

It was lunchtime and a large queue was waiting by the sausage grill. The glazed area at the front was full, but they defended their table with broad elbows.

'I agreed to this meeting at short notice,' Heinzmann began, 'because it's crucial for me to correct a false impression you may have gleaned from our conversation.'

'What false impression?' Jonas asked.

'That I might have my doubts that Paolo committed suicide. You see, I don't.'

'Frau Contini certainly does.'

'You have to understand her. Committing suicide without leaving a note is the most radical way to wilfully abandon your family. It would be easier for Barbara if she knew he hadn't done it himself.'

'I can understand that. Especially if she can't see any sort of motive.'

'It's hard for all of us.'

Jonas dipped his bratwurst into the mustard and took a bite. Heinzmann did likewise.

When Jonas had finished swallowing he said, 'But is there really no motive?'

Heinzmann looked at him expectantly. 'Can you see one?'

'Is it possible that a massive trading loss was discovered prior to his death?'

Heinzmann's reaction was rather stilted. 'Not that I'm aware of.'

'And you would have been aware of it had there been one?'

'Not necessarily. It depends where the loss originated from. Are you suggesting that Paolo killed himself because he'd made enormous losses?'

'It's a possibility, isn't it?'

'I've already told you, I'd have known about it.'

'Maybe steps were taken to ensure you didn't find out.'

'Impossible. Some of us would have found out.'

'Including you?'

Heinzmann bit off another piece of sausage and ate it. Then he said vaguely, 'Not necessarily.'

'Who would definitely know?'

'Bühler. The boss.'

Heinzmann dropped the subject and ate his sausage. As he left he said, 'Do me a favour, Herr Brand. We've never spoken, OK?'.

*

The sort of journalist that Jonas wanted to become sometimes had to resort to unorthodox methods.

He was searching for a way to interview the head of the trading floor, Hans Bühler, without being put off by the bank's very own dragon, Frau Hofstettler. Jonas found Bühler on Facebook, where he came across a post revealing that he was a member of the seniors team at a handball club. Jonas was fortunate: the club trained every Monday and Thursday at seven pm in the Gelbtal sports hall.

Jonas called the trainer, said he was working on a piece about amateur sport and requested permission to film the training session and put a few questions to some team members.

Now he was standing by the subs bench between two sets of wall bars. His ears reverberated with the sound of footsteps, shouting and balls bouncing; and his nose was met by the odour of sweat, cork and detergent. From time to time he interviewed the players being substituted, as soon as they'd stopped wheezing.

Bühler played right backcourt; Jonas remembered the positions from his childhood when his father sometimes took him to watch handball matches.

The trading floor boss was tall and wiry, with unruly blond hair and a rather idiosyncratic style. 'Pass, pass!' his teammates kept shouting. When he was finally substituted Jonas asked him the same questions he'd put to the others: how long he'd been playing and why he chose a team sport over individual forms of exercise such as jogging or going to the gym.

'It promotes team spirit,' was Bühler's predictable answer.

This gave Jonas the opportunity to ask, 'What job do you do?'

'I run the trading floor of GCBS,' Bühler replied with casual pride.

'Really? In that case I'd like to ask you quite a specific question if you don't mind.'

'If I'm able to answer it,' he replied, adding with a smile, 'And allowed to.'

Jonas took a deep breath. 'Can you explain why Paolo Contini took his own life?'

Bühler froze.

'I mean, life was good for him. Successful, happily married, two sweet children.'

'This is something we're not going to talk about. It's a question of decency. Do you know what that is?'

'Alright, a different question: did GCBS suffer large trading losses last September? I mean really large ones?'

Bühler looked at him frostily. 'I assume you've asked all

your handball-related questions. Regarding the others, please contact our press department.'

Bühler sat on the bench, but was called back onto the court shortly afterwards.

*

They'd got into the habit of meeting at the flat of whoever got home earlier. On 23 December it was Marina.

She sat beside him on the sofa, her feet up on the coffee table, and wearing a comfortable black tracksuit with three stripes. The television was on.

A tray with the leftovers of their supper was on the table too. Both of them were too lazy to take it away.

He'd told her about his encounters with Heinzmann and Bühler. Perhaps, she said, he ought to focus back on the incident rather than the motive. After all, he wasn't an investigative journalist. 'Or is that what you'd like to be?'

'No, but it's what happens in this profession. You're researching something and during your research you stumble upon something else. You can't just then say, I'm not interested, it's off-topic.'

Marina took a sip from her can of beer and nodded.

'Maybe I've stumbled upon something really big.'

'Maybe something too big. Given the way they're all responding to your questions.'

'Maybe.'

Marina hopped through a few channels. 'Aren't you afraid?'

'Of what?'

'Of being gagged.'

'Gagged?' Jonas's mouth froze as if it had just been gagged.

Marina laughed and kept channel hopping until she

happened upon the repeat of the latest Highlife broadcast. A presenter briefly outlined the contents of the programme. The next item but one would be the piece on Gstaad.

They let a report about the inauguration of a fitness studio featuring a whole host of VIPs wash over them, then came the lead-up to the Gstaad piece:

'Yesterday, Gstaad's Palace Hotel hosted its traditional pre-Christmas ball, attended by a host of international celebrities. The climax of the event was an exclusive appearance by Theophania Tau. Jonas Brand will now tell us whether she showed up or not.'

There were the comments about Theophania's cancellation. Hotel management, head of the sponsor firm, lead guitarist, guests as they were arriving. And the young couple from fashionable society who left again immediately.

They saw the images of the rain-swept airstrip, the horses and carriages, the chalets decorated with lights. The report ended with the comment from the carriage-driver: 'If everyone does it, then it is a bit obligatory.'

The scene in which Just and Stimmler looked as if they were toasting the camera was missing.

*

The following morning Jonas arrived at his studio early. It was 24 December and if he wanted to get in contact with anyone it would have to be in the morning. Most people took the afternoon off.

It took him almost two hours to get through to the chief editor of Highlife. She was always either in a meeting or on the phone or not at her desk. No, Jonas kept saying, you can't take a message; I must speak to her personally.

When he finally reached her he was so livid that without even a hello he asked, 'Who applied the pressure: GCBS or the SBSA?'

'Who is that?'

'Jonas, and I want to know at whose request you binned the scene with Just and Stimmler.'

'It was my own decision. It didn't fit. We're not a political programme.'

'If you cut all those scenes from the reports that didn't fit you wouldn't have much of a programme left.'

'Did you want anything else? We're up to our ears in Christmas stress here.'

Jonas wished her happy Christmas stress and hung up in fury! Not a political programme!

He dialled Max's number and told him about the censorship, as he referred to it. 'Can you ask around to see whether there was a call from the bank or the SBSA?'

'I certainly can,' Max said, 'but you can assume that there was one. Maybe even from both parties.'

The next person he telephoned was Barbara Contini. After a number of rings she answered with a quiet 'Hello?'

'Frau Contini?'

'Who is that?'

'Jonas Brand. I came to see you last week. With Herr Heinzmann. Do you remember?'

'Oh yes. How can I help you?'

'I'd like to ask you a few more questions. Is it alright if I come round again?'

'What sort of questions?'

'About your husband's death. About whether it was suicide or not.'

The line went silent. A few moments later she said, 'There's no more to say on the subject. I'm absolutely sure now that it *was* suicide.'

'I see,' Jonas muttered in surprise. 'Have there been new developments?'

'Yes.'

'What?'

'It's personal.'

'Was a suicide note found?'

'Like I said: it's personal. Please don't call me again.' She hung up.

Jonas went into the kitchen and made an espresso. Either the bank had put pressure on the widow or a suicide note *had* actually turned up, or some other proof that he'd killed himself. In any event, the possibility of an accident or the widow's bold theory that it had been murder must now be eliminated.

The question of the motive was still outstanding.

The other issue still outstanding was whether the star trader Paolo Contini had gambled away a fortune at the bank.

He rinsed out his cup, put it on the draining rack and returned to his studio.

There were two new emails in his inbox. Both marked high priority with an exclamation mark.

The first was from a lawyer's office – Nottler & Kauber – containing the scan of a handwritten letter, copied to Karin Hofstettler, GCBS press office, and to the Highlife editorial team.

The lawyers said that this email was by way of advance information and that the attached letter was in the post. The letter stated that Nottler & Kauber's client, the General Confederate Bank of Switzerland, GCBS, would view any further investigation into the tragic demise of their employee, Paolo Contini, as a violation of his and his family's right to privacy, and would take legal action if any of the existing footage were to be broadcast.

The second email was from Jeff Rebstyn.

Rebstyn was a film producer and head of Nembus Productions, one of the country's leading production companies. Nembus was one of the firms to which Jonas had unsuccessfully submitted his *Montecristo* project. Although Rebstyn, like the other production companies, had not rejected the proposal outright, he'd deflected every enquiry with different excuses: too expensive, too derivative, too big for a first directing job.

Rebstyn wrote:

'Dear Jonas,' – he didn't recall them being on first-name terms – 'I know it's very short notice, but if you happen to be free at lunchtime today or can take some time off, then I'd love to invite you to lunch. For a Christmas surprise! Is half twelve in the Silbere Frosch OK? Hope to see you later – Jeff.'

*

The Silbere Frosch was a bit too trendy for Jonas. He'd only been there once, for its opening two years ago, on a job for Highlife which wanted a short feature about the place. The usual celebs had been in attendance, saying the usual things and pulling the usual faces. Even Jonas's piece had become the usual mass-market offering.

Back at the time he hadn't given the restaurant more than a year, but evidently it had got its act in order and since then, probably more down to its location than cuisine, had attracted a healthy mix of guests comprising business people, academics and the in-crowd.

Tablecloths and napkins were white with an embroidered frog, while the heavy stoneware crockery was decorated with a silver frog too – the theme pervaded the entire restaurant, although fortunately the chef possessed sufficient tact to avoid putting it on the menu as a starter.

Jeff Rebstyn was clearly a regular at the Silbere Frosch. The management had reserved a four-person table by the window just for the two of them. He was already sitting there when Jonas, a little early himself, came through the old-fashioned felt curtain with leather trim. Jeff waved at him animatedly, as if it were possible to miss him.

Rebstyn was tall and lean, with a long, narrow head crowned by a shock of white hair. And he always wore a yellow scarf, made from different material depending on the season.

'Excited?' he asked with a smile when Jonas arrived at the table.

Jonas was not someone to show his feelings so easily. Of course he was excited; he was almost bursting with anticipation. After so many years of indifference from all producers, if there was one suddenly wanting to see him urgently, promising a Christmas surprise, it would have been very strange if he hadn't been excited.

'A little,' he admitted, sitting down. Now he noticed the champagne bucket on the table, heightening his excitement even further.

Jeff filled Jonas's glass and replenished his own, which had had a little left in it. Then he raised his glass and waited for Jonas to do the same.

They clinked glasses and drank.

'Go on, ask,' Rebstyn grinned.

'What have we just toasted?'

'*Montecristo*! We're going to make it!'

Jonas could feel the blood coursing into his cheeks. 'Are you being serious?'

'Do I look as if I'm joking?'

Jonas looked at the producer wearing a broad grin. 'To be honest, yes.'

Jeff let out a loud laugh and clinked glasses with Jonas once more. 'I'm laughing because I'm happy for you. For us. It looked for ages as if we had to abandon all hope. But you know I always believed in *Montecristo*.'

Well, you did an excellent job keeping it hidden from me, Jonas thought. But stifling the comment he asked, 'What's brought about this sudden change?'

'Money, of course. As always. You won't believe it, but Moviefonds stumped up the cash.'

'Moviefonds? But they rejected it.'

'It was a close decision. Sometimes they have another think about it.'

Moviefonds was a part state-owned institution which – so the industry thought – distributed funding based on opaque criteria to Swiss film projects with 'international potential', as it said in their statutes. Some of the money came from the coffers of the National Office for the Arts, and some from the arts budgets of a number of unnamed firms. The fund only gave out money at irregular intervals of two, three or more years, but the sums were always generous.

'How much?' Jonas asked.

'One point six.'

'Wow!'

'That means I can unlock other funding – federal, television, City of Zürich etc. Maybe not the entire 3.4 million, but if there's any missing I'll rustle it up. Even if I have to put my hand in my own pocket. Shall we order?' He waved to the waiter, who he called Vittorio, and asked him to bring the menus and top up their glasses.

As Jonas raised his refilled glass to his lips, his hand was trembling. In the few minutes since he'd sat down at this table his life had completely changed. His great dream, which he'd only clung to out of habit, had suddenly come true. He was getting the chance to become what he'd always wanted to be: a filmmaker!

'I'll have what you're having,' he said. 'I'm too excited to choose for myself.'

Rebstyn ordered the lunch menu – stuffed breast of veal with potato puree and brussels sprouts – opened the battered briefcase that was on the chair beside him, took out a folder entitled 'Montecristo (working title)' and said, 'Let's go!'

They weren't the only people to stay in the Silbere Frosch until late that afternoon, but they were the only ones who were working. The others were enjoying a leisurely afternoon before being expected by their families beside the Christmas tree.

Jonas and Jeff – Jonas had already got used to calling Rebstyn by his first name – discussed the key positions on the team – head of production, cameraman, set, costume, script – drew up their ideal cast and worked out a provisional schedule.

Top of their list was researching locations in Thailand, especially Bang Kwang Central Prison, where the lead character languishes for years. The screenplay for these scenes was still pretty vague.

'When could you do that?' Jeff asked.

'Soon,' Jonas replied. 'I've just got to finish one or two jobs, then I'll be ready.'

'What sort of jobs?' Jeff asked with a hint of irritation.

'Reportages. I'm a good way through them.'

'Jonas, making feature films is a full-time job. What am I saying? It's a 150 per cent job. You can't slot them in between reportages. You've got to make a decision.'

'I already have.'

Rebstyn's forehead smoothened out. 'So, when?'

Jonas thought about it.

'Why not between Christmas and New Year? You can take advantage of the time when the entire film business is on holiday and get some good deals. Despite the Moviefonds money, our finances are not unlimited. Do you need a visa for Thailand?'

Jonas shook his head. 'Just a passport, which has to still be for six months on your day of arrival.'

'And yours is?'

Jonas nodded.

'So what are you waiting for?'

*

Marina was spending Christmas Eve with her mother. She was desperate to take Jonas with her, but he'd fought against it tooth and nail. For him, family Christmases were a horror that he'd only been able to avoid since his mother had retired to Tenerife and he'd divorced his wife.

But now he was almost regretting not having gone. Her mother lived in Geneva. Marina was going to spend the night there and come back on Sunday morning at the earliest. He couldn't wait to ring her at least and tell her the sensational news.

But he didn't want to stay at home on his own either, so he went to Cesare's, where every 24 December the hardcore Christmas-haters of the area met and did their best to ignore the festivities.

There was a good crowd at Cesare's. A CD was playing at full volume the winning entries from the San Remo Festival della Canzona Italiana, and the air was thick with the aroma of the house speciality: ossobuco alla Milanese.

Jonas was scouring the place for a seat when a waiter noticed him and motioned him over to a table where one was free. Here it was custom to join someone else's table even if you didn't know them. But he could see from the faces of the three customers at this table – two women and a man – that his presence was regarded as an intrusion.

And Jonas soon realised why. He was together with a couple and a woman whose absent partner or ex-partner was the subject of their conversation. She was knocking back her drinks, hardly touching the ossobuco and permanently on the verge of tears. The two others were trying to comfort her by picking to pieces the man who wasn't there.

Jonas pretended he wasn't listening to anything they were saying, so his presence was soon forgotten, as were all last vestiges of discretion on their part.

In truth he didn't catch much of what they were saying as he was deep in thought about *Montecristo*. The excitement about his forthcoming work was now joined by the first signs of worry over making a flop. He'd always been up to his dream, but was he also up to the task of realising it? For the first time he asked himself the question that producers had posed for the past six years: wasn't this project just a little too big for him?

Nonsense! If Jeff Rebstyn had faith in him, then Jonas had faith in himself too. The man even had an Oscar in his boardroom. Admittedly, it was from a number of years back, but producing films wasn't something you forgot with age. Quite the opposite – look at Clint Eastwood.

Jeff was one of the few Swiss producers with international flair. Who else would have been able to get Moviefonds to fork out 1.6 million for the film project dreamed up by an unknown quantity? Jonas couldn't think of anyone.

The waiter brought the ossobuco and Jonas ordered a bottle of Tignanello to celebrate the day – no, to celebrate all the days to come.

The veal shank was just as it ought to be: tender and with freshly grated lemon zest in the gremolata. The Tignanello had the bouquet of carefully preserved antique furniture, Claudio Villa sang 'Corde della mia chitarra', the surge of voices ebbed and flowed and the inconsolable woman opposite him cried silently to herself. Only Marina was missing.

Jonas took his mobile from his pocket and dialled her number. She answered immediately.

'Am I interrupting the presents?'

'No, we're having dinner.'

'What are you having?'

'Fondue chinoise.'

'That's one of the reasons why I don't like Christmas.'

She laughed but didn't reply.

'Do you want to know the craziest thing that's ever happened to me?'

'If you can be quick about it.'

'I'm going to be doing *Montecristo*.'

'What?'

'I had lunch today with Jeff Rebstyn.'

'From Nembus?'

'Exactly.'

'Are you pulling my leg?'

'No… but I wouldn't mind rubbing my hand up it.'

When he hung up he noticed that the inconsolable woman was no longer crying and had been listening in to his conversation. Feeling caught in the act, she gave him an embarrassed smile and said, 'I'm sorry, you just sounded so happy.'

'I am,' he replied to his surprise.

She raised her glass and they toasted. 'Congratulations,' she said, before weeping again.

*

His happiness was somewhat muted by the after-effects of the Tignanello. He'd got into conversation with the people at his table and ordered a second bottle. Then they'd splashed out and bought another. It wouldn't have been half as bad if the waiter, seeing the size of the bill, hadn't treated them all to a round of the house grappa. At any event, they wished each other 'Happy Christmas' as they went their separate ways.

It was snowing when he left Cesare's. Snowflakes spun in the light of the spherical streetlamps and the posts of the garden fences wore little white hats.

Jonas sauntered home a happy man, catching the snowflakes on his tongue like a child and trying to hit the streetlamps with snowballs.

He was woken by the telephone and looked at his alarm clock: 10:12. The display said 'Max' rather than 'Marina'.

He cleared his throat. 'Max?'

'Did I wake you?'

'Yes. I was out celebrating.'

'The baby Jesus?'

'No, *Montecristo*.'

'Your failed film project?'

'My *live* film project. Rebstyn's going to do it. He's secured the money. Why are you calling?'

'I've been doing some research into Paolo Contini.'

After a pause, Jonas said, 'To be honest, Contini isn't my top priority any more after yesterday.'

'I understand.'

'Doesn't sound like it.'

'I was always told to finish something before embarking on the next thing.'

'That's precisely what I intend to do. *Montecristo* is my old project and Contini my new one.'

'I see. Don't you even want to know what I found out?'

'Tell me.'

'Paolo Contini was known as the daredevil of the trading floor, forever gambling at the highest odds. He didn't care for risk management and only survived because he made unbelievable profits. My source says it was only a matter of time before he made an equally unbelievable loss. It's possible his death prevented a catastrophe for the bank.'

'Who is your source?'

'I'll tell you when Contini becomes your top priority again.'

'When I'm back from Bangkok, in about ten days' time. It'll have to wait till then.'

'You're going to Bangkok?'

'Research, reconnaissance, scouting.'

Max didn't respond.

'Max? Are you still there?'

He spoke again. 'Do you know what it looks like to me? As if someone were trying to sidetrack you from the Contini affair.'

Jonas thought about it. 'Do you know what? If that same person's going to finance my film in return, then I don't have a problem with that.'

*

But he wasn't able to shrug off his mentor's suspicions quite that easily. The thought had occurred to him as well: it was a remarkable coincidence that his greatest dream should suddenly come true while he was working on the most explosive investigation of his career. He couldn't begin to imagine how the two might be related, but to exclude the possibility it might be neater to bring the Contini affair to a conclusion before setting off for Bangkok.

He was busy mulling over these doubts when the doorbell rang. It was just after eleven o'clock the following morning and he was sitting in the kitchen in his pyjamas with his second glass of mineral water and third espresso.

Even from a distance he could see through the frosted glass of his front door a silhouette that he recognised as Marina. She couldn't let herself in as his key was on the inside of the lock.

He opened up and she fell into his arms. Then, holding him away with her arms outstretched, she gave him a good stare. 'You obviously took your celebrations into your own hands,' she declared. 'Give me a coffee; I've been on my feet since six o'clock.'

In the kitchen Jonas told her about Jeff Rebstyn and Moviefonds, their schedule and Rebstyn's suggestion that he should go straight to Thailand for research, as everyone else who might be involved in the production would be on holiday.

'Sounds logical. When are you flying?'

'We.'

Marina put an arm around his neck and kissed him. 'That's such a sweet idea, but it's impossible; I've got two events inked into my diary.'

'I'm not sure whether I'm going to go either.'

'Why not, for God's sake?'

He told her about Max's scepticism and his own doubts.

Marina was sitting opposite him at the kitchen table, holding his hand all the while. When he'd finished she said, 'I think Max is seeing ghosts. Didn't you say he drinks?'

'Max is the clearest-headed alcoholic I know.'

'Does he seriously believe that the bank's trying to distract you from your investigation by somehow influencing the financing of your film? Jonas, don't let your dream get ruined by a discredited conspiracy theorist. For Christ's sake do your film!'

3

THE BOATMAN CUT THE engine and manoeuvred the long-tail boat to the pier with the driveshaft. Jonas paid him and climbed onto the platform.

It was afternoon, the grey sky hung low and the air was hot and sticky.

He could already see the watchtowers from the pier. Light-grey, slender, and slightly tapered with delicate, wide-projecting roofs, almost like rice hats.

He went into the prison via the visitors' entrance and made his way to the reception desk, where he gave the name of the inmate he wished to see: Cameron Busbar, a British prisoner who'd been there for eleven years. Jonas had found the name on the internet. He could have easily chosen any one of the almost three hundred foreign prisoners. But Cameron had maintained his innocence, insisting that the hundred grams of heroin they'd found had been planted on him.

Busbar had been sentenced to death. Later his punishment was reduced to sixty years imprisonment. He was thirty-six years old and forty-nine years still lay ahead of him.

They took Jonas's passport and indicated the building where he was to go. There he had to hand over everything he had on him, including his camera.

He argued that he was making a film and had come here specially to take some footage, but to no avail. 'No cameras,' the officer repeated. And that was that.

He was led through an iron door into a sticky room, lit only by a few bare bulbs on the ceiling. It stank of faeces and the disinfectant that was supposed to mask the stench. Jonas gave a guard the presents he'd bought with him: a shopping bag with fruit, biscuits, a few books, four Toblerones and a Swiss salami. He was frisked again by a prison guard, then another guard unlocked a further iron door. Jonas entered a courtyard and from there the visitors' room.

He wasn't the only visitor. These days there were travel agencies which organised visits to Bang Kwang. Tourists from throughout the world sat in front of a wall of metal bars spanned with wire mesh, chatting through a narrow passage to inmates who sat behind a second wall of metal bars, likewise spanned with wire mesh.

He was led to a chair and ordered to sit down. The chair on the other side of the bars and the passage was still empty.

While waiting for Cameron Busbar, he listened to the hubbub of the visitors and inmates. There was an odd excitement on both sides. Everyone was speaking loudly to make themselves heard above the din, which gave the conversations a chirpiness that didn't match the prisoners' situation or what they had to say.

One of the inmates stood up and was led away. Jonas could see that he was chained in leg shackles. He'd learned that new prisoners were obliged to wear them for the first few months.

As well as those sentenced to death. These had them welded around their ankles and the shackles were removed only after execution. Along with the feet, so they said.

A guard brought in a prisoner and told him to sit on the chair opposite. It had to be Cameron Busbar. Jonas had a different recollection of him from the photograph. Cameron now had a beard and the sunken cheeks of someone missing a large number of teeth.

'Hi,' Cameron said.

'Hi,' Jonas replied. 'My name is Jonas. I'm a filmmaker.'

'So why are you here?'

'Research. I'm making a film about an innocent man who ends up here, but then escapes and takes revenge on those who got him arrested.'

Busbar bared the few teeth left in his mouth and laughed out loud. 'Oh I see, you're filming fairy tales.'

'Fiction,' Jonas corrected him.

'Are you going to let me in on the stunt that gets him out of here?'

Jonas tried humour: 'I'd better not; far too many witnesses around.'

But Busbar became serious again and his gaze dulled. 'There are few innocents here. Do you know why?'

Jonas shook his head.

'If you admit your guilt they reduce your sentence. From death to life imprisonment. Or to ninety, fifty, thirty years. It depends.'

'On what?'

'The mood of the judge.'

Their conversation petered out into silence and other people's chatter dominated again. It was the prisoner who started talking again.

'In the past prisoners here were executed with a machine gun. Tied up and shot in the heart from behind. Now they use lethal injection. Because it's said to be more humane.' Another short, toothless laugh. 'The condemned man finds out an hour before, mostly in the middle of the night. Then he has an hour to write his will and a minute to make a phone call.'

The general hubbub took over once more.

Out of the blue Busbar asked, 'What did you bring me?'

Jonas listed the contents of his bag.

The man without a future nodded knowingly. 'I'll get a little of the chocolate. And a few of the biscuits. Some of the books too. But you can forget the salami.' He cast a look at the guard and stood up. 'I hope I get to see your film one day. But I sincerely doubt they'll show it in here.'

Once more Jonas saw this young man's old grin. Then he ambled away with his guard, two men thrown together by fate.

Jonas returned through the gloomy, stinking room, then back to the reception desk, where his possessions had been taken away. Beneath the mocking gaze of the officer he checked that nothing was missing, acknowledged receipt of his things and felt a sudden urge to make for the exit.

A few of the tourists from the visitors' room were chatting animatedly on the pier as they waited for their chartered boat. When it arrived they invited him to come with them. But Jonas did not fancy it and waited for the next water bus.

When finally one arrived that was going in his direction it was already dark.

*

The lobby of the Mandarin Oriental was as tall as a cathedral and decorated with lavish floral arrangements of orchids. But the stench from Bang Kwang of faeces, urine, disinfectant and sweat followed Jonas as far as the lift.

The dapper lift boy in his exotic uniform greeted him with a ballet-grade low bow and called him 'Mister Brand, Sir'.

Jonas went up to his floor. In his room a plate of satay skewers with a variety of sauces was waiting for him on a wreath of orchids.

He stood beneath the drencher shower for ages, scrubbing away the squalor of that terrible place from his body. Then he wrapped a towel around his waist and went over to the balcony. When he opened the door he was hit by the warm tropical air. Beneath him flowed the busy Chao Phraya, on which hotel boats cruised looking like graceful garlands of light. The sound of a jazz band rose up from the hotel's riverbank terrace.

He'd chosen this hotel because Montecristo, the eponymous hero of his film, had also stayed here before he vanished into Bang Kwang. The room cost six hundred dollars per night, and without batting an eyelid Jonas had handed over Nembus Productions' company credit card, which Jeff Rebstyn had hurriedly had issued for him.

The river was carpeted with aquatic plants and collections of rubbish that were fished out by men on long-tail boats. It smelled of river, not much different from a hot summer's day by the River Sihl in Zürich, where he'd grown up and spent almost his entire life.

Gripped by the sudden transition his life had taken, he lingered on the balcony, gazing at the hustle and bustle below.

When he went back into his room he was met by the chill of the air conditioning. Shivering, he got dressed and went downstairs to the terrace. The maître d' showed him to a small table beside the railings. At the neighbouring table sat an elderly Englishman with his young Thai companion. Having run out of conversation, they were silently staring past each other into the distance.

Jonas ordered a beer and a red beef curry. He looked at the hotel boats decorated with lights, which were dropping off and picking up guests at the jetty. A police speedboat was anchored there too. Two uniformed policemen were waiting for their officers; Jonas had seen them in the bar as he'd walked past.

Beneath him fish were tussling over some leftovers that a group of tourists a few tables further along had chucked into the river.

Jonas listened to the band knock out their stylish tunes. The only reason he wasn't completely happy was that Marina wasn't beside him.

*

He could have stayed sitting for ages on the river terrace, but he'd ordered a long-tail boat at six o'clock the following morning. He wanted to sail along the khlongs with his camera at first light, filming a few locations that might be suitable for Montecristo's escape from Thailand. So he came to a compromise with himself: he'd go back up to his room and drink one last beer from the minibar on the balcony before turning in.

As he passed the reception, he was beckoned over by the night duty manager, a smart-looking man in a dark suit around forty years old. His thick, prematurely grey hair had been carefully parted and he wore round-rimmed glasses. He handed Jonas a card which he was to give to the hotel employee on the jetty the following morning. He would then explain to the boatman what Jonas wanted.

He thanked the manager and went to the lift, where there was no boy at this time of night.

No sooner had Jonas made himself comfortable on the balcony than his mobile rang.

'Were you already asleep?' Max's voice asked.

'Almost. It's just before midnight here.'

'I know. I wouldn't have rung unless it was important, Jonas. Very important.'

'What's up?'

'Moviefonds is GCBS.'

Jonas was speechless.

'Are you still there? Jonas?'

'Yes, yes.' He sounded slightly irritated. 'I heard you. Moviefonds is a part state-owned institution for the promotion of Swiss films with international potential.'

'Part state, part GCBS. Most of the funding comes from the bank's arts budget.'

'How did you find that out?'

'A reliable source. Although the bank isn't represented on the jury and doesn't have a say in the decision-making, it does provide the cash.'

'What about the other private backers?'

'They're all anonymous. And their involvement is just a formality, my source says.'

'What else does your source say?'

'Do you really want to know?'

'Yes.'

'Your film didn't even make it onto the shortlist.'

Jonas fell silent. Two water buses, still carrying plenty of passengers, hooted each other as they crossed paths on the Chao Phraya below. He felt that the world of unreality he'd been inhabiting since Christmas was vanishing before his eyes. 'Why are you ringing to tell me that in the middle of the night? Just to be spiteful?'

'I just wanted you to know that the reason you're in Bangkok is that someone wants you out of the way.'

'Alright. Armed with that knowledge, what do you think I should do here then?'

'Watch out.'

'For what?'

Now Max sounded stroppy. 'I don't know myself. All I know is that the Contini story is huge. Just take good care of yourself.'

'Marina's right.'

'Who's Marina?'

'My girlfriend.' This was the first time Jonas had referred to her in this way.

'What's she right about?'

'That you're a conspiracy theorist.'

*

He plugged his mobile phone into the charger beside his bedside table and set the alarm for five o'clock. The balcony door was still open. With its odours of blossom and decay, the tropical night air mingled with the climatised air of his room.

He sat on an armchair and drank the beer which had already turned slightly warm. Just take good care of yourself, Max had urged him. It was perfectly possible that he *was* a conspiracy theorist. But he was also a highly experienced journalist with a profound insight into the power structures of the business world. Maybe he ought not to dismiss the warning outright.

He resolved to be on his guard against whatever might be threatening him. Then he got into bed and turned out the light.

He'd left the curtains open. The illuminated boats cast their beams onto the ceiling. Sometimes he heard a distant hooting or a police-car siren from afar.

On the sofa he could see the outline of his camera bag, packed ready for his excursion.

Two green LED lights shone out from the small desk – his camera battery charger. He'd left the two batteries in there. The lights showed that both were fully charged.

To make sure that he didn't forget them in the morning he got up again and took the batteries from the charger. Without switching on the light he unzipped his camera bag and felt for the inside pocket he kept them in. He happened upon a plastic bag that he didn't recall having been there before. Jonas took it out and turned on the light.

On the desk in front of him was a clear, sealed bag containing a white powder. About half a kilo in weight.

He knew at once what he had to do. Grabbing the bag he ran to the bathroom, flipped up the loo seat, ripped open the plastic above the toilet bowl, shook the contents of the bag into the water, flushed and watched the stuff swirl away.

While the cistern was refilling he knotted the empty bag several times until it became a hard lump and then flushed this away too. Jonas washed his hands thoroughly, flushed a third time and went back to inspect his bag. He took everything out and made sure that nothing else was inside. Then he searched his suitcase, wardrobe, bed, every chest and drawer. He found nothing.

He went back into the bathroom, tore off a few metres of loo paper, wiped the inside of the toilet bowl and flushed one final time.

Jonas took another look around, switched off the light and lay in bed with his pulse racing.

*

It didn't take long for them to come.

The door opened without any warning, four uniformed policemen stormed in with their weapons at the ready and screamed at him in Thai. Dragging him out of bed, they motioned for him to hold up his hands and frisked his pyjamas.

Behind them the two officers he'd seen in the bar had now entered the room. They were followed by the well-groomed night duty manager gesturing apologetically.

One of the two officers spoke to him in English and allowed him to put his hands down. He requested to see his papers and, when Jonas said they were in the safe, asked politely for the code.

A policeman opened it and brought out the contents: his laptop, passport and wallet. He placed everything on the small desk.

The officer gave an order and three policemen started searching the room. The fourth stood guard over Jonas; the second officer sat in a chair and lit a cigarette. Judging by the insignia he was the highest-ranking man in the room. The night duty manager stood awkwardly by the door. Jonas wondered what role he played in all this. Accomplice or witness?

The number two officer picked up the passport from the desk and leafed through it slowly. Eventually he asked, 'Mr Brand, why did you visit Cameron Busbar in Bang Kwang?'

'Research,' Jonas replied. 'For a film.'

'I see. And why did you rent a long-tail for tomorrow at six in the morning?'

'Research.'

'I see.' Slipping a small notebook from his breast pocket, he took the hotel biro from the desk and jotted something down.

'Do you have any category one substances in your possession?'

'I'm sorry, what is a category one substance?' Jonas asked.

'Heroin, amphetamines, methamphetamines, ecstasy, LSD.'

'No, Sir. Definitely not.'

'I see.' He made another note. Then he uttered the sentence that Jonas knew from his research into the Thai drug laws, and which gave the police the right to search him and his room: 'We have reasonable grounds to believe that you are carrying or hiding illegal drugs.'

Jonas could feel himself going weak at the knees. 'What grounds?'

The police officer declined to answer. He sat in the second armchair and also lit a cigarette.

Jonas watched the policemen search his room. They were most thorough in their approach; it was clear that they had expertise in this task.

'May I sit down?' Jonas asked.

The officer nodded. 'Please.'

Jonas took a step towards the sofa. The policeman guarding him raised his automatic pistol and screamed at him in Thai.

He froze. The officer gave an order, the policeman lowered his weapon and his superior said again, 'Please.'

Jonas sat down. The beads of sweat that had formed on his forehead started running down his face. His heart was pounding and he felt as if he was about to throw up.

Two of the policemen now set to work on the camera bag. Emptying it out completely, they searched every last corner of every inner pocket. Jonas thought he'd glimpsed the English-speaking officer raise his eyebrows at one of his subordinates.

After more than an hour the policemen gave up. The highest-ranking of them stood up and left the room brusquely without saying a word. The armed policemen followed him. The second officer condescended to venture an apology before touching his cap with his hand and leaving.

The night duty manager said, 'I'm very sorry about this. Shall I send somebody to help you clean up the mess?'

Jonas declined the offer. He'd sort it out himself.

As soon as the night duty manager had left, Jonas yanked open the door to the balcony to let out the stench of sweat, cigarettes and boozy breath. Then he dashed to the bathroom and vomited into the toilet bowl that had saved him.

*

It was not yet five o'clock the following morning and he was already in a taxi to the airport. In the night he'd gone on the internet and booked the first flight to Phuket via Chiang Mai. Jonas assumed that passengers on domestic flights were not monitored, or hardly at all, and that he'd find it easier to get away from a tourist destination such as Phuket.

The night duty manager had not been surprised by Jonas's premature check-out; 'I completely understand,' he'd assured him. The man had been most helpful and had accompanied him to the cashpoint in front of the hotel, where Jonas took out some money. The dollars, Swiss francs and baht which had been in his wallet had disappeared along with the policemen.

But however kind the night duty manager had been, when Jonas asked him to order a taxi, he said he was going to Hau Lamphong station, just to be on the safe side.

He landed punctually at twenty to ten that morning in Phuket. With Jeff's credit card he bought a Qatar Airways ticket to Zürich via Kuala Lumpur. Just before eleven o'clock he was at passport control, his shirt drenched through and his heart thumping.

As ever, he'd joined the slowest queue. The border policewoman at her shiny desk was a stickler for detail. Jonas was tempted to change queues but, afraid of sticking out, he decided against it.

The woman did not return his friendly greeting. She gave him a severe look, comparing his face with his passport photo, his passport photo with his face, and his face with his passport photo. She placed the passport on the scanner and stared long and hard at the screen. Then she slowly leafed through the passport, examining every page. 'What was the purpose of your visit?' she asked.

'Tourism.'

Now she looked at the entry stamp for Thailand. 'Why only three days?' she asked.

Jonas felt the air from her fan cooling the sweat on his brow. 'Family business,' he told her.

She gazed back at the screen.

It was eleven o'clock. The police could have discovered that he'd left the Mandarin Oriental hours ago – that's if the night manager hadn't notified them. Maybe they'd already organised a manhunt for him.

The policewoman leaned over to her colleague who was working his way through the other queue and asked him a question. She turned her screen so he could see.

The same nausea that Jonas had felt in his hotel room now rose from his stomach again.

The border colleague said something and the two of them laughed. She stamped the passport, handed it back and called out, 'Next!'

All he had to do now was survive six hours in the departure lounge, then he'd made it.

*

The tourists in the departure lounge were either frustrated that their holiday was over or gloomy about the long flight ahead of them. Others were prolonging the holiday spirit with the drinks they'd been knocking back over the past weeks. Many were showing off their tattoos as well as their new tans, and were dressed for high summer, as if they could take the weather back with them to Birmingham, Frankfurt or Stockholm.

But Jonas was in harmless, innocent company here. He didn't believe he was in danger any more. All the same, he didn't dare call Max or Marina; he'd wait until he got to Kuala Lumpur. There he had a seven-hour stop-off until his connecting flight to Doha.

He found an empty seat beside a family with two small, fat children, and a group of loud young Swedes who were drinking beer and bellowing out something that sounded like toasts or Viking battle-cries.

For the first time since the raid on his room he was able to get his thoughts back into some sort of order again. Was Max right about his conspiracy theory, as Marina called it? Did GCBS really lure him to Bangkok with funding and did its tentacles reach so far that they could have half a kilo of heroin smuggled into his luggage? Were certain individuals from the bank or its associates so treacherous that they could have him sink into obscurity exactly like the protagonist of his film they were helping to finance?

He couldn't believe it. For him it looked more like a coincidence, a particularly crass case of fate's irony.

Part Three

1

ALMOST FORTY HOURS AFTER he'd checked out of the Mandarin
Oriental he put the key into the lock of his front door. Jonas
had barely had a wink of sleep throughout the entire journey.
He'd been too shaken by what he'd gone through, while the
flights from Kuala Lumpur to Doha and from Doha to Zürich
had been too unpeaceful. He was in a state between semi-
consciousness and euphoria, and the solid ground felt as if it
were wobbling beneath his feet.

As he stepped into the hall he could immediately smell
sandalwood incense sticks. Music was coming from the sitting
room, Marina's music: 'Flume' by Bon Iver.

Putting down his luggage, Jonas went into the sitting room.

She was sitting on the floor, her head on the leather armchair
covered with the kanga from Tanzania, and had fallen asleep.
Her face looked so calm, peaceful and beautiful that he burst
into tears. He dried them with his forearm and when he was
able to see again she was on her feet. She threw her arms around
Jonas and pulled him towards her.

'What happened?' she whispered.

'Later.'

She started undressing him.

'I've got to have a shower first.'

'Later.'

*

When he awoke it was night time. It took Jonas a moment to orient himself. He was lying in the dark of his own bedroom and the noises he could hear were coming from his own kitchen. He could still feel the gentle rocking of his long-distance flights.

The scent of the incense sticks had dissipated and given way to the aroma of tomato sauce.

Jonas went into the bathroom and took a shower with his eyes closed. The images came straight back to him: Bang Kwang, Cameron Busbar, the prison tourists, the boats lit-up on the river, the white powder in the toilet bowl and the policemen in his hotel room.

He kept soaping himself and rinsing off until he felt he'd washed the entire Bangkok episode from his body. Then he rubbed himself dry and shaved the stubble from his face and head.

It was only now that he caught sight of Marina in the mirror. She was standing in the doorway, watching him and wearing her makeshift apron from two dishcloths, showing a few spots of tomato.

'When you're done with your depilation we can eat,' she said. When she turned round to go back to return to the kitchen he could see that the apron was all she was wearing.

He slipped on his dressing gown and joined her. Two candles were lit on the table. For dinner there was green salad and spaghetti Napoli. Jonas hadn't realised till now just how starving he was. He'd barely eaten a morsel on the entire journey home.

Marina watched with amusement as he devoured two platefuls of spaghetti. She waited for him to wipe his mouth and down a glass of red wine before asking, 'So, what happened?'

Jonas described how by the skin of his teeth he'd escaped being arrested and imprisoned for decades, maybe even sentenced to lethal injection. Marina listened with increasing horror. When he'd finished she stood up and hugged him. He could feel her quivering and when she moved away from their embrace he saw her tears.

'Why do they do that?'

'Because someone pays them to.'

'Who?'

'Max would say it's the people who don't want me investigating the Contini story any longer.'

'Max, the conspiracy theorist.'

'Listen, GCBS is funding my film on the quiet. The first thing on our production schedule is for me to fly out to Bangkok to do some research. The same thing happens to me as to the hero of my film – heroin gets planted in my luggage. I tell you, it's bloody hard not to believe in a conspiracy.'

Marina poured them both some more wine. 'How do you think they did that?'

'GCBS is an international concern; they've got a worldwide network. Do you think organising something like that's a problem? In a country where policemen earn three hundred francs a month and have to pay for their own uniforms and service weapons?'

Marina held her glass in both hands and thoughtfully took a sip. 'But to take it so far!'

'Which means Max is right again. The Contini affair is

enormous. Bigger than we could have ever imagined. Much bigger.'

'So what now? What are you going to do now?'

Jonas shrugged.

Marina sat on his lap and put an arm around his shoulder. For a while she stayed like this, in silence. Then she said, 'Jonas, I'm scared.'

*

There was a new note stuck to Max's office door: 'Cleaners – don't touch anything!! Just empty wastepaper basket and ashtray!!'

Inside it looked as if his orders had been obeyed. The piles of paper were in their old places, they'd just grown a bit. You could still only get to the desk and visitor's chair via a narrow path between a combination of rubbish and documents. To Jonas it seemed as if the quality of the air in the room had deteriorated, as had Max's shape.

'Back already?' Max sounded surprised. 'Weren't you intending on staying longer?'

'I almost stayed forever; it was a horribly close shave.' Jonas told him what had happened.

Max listened attentively, moving only to stub out his cigarette and light a new one. When Jonas had finished he said, 'I did warn you.'

'Maybe that's why I was a little more prudent. Thanks for the call.'

'My pleasure. The television company paid for it.'

'Do you think it was GCBS people?'

'Don't you?'

'Somehow I still can't believe that they'd go to such extremes.'

'If what I've found out is true, I'd say they'll go even further.'

'What have you found out?'

'It's possible that Contini lost billions, even tens of billions.'

'My God! How?'

'I don't know exactly. With some sort of Russian speculation.'

'And no one noticed?'

'He must have neutralised the losses with bogus derivatives.'

'What?'

'He made fictitious profits with derivatives, which offset the real losses with the Russian securities. And this is the thing: the bank is carrying on with the pretence. Why?'

Regarding the question a rhetorical one, Jonas didn't reply.

Max continued: 'Because a loss of between ten and twenty billion francs would unleash a momentum that would bring it to its knees.'

'But then the state would bail it out, as it always does.'

'No, the state wouldn't come to its rescue this time, precisely because it has done so in the past. No politician would go anywhere near it. The state would let the bank fail, you can be absolutely sure of that.'

'But I thought the banks had a better capital cushion these days. Surely they could swallow a loss like that.'

Max's laugh turned into a coughing fit, which he managed to overcome without taking the cigarette from his mouth. With a token flick of the ash from his dark jacket, he continued: 'Do you know what the equity ratio of GCBS's total assets was at the outbreak of the financial crisis? One point four per cent! None of us would ever get a mortgage with any bank with as little equity as that.'

Max had talked himself into a fury.

'Did you know that during the last financial crisis a substantial proportion of risk-weighted assets of certain big international banks consisted of so-called sub-prime securities? That in some cases these even exceeded the banks' core capital? Sub-prime securities! Such securities are a cocktail of mortgages belonging to a few solvent borrowers and many others who can hardly meet the interest payments. And the internal risk models rated these securities as highly as safe assets such as US government bonds! This is how they brought themselves and us to the verge of ruin.'

'But I thought the banks had to have a greater equity ratio these days,' Jonas argued.

Max grinned. 'Four per cent. GCBS would have to have a core capital of at least thirty billion. Just imagine there was a crash in the housing market – not an inconceivable scenario. So, with a write-off of between fifteen and twenty per cent of their mortgage portfolio the entire core capital would be down the drain.'

Max gave Jonas a combative look, as if he were expecting to be contradicted. But when Jonas remained silent, he continued: 'Did you know that there are some big banks who with their right hand take money from investors to bulk up their equity, on the condition that with their left hand they provide the same investors with the same sums as credit?'

'How come the public doesn't know about this?'

'Because it would only aggravate the crisis.'

Max slapped his forehead and bellowed, 'Can you believe it?' Once more his exclamation turned into a coughing fit.

When it was over Max said calmly, 'That's why GCBS is as dangerous as a wounded grizzly bear.' He lit a fresh cigarette with the butt of the old one.

'So what do you recommend I do? *Montecristo* or Contini?'

Max puffed a column of smoke up to the ceiling. 'Do you mean: should you work for or against GCBS? For me it's clear cut. But you have to decide for yourself. Perhaps you'll return to popular journalism. Less controversial.'

*

That evening he met Marina in the Losone Bar, a rather old-fashioned place in Niederdorf with a jukebox full of musical rarities and walls painted with scenes from Ticino.

Nothing really kicked off at Losone until close to midnight. Now, not even five o'clock and before happy hour, there were few customers. Marina had an event from which she wouldn't get back home until late. They were meeting here before her evening's work began. She didn't want to have to wait all that time to find out what Max had advised him.

The event was on the fringe of a ball, and Marina was dressed fittingly. Wearing a floor-length, low-cut strapless dress and plenty of make-up, she attracted a lot of attention from the few customers in the bar.

'Work gear,' she said, as he helped her out of her coat. Jonas felt proud of her.

He drank a beer, Marina sparkling water. The guests should be drunk at an event, she'd said, not the organisers.

Jonas had told her about the possible sums involved at the bank and how Max had explained it was as dangerous as a wounded grizzly.

'Keep well away, Jonas. Promise me.'

He nodded. 'I just wish it weren't so cowardly.'

'Cowardly, brave – precisely those male attributes that create widows, orphans and weeping mothers.'

'Who said that?'

'Marina Ruiz.'

He kissed her.

'But I can't do the film either.'

'Some of the greatest films were made with dirty money.'

'Really? Name me one, then.'

'I can't say off the top of my head. But there's certainly not as much clean money around as there are good films.'

Jonas laughed. 'Another Marina Ruiz quote?'

She nodded.

'I'd love to meet her.'

*

Rebstyn's personal assistant had made him wait for more than half an hour. Herr Rebstyn was busy, she'd said, would Herr Brand be so kind as to take a seat for a moment? Be so kind!

Now Jonas stood up and barged straight past the startled assistant into Jeff's office.

The producer was sitting in front of his flat-screen monitor, watching a film. *Magnolia*, if Jonas wasn't mistaken.

An irritated Rebstyn swivelled round in his executive chair. As soon as he realised it was Jonas the irritation gave way to surprise. 'Why are you back already?'

'To save my life.'

Jeff got up and motioned for Jonas to take a seat at the conference table. 'Please excuse me; I said I wasn't to be disturbed. Obviously I wasn't expecting you to turn up. Save your life? Coffee?'

Opening the door a notch, he ordered two espressos. Then he sat down opposite Jonas. 'Tell me all about it, for heaven's sake.'

'A question first: Did you know that GCBS is behind Moviefonds?'

'I've heard that GCBS is one of the anonymous sponsors. One of many. Why?'

'When did you find out about the Moviefonds money?'

'I'd have to look up the precise date. A day before we met up in the Frosch. Why?'

'I'll tell you after I've told you what happened in Bangkok.'

Jonas described his adventure. When he'd finished, Rebstyn uttered, 'But that's just like the film.'

'And now the bombshell: GCBS wants me out of the way.'

Jeff smiled sceptically. 'What makes you think that?'

'I was working on an exposé that would cause huge damage to the bank. I believe they decided spontaneously to finance the film to entice me away from the other project. And when they found out I was doing research in Bangkok they had the witty idea to get me out of the way in exactly the same manner as the hero of my film.'

Rebstyn shook his head in disbelief. 'No offence, Jonas, but I think your imagination's got the better of you. We're talking about Switzerland here.'

'Indeed. But be honest with me. Weren't you surprised when Moviefonds told you they were coming on board?'

There was a knock at the door and the assistant brought in two espressos. The interruption gave Rebstyn the opportunity to give his answer without embarrassment. 'A little, yes. But personally, I've always believed in *Montecristo*, Jonas.'

'Have you ever had funding from Moviefonds in the past?'

'Twice.'

'And were either of those reconsiderations?'

'No. But they can reconsider a proposal; it says so in their statutes. If new angles come to light.'

'So what were the new angles on *Montecristo*?'

'Maybe that I stuck with it. I was constantly in contact with Serge Cress, the chief executive. Look, are you seriously thinking of chucking the whole thing in?'

'If what I suspect is true – how could I possibly go on?'

Shaking his head, Jeff reached for the telephone. 'Get Cress on the line,' he said. And to Jonas, 'We'll soon see.'

When the phone rang, Jeff picked it up, nodded, cast Jonas a conspiratorial glance and said loudly and cheerfully, 'Serge! What luck to catch you! How are you, old chap? Me too, thanks. Listen, I've got Brand with me in the office, you know, the guy who's doing *Montecristo*. He's just back from Bangkok and not here for very long…' he winked at Jonas. '… but he'd love to meet you. Tell me, how flexible are you?'

Cupping his hand over the mouthpiece he whispered to Jonas, 'Civil servant: very flexible.' Then back into the phone, 'Diary? No, no, I'm really flexible. Completely. Listen, can I book a table at the Silbere Frosch? Lunch? Today?'

Placing his hand over the mouthpiece again he said to Jonas, 'Got to look at his diary. What are the odds he can make it?'

'You can? Excellent. Half twelve? A couple of hours! Looking forward to it!'

'Right then. You can ask him how it all came about. And you'll see – everything above board. Shall we meet there? I've one or two things to sort out first.'

Jonas got up and went to the door. Before he'd opened it, Rebstyn said, 'Jonas, you just wanted to meet the man who's enabled your dream to come true and find out what made them change their mind. You keep your cock-and-bull story to yourself, OK?'

*

He liked Cress straightaway. Not at all the typical civil servant type he'd imagined from Rebstyn's remarks, but a casually dressed chap in his late thirties with longish hair and glasses with white transparent frames that gave him something of an American East-Coast intellectual look.

He was already sitting at Jeff's preferred table when Jonas entered the Silbere Frosch. The host wasn't yet there, maybe deliberately so.

'You must be Herr Cress,' Jonas said. 'Seeing as you're sitting at this table.' He sat down and ordered a sparkling water, like Serge Cress.

'Delighted to meet you in person,' Cress said. 'I'm a huge fan of *Montecristo*.'

Jonas still had to get used to such praise for his screenplay. He'd had precious little of it over the past six years, which is why he responded with a wary 'Why?'

This didn't appear to embarrass Cress. '*The Count of Montecristo* was my favourite book as a boy. And revenge for an injustice is one of the most infallible dramatic formats there is. Then you've got the combination between the archaic and the high-tech, plus the ages of the protagonists – all the same generation as the main cinema target group. Yup, I think the material has all the makings of a blockbuster. Now you just need the right cast. And good direction.'

'That's what I'm most worried about too.'

Cress laughed. 'Not the sort of thing you should tell a financial backer.'

'I've no experience of that either.'

The two of them laughed. 'We trust you,' Cress said.

'That's the reason I badly wanted to meet you. I don't know many people who trust me. Not in this field at any rate.'

'Well, one of them's sitting right here.'

Jonas looked at him thoughtfully. 'May I ask why?'

Cress didn't need long to muster his reply: 'Someone who pursues an idea so doggedly for so long isn't going to cock it up when he finally gets the chance to turn it into something.'

Jonas was amused by this rationale. But he remarked, 'Great films need genius, not doggedness.'

'Maybe you possess both.'

'Excuse me for interrupting.' Jeff cast his long shadow onto the table. Cress stood up to greet him, whereas Jonas remained seated because they'd already said hello earlier on. But then he felt a little awkward, so half stood up and waited in a position between sitting and standing until the producer took his seat.

'Have you discussed everything already?' Rebstyn asked when he finally sat down.

Cress smiled. 'I don't know. Have we, Herr Brand?'

'Together for a quarter of an hour and still calling each other by your surnames?' He looked at the two water glasses. 'Oh, I see. You've got the wrong drinks.' He gestured to the waiter, who immediately brought a bottle of Jeff's favourite champagne. Jeff tried it, let the waiter fill the glasses, and they toasted.

Now that Jonas was on first-name terms with the boss of Moviefonds he found it easier, as he tucked into his côte de boeuf with risotto and chard, to ask the question that had been troubling him.

'I've heard that GCBS is Moviefonds's chief backer,' he remarked casually.

'Artists!' Jeff laughed, turning to Serge. 'Don't they just love looking gift horses in the mouth?'

'I can well understand. I would do the same in your shoes. The fact is, by statute Moviefonds is a horse with clenched teeth. I'm not allowed to answer your question.'

'OK, but maybe you could answer this at least: am I right in thinking that by statute the financers have no say in the allocation of funding? And what about in practice?'

'So long as I'm at Moviefonds I won't allow any differentiation between theory and practice.'

Rebstyn washed down a mouthful of meat with a swig of claret, raised his glass and said, 'Big words!'

Jonas took a mouthful too and braced himself for the critical part of the conversation. The lunch was excellent, and the champagne and wine had put him in that same convivial mood he sometimes felt in good company when he knew everything would fall into place.

'Tell, me Serge, what happens when a film proposal is reconsidered?'

Bringing his glass to his lips, the civil servant took a sip, relished the sensation of the wine swirling around his mouth, then said, 'In one of our regular committee meetings someone will raise the issue, explaining why they think a project deserves to be reconsidered, and then a decision is taken.'

'A vote?'

Serge shook his head slowly. 'Discussion followed by a decision.'

'And the person who proposes the reconsideration, do they do it off their own bat?'

'Either off their own bat or because someone's convinced them to.'

'What about with *Montecristo*?'

Cress and Rebstyn exchanged glances. 'Both.'

'Can I assume that I know both advocates, that I'm on first-name terms with the two of them and that I'm sharing a fantastic lunch with them in the Silbere Frosch?'

Cress smiled. 'We don't give details of the decision-making process at Moviefonds.'

'Just like the government,' Rebstyn interjected.

'Only more secret,' the civil servant said.

With his knife Jonas pushed some sauce onto a fork of risotto, chewed it carefully and took a sip of wine before asking the crucial question: 'How long does it take from the decision being taken to informing the lucky beneficiary?'

'Two, three, four weeks, sometimes longer. Depending on the bureaucracy involved.'

'When was the key meeting for *Montecristo*?'

Cress took his mobile from his inside pocket and consulted his diary.

Jonas had to put down his glass because he was afraid his hand might shake.

Switching the mobile back off, Cress returned it to his pocket. 'Wednesday, 10 December.'

Jonas nodded and took another mouthful to avoid having to say anything.

Wednesday, 10 December. More than a week before he'd started his investigation into the Contini affair.

*

The offices of the event agency where Marina worked were on the second floor of a converted industrial building. Above the windows stood a neon sign: Eventissimo!

Jonas was standing beneath the awning of an electrical shop, beside the window with its chaotic display. It was just after six o'clock and the light rain which had been falling all day was starting to turn into snow.

Eventissimo!'s windows were still all lit, and sometimes he could see Marina's tall figure passing by them. She had no idea he was waiting down here for her, it was meant to be a surprise. Just like what he had to tell her. He was still feeling the effects of the good news, the heavy wine and the seven hours' jetlag, and could have stayed standing there for ages.

Once more he saw Marina's figure by the illuminated window. But this time she stopped and looked out. Resting her elbow on her left hand, she seemed to be on the phone.

His mobile rang. Marina.

'I'm finishing up now. Shall we meet?'

'You bet.'

'How was your chat with Rebstyn?'

'I'll tell you soon.'

'Where shall we meet?'

'Outside your office.'

'When?'

'Now.'

He watched her move right up close to the window pane, shielding her eyes from the reflection of the light. Now she raised her arm and waved. He waved back.

'What a lovely surprise!' she said.

'Bring a brolly; it's snowing.'

Three minutes later he was holding her in his arms.

'You've been drinking,' she said when she moved away again. 'Is that a good sign?'

'Not always, but today it is.' He took her umbrella, she held onto his arm and they made their way through the snow which was falling more heavily. 'Spill the beans,' she pleaded.

'I had lunch with Jeff and Serge Cress.'

'Serge Cress?'

'Moviefond's boss. Although he wouldn't say where the money came from or how it was decided that *Montecristo* should receive funding, he implied that *he* – urged on by Rebstyn – had suggested my proposal be reconsidered. And the key thing is that the decision was taken on 10 December.

Before I started researching the Contini story.'

Marina stopped. 'Which means the decision was made on the strength of your screenplay and *not* as an attempt to get rid of you.'

Jonas grinned. 'Seems like it.'

She threw herself so violently around his neck that the umbrella was knocked away, and they kissed, exposed now to the thickly falling snow.

'Doesn't that also mean that it wasn't the bank who set the trap for you in Bangkok?'

'Well, by then they *did* have a reason for getting rid of me.'

They started walking again. 'I looked on the internet,' Marina said. 'It seems as if one of the Thai police's favourite methods of getting money is to plant drugs on unsuspecting tourists and only let them off after a hefty bribe's been paid.'

'I know. But it's hardly going to happen in the Mandarin Oriental.'

'Why not? That's where the tourists with the most money stay.'

'You're right there,' Jonas conceded, only too willing to exonerate his financial backers.

A police car drove by, its blue lights flashing and siren wailing. Not especially fast as the road was already slippery.

'Do you realise where we're going?' Marina asked gleefully. Without coming to any arrangement they'd set off in the direction of her flat.

'Because I've got nothing in,' Jonas explained.

'But nor have I.'

Putting his arm around Marina, he drew her towards him and said, 'I'm sure I'll find something.'

They'd increased their pace as the snow was making their shoes and trousers wet. Ahead of them was the police car with its blue flashing light. The traffic was starting to tail back; a pile-up, perhaps.

'Jonas, doesn't all this mean that you *can* do your film now after all?'

His heart leaped. 'Exactly! But maybe in Bali instead of Thailand.'

Again they stood in a tight embrace in the driving snow, the umbrella hanging from Jonas's hand.

*

As expected, Max reacted more soberly to the news. Jonas had met him at the Schönacker over a knuckle of pork, one of the house specialities.

He'd told him about his meeting with Cress; Max had listened to him sceptically with his cheeks full.

The short time it took for Jonas to tell the whole story was sufficient for Max to put away the entire pork knuckle. Now he wiped the plate clean with a piece of bread, leaving it unusually neat and tidy by his standards.

'So now,' he chomped, 'you think you can make your film with a clean conscience and drop the Contini story.'

'And of course you don't think that.'

Max prized a toothpick from the cruet stand and started poking around inside his mouth. 'I wouldn't be satisfied by Serge Cress's explanation. Although he didn't say that GCBS is financing the project, he didn't deny it either. And,' he added, holding his free hand carefully over his mouth, 'although he said that the financiers don't have a say in the decision-making process, he didn't say how the decision was reached. Apart from the fact that it wasn't a simple majority vote.'

'However the decision came about and who made it,' Jonas

countered, 'its aim wasn't to divert me from the Contini affair. I only started investigating it after the funding decision was already made.'

Gantmann swallowed the yield from his poking around and took a large gulp from his glass of dark beer. Breathing out deeply, he said, 'But the banknote business *was* beforehand.'

'The banknote story was a flop, you know that.'

'I still find it quite fishy. Maybe GCBS caused your story to be a flop.'

'Even if it did, what has that got to do with Contini?'

'I don't know. Not yet. But I've got an inkling. If the hole Contini made is really as enormous as I suspect – and it *is* huge – then the banknotes could have been part of the measures the bank took to protect itself.'

'I don't understand.'

'I don't quite understand yet either. But I'll get there. I sense I'm quite close.' He finished his beer and waved with the empty glass. 'If you're giving up and devoting yourself to art, will you at least allow me to stay on the case?'

'Yes, of course.'

'Will you give me the material you've gathered till now?'

'Sure.'

'All of it? Including the banknotes?'

'All of it.'

*

Blauwiesenstrasse 122 was in the Seefeld district of the city, not very far from Brand's flat in Rofflerstrasse. A yellow brick building from the 1920s, its large windows were bordered by an ochre brick trim. Nembus Productions was on the ground floor.

It was a stirring moment when Rebstyn's assistant took him to a door with a sign saying 'Montecristo'. She unlocked it and gave Jonas the key. He entered a large, bright room with a tall ceiling, whose window gave onto the rear courtyard. There were four desks, a conference table, cupboards, shelves and filing cabinets. Next to the window and set aside from the others was a larger desk with an office chair and visitor's one opposite. On the desk were a flat-screen monitor, a keyboard and a computer mouse. 'That's your desk, Jonas,' the assistant explained. As soon as they'd met she'd said, 'We call each other by our first names here, and you're on board now.'

Jonas tried out the office chair, making a half-turn in either direction and adjusting the seat to his height. Opening the drawers to his desk he found them empty apart from a shrivelled-up apple, which rolled towards him from the back of one drawer when he yanked it out with a little too much force.

'Ooh, sorry,' the assistant said, making to remove the apple.

'No, leave it. Schiller used rotten apples for inspiration. Maybe it'll help me too.'

She wished him luck with his inspiration and reminded him that the first production meeting with Jeff would be here, in just over an hour.

Unpacking his laptop, Jonas put it beside the keyboard and sat down. So this would be his workplace for the coming months. Gradually he'd be joined by more colleagues. The production assistant, head of production, location scout and all the others.

Only now did he notice the clapperboard on the window sill, leaning against the glass. 'Montecristo' was written in large letters beside 'Title'. In the 'Production Co.' slot, someone had written 'Nembus' in beautiful handwriting with an indelible marker. Next to 'Director' stood 'Jonas Brand'. There was still no name beside 'Cameraman'.

On the wall was a plastic whiteboard with the title 'Montecristo – Production Sequence.' In the top left was written 'When', next to it 'What', then 'Who', then 'Comments'. Beneath 'When' someone had put today's date. Beneath 'Who' it said 'Brand/Rebstyn'.

Jonas clenched his fist and let out an inaudible yelp of delight.

*

Snow lay on the balcony of the Dragon House. More had fallen that afternoon; the sandstone parapet was decorated with at least twenty centimetres. It was dark and the lights of the city were reflected in the River Limmat.

William Just stood smoking in the balcony doorway. He didn't want his custom-made English shoes, which he'd now worn in, to get wet; they had leather soles. Given how cold it was outside he was also enjoying the cosy warmth of the room on his back.

In the glass of the open door he could see his reflection against the background of the Gentlemen's Room. He held the cigarette in his brown hand with its blue signet ring, contrasting with the white of his cuffs, just as his tanned face and neck stood out from the crisp white collar. Between Christmas and New Year he'd taken a few opportunities to enjoy some Gstaad sun, reinforcing his tan afterwards on the sunbed in his home gym.

Just took a final drag and flicked the half-smoked cigarette over the parapet. Imagining it falling down the four floors made him shudder briefly.

Going back into the Gentlemen's Room, he closed the door and drew the curtains. The pendulum clock said a quarter to six. Fifteen minutes until his guest's arrival.

He left the room and crossed the parquet corridor to the

room he used as a study. In contrast to all the other rooms on that floor it was minimalist in appearance. White walls and ceiling, hidden, dimmable lights and the furniture deliberately scaled back.

He stood at a high desk, on which stood a flat-screen monitor and a wireless keyboard and mouse. With a click the home screen appeared and he typed in his password. The monitor was filled with figures. He studied them for a few minutes and smiled; he was happy with what he saw.

This hadn't always been the case over the past few months. GCBS, his supertanker, had come within a whisker of disaster more than once during this time. Just could pride himself that it was purely down to his flexibility, imagination and presence of mind that it was still, or back, on course. As well as his willingness to try out unconventional solutions.

He heard the muffled ringing from Herr Schwarz's office. His visitor must be here. A little early: typical civil servant.

Returning to the Gentlemen's Room, Just stood by the fire. He didn't intend to spend long with his visitor; he was off to see a première that evening: *La Sonnambula*.

Herr Schwarz had put two bottles of Krug 1998 on ice, the second as a reserve in case the first was corked. There were some puff pastry canapés to go with the champagne, and that was it.

Although his visitor had turned out to be surprisingly undogmatic and accommodating, what Just had laid on here was perfectly sufficient. He didn't want to go over the top. That might induce the man to overestimate the significance of how helpful he'd been.

There was a knock at the door.

'Come in!' Just called out.

Herr Schwarz opened the door. 'Herr Cress is here to see you.'

2

PREPRODUCTION FOR *MONTECRISTO* HAD been ongoing for more than two weeks. Jonas had decided on a cameraman, a costume designer was under contract and two set designers were on the shortlist. He'd already had a meeting with the woman who, in his opinion, was the best casting director in the country, while the best script doctor, according to Jeff, had offered his initial feedback.

Jonas had settled into his role as the man calling the shots, and was now playing it with an assurance that was new for him. His moments of doubt had become more infrequent and were quickly overcome each time they surfaced.

He was living a joint-residence relationship with Marina. Both of them kept a few of their things in each other's wardrobe, they sometimes slept at his, sometimes at hers, depending on who got home later. They'd discussed on a couple of occasions – half in jest – the possibility of moving in with each other.

One evening when they were due to meet at Marina's flat and

he'd just popped back home to fetch a few things, the doorbell rang.

Jonas wasn't expecting anybody and was just about to leave, but as there was no intercom in his flat he simply pressed the button to open the door.

Hearing leaden-footed steps in the stairwell, he went out onto the landing to look down. All he saw was a man's hand on the banister, hauling up a figure in a dark coat. It was only when this character turned the final corner on the stairs that Jonas recognised him: Herr Weber, his account manager at GCBS.

When Weber had finally made it up and was standing beside him, Jonas could see that he was drunk. He raised his index finger to his lips. Shhhh. Then he pointed to Jonas's door. He didn't say a word until they were inside the flat, and even then his voice was hushed. 'Is this a bad time?'

'I was just about to go out,' Jonas replied, realising that he was practically whispering too.

'I won't be long, but it's important.' He started taking off his coat with great difficulty. Jonas helped him out.

Herr Weber stood facing him in the hallway, expectantly. Jonas had no option but to invite him into the sitting room.

With a sigh, he sank into Jonas's favourite armchair and, with a nervy wave of his hand, invited Jonas to take the chair opposite. Jonas sat.

'I don't want to sound rude, but you wouldn't have a beer for me, would you?'

Jonas went into the kitchen and returned with two cans of beer. To emphasise how short he was for time he didn't bother bringing glasses.

Herr Weber pulled open the can and took a few large gulps. Putting the beer down with another loud sigh he said, 'I'm already... er... a little... tipsy. Cheers!'

Toasting Jonas, he took another swig. Jonas did likewise. 'I haven't been to the bank in a while, but I often pay a visit to your automatic colleagues beside the entrance.'

'Even if you did go in you wouldn't see me.' Herr Weber tried in vain to disguise his slurred words.

'Why not?'

The account manager drew his index finger across his throat. 'All over. Finito.'

'You got the sack?'

'Exactamundo, as the Spanish say.'

'I'm sorry.'

'Me too. And my family. It's not easy being an unemployed head of the family.'

'I'm sure you'll find something soon, what with your experience.'

Herr Weber drained the can. 'Oh sure. These days people are crying out for fifty-three-year-old bankers who've been given the boot.' He crumpled the can.

Jonas went to the fridge and brought him a new one. 'I'm afraid it's my last,' he lied.

'Thanks. Anyway, I don't mean to keep you for much longer,' he said, having trouble with the ring pull. 'There's just something I wanted to tell you.'

Herr Weber turned his attention back to the ring pull. Jonas felt sorry for this small man with his high hairline. The worried concentration made his face look even more monkey-like.

Jonas was about to offer his help when the can opened with a hiss, spraying out a little beer.

'The hundred note was genuine,' Herr Weber said, before taking a sip. 'As genuine as the other one.' He put his finger to his lips again. Shhhhh.

'So why did you say it was a forgery?' Jonas asked, surprised.

'The second time, you mean? The second time it was a forgery. Someone swapped it.'

'Who?'

Finger to his lips.

'I thought the deposit box could only be opened with two keys. The bank's and mine.'

Herr Weber took a sip before answering. 'Except in emergencies.'

'And that was an emergency?'

Weber gave a mysterious smile. 'Obviously it was.'

Jonas was unsure whether Weber was telling the truth or whether he was merely listening to a drunkard's waffle. 'I was assured that it's impossible for two Swiss banknotes to bear the same number accidentally.'

'It's true.' The mysterious smile again.

'So…?'

Herr Weber took his time. Sipped, burped, apologised. Then, with a wag of his finger, he informed Jonas, '"Accidentally" is right. But deliberately…'

'You believe Coromag deliberately printed the notes with duplicate serial numbers.'

'No, I don't believe that.' Rummaging in his inside pockets, Weber found a wallet and dropped it, causing some of the contents to slip out. Jonas wanted to help him, but Weber shouted, 'Stop! I'll do it!'

Lifting himself from the chair, he squatted down uncertainly, gathered up business cards, scraps of paper, banknotes and documents, and stuffed them back into his wallet, save for one piece of paper which he kept in his hand.

He stood up and handed it to Jonas.

On it was written 'Gabor Takacs' and a mobile number.

'This chap believes it,' Herr Weber said, finishing the can. 'He used to work in consignment where they print the banknotes. But now he's also,' Weber said, repeating the throat-slitting gesture, 'finito, kaput.'

Weber offered Jonas his hand. 'Right, I'll leave you in peace. Thanks for the beer.'

Jonas shook the small hand and accompanied him to the door. 'Do you want me to call you a taxi?'

'No need, I just live round the corner.' Then he added, bitterly, 'Within walking distance of work.'

Jonas accompanied him down the stairs.

At the front door Herr Weber pointed to the piece of paper Jonas still had in his hand. 'I told him you'd ring.'

When he got to the garden gate he turned around again to Jonas, who'd stayed in the doorway, and put his finger to his lips once more.

Jonas did the same.

*

Gabor Takacs, the man with the Hungarian name, spoke German with a broad Zürich accent. He'd been born in Schwamendingen in 1966, ten years after the Hungarian Uprising, the third child of Hungarian refugees. He told Jonas all of this in the first few minutes after they met.

Fully occupied with preliminary work for *Montecristo*, Jonas was no longer really interested in the banknote affair. But as soon as Herr Weber left he'd telephoned Max and told him about the peculiar encounter. Max became very excited, insisting on a word-for-word account of the conversation, and demanding Gabor Takacs's number.

The following day he called Jonas on his mobile. When the latter rejected the call because he was in a meeting, Max pestered Rebstyn's assistant for so long that she finally put him through.

'Takacs refuses to talk to me, Jonas. He'll only talk to you. That Herr Weber chap must have made it quite clear to him that you're the person directly involved, because it was you who discovered the notes with the same serial number.'

'Look, Max, I'm in the middle of a location meeting. As far as I'm concerned, the banknote affair's over. I'm done with it.'

'Then I'm done with you,' Max had said, hanging up.

After ten minutes of defiance Jonas had called back and agreed to meet Takacs.

The man who opened the door of the 1980s terraced house wore pyjamas that were too big for him. A bald head and a pair of low-set eyes circled by dark rings protruded from the neckline. 'Please excuse me, I've got cancer' were his opening words. He led Jonas into what had once been a sitting room. Now the sofa and chairs had been pushed together to make room for the tall hospital bed by the window. This gave onto a snow-covered back garden which bordered on the back garden of another terraced house.

Two large flat screens were on, showing different offerings of German afternoon television. The room smelled of hospital. On a bedside table on wheels sat the leftovers of a meal in a divided plate covered with a transparent lid.

Takacs climbed into bed and turned down the volume of both televisions. 'Excuse me, I always watch these things. It does me good to see I'm not the only one with a shit life. Sick *and* a wife who's buggered off.'

The following year he would have been celebrating twenty years at Coromag, but he'd fallen victim to restructuring.

'Not because the company was having a tough time, I mean, a firm that prints money can't get into difficulty, can it? No, but because thanks to technological and economic developments,' he explained, sounding as if he were quoting from a press release, 'there was a review of certain processes and procedures.' He paused for effect. 'Do you know what that means? The same work that used to be done by two men in consignment is now being done by just one. He's fifteen years younger and therefore cheaper. Not much to review there. And they were lucky to boot: I was only diagnosed three months after being made redundant.'

'I understand,' Jonas said. He understood particularly why Weber and Takacs had been talking and were prepared to blow the whistle on their former employers.

'Hans – Herr Weber – told me you came across two banknotes with the same serial number, both of them genuine. Although I don't know how that could have happened, I *do* know that both of them were printed by us. You see, I still say "us".'

'Would you mind if I filmed you?' Jonas asked.

'No, be my guest. I've got nothing left to lose. Married for twenty-five years and now that I'm ill I'm being looked after by home care.'

Jonas set up the camera and two small LED lamps. He asked Takacs to switch off the televisions completely and start with: I know that both the banknotes with the same serial number were printed by us.

Takacs repeated his statement.

'How do you know that? In your department you didn't have anything to do with the manufacture of notes, did you?'

'But I know people who do.'

'So someone in production told you that notes were being printed with serial numbers that already existed?'

'It happened like this. When a consignment's ready to go to the National Bank, armoured cars and police come to escort it. But we... er, *they* also print for other countries – Malaysia, Jordan etc. – and far less fuss is made over these. The lorry docks, the palettes are loaded on, one security guard travels in the cargo area and a second one up front with the driver.' Takacs closed his eyes as if he were waiting for pain to subside. When he opened them again he went on speaking as if nothing had happened.

'All these transports go to the airport. As my house is on the way there, one of the security guards – I've known both of them for ages – would sometimes give me a lift. My driving licence had been taken away for a year, just so you know, dear viewers.'

'We can cut that bit out if you like.'

He ignored the comment. 'In late summer these transports became more frequent, and once when I asked the security man if he would let me come along, he said, "That's fine, but we're not going to the airport, we're going to Nuppingen".' Takacs looked expectantly at Jonas, but he didn't react.

'Nuppingen! GCBS's cash depot! With eighteen palettes of banknotes! Do you know how many notes there are to a palette? Forty-eight boxes each with ten thousand shrinkwrapped notes. If we're talking about hundreds, that's one million francs per box, 48 million per palette. If we're talking about thousands then it's 480 million. Per palette! Which in a single lorry comes to 8.64 billion!'

'And you're saying the money was taken directly to GCBS. Is that unusual?'

'Unusual? You bet! It never happened before in my nineteen years. I asked a friend of mine in production – I'm not going to say his name – what sort of consignment it was, and he said duplicate numbers. He said the National Bank had recently been printing notes with duplicate numbers. For some sort of tests. I didn't tell him that the consignments were going to Nuppingen.' Takacs closed his eyes once more and again it looked as if he were waiting for a wave of pain to pass.

He opened them again. 'So, now you know how you came to be in possession of two hundreds with duplicate numbers.'

*

Max's flat was on the top floor of a dirty-yellow, four-storey building from the sixties. When Jonas rang, the curtain at the window above the entrance twitched. A leisurely lift took him upstairs.

Max had been fairly reticent about suggesting his flat as their meeting point. 'You know the reasons why.' Although Jonas had no desire for a closer glimpse into the private life of Max Gantmann, he was in a hurry to put this banknote business behind him, so he could turn his attention back to the important things in his life: *Montecristo* and Marina.

Max's office was neat and tidy compared to his flat. The front door could only be opened two-thirds of the way because the chaos had spread that far.

The walls in the hallway were lined with removal boxes, piles of newspapers, archive boxes, rubbish bags overflowing with women's clothes, and banana crates full of household stuff, ladies' shoes and cosmetics. The flat was overheated and unventilated.

Max greeted him with his sleeves rolled up, and a waistcoat over his shirt. Pointing to the mess everywhere he said, 'Effie's things. I'm just…'

He took Jonas past a kitchen where the dirty plates were piled up. On each surface sat empty pizza boxes and Styrofoam packaging for burgers and other junk food.

The door to the bedroom didn't close either. Jonas saw an unmade bed full of laundry and items of clothing. On the floor were boxes of fabrics, and there were books and papers piled up everywhere.

His study had presumably once been the sitting room. Now, just as at Gabor Takacs's, all the furniture had been pushed into one corner to make way, not for a bed, but two desks. There was a computer on each of them, partially buried beneath paper, newspapers and rubbish.

'The flat's not really meant for visitors,' Max explained, tipping a heap of stuff from the seat of a chair and setting this beside the office chair he must have been sitting in when Jonas had rung the bell.

Jonas sat down. He was pleased Max didn't offer him anything. He handed him the memory stick. Max inserted it into the computer and watched the video without saying a word.

When the screen turned black Max whistled noiselessly past his cigarette. 'So. Coromag printed duplicate banknotes for GCBS. By the palette! And the consignment was disguised as an order for Malaysia! This is fantastic support for my theory.'

'What theory?' Jonas asked.

'That Contini and the banknotes are connected. The hole that Contini's speculation blew into the balance sheet was so cataclysmic that GCBS would have to fear a run on the bank if the matter ever came to light.'

'What's a run on the bank?'

'It's when customers rush to withdraw their money from a bank that's got into trouble. A little old-fashioned, I admit, but it does still happen. GCBS wouldn't have had enough cash to survive.'

'So a bank can simply print cash like that?'

'Of course not. They have to do it in secret. And what's more they must have very, very close relations with Coromag, the only firm that prints Swiss francs.' Max whistled past his cigarette again. 'No wonder Dillier got so nervous when he saw the two notes.'

'But why duplicate numbers? Why run the risk?'

Max tried to whip the cigarette from his mouth with his index and middle fingers, but it stuck to his top lip and he burned his finger on the lit end. It fell to the paper-strewn floor, where he ground it out beneath his foot, cursing.

'Why duplicate numbers? It's quite simple – because it's more secure than using serial numbers that don't exist. These would be identified by any electronic check, but not duplicate numbers. And the probability of someone getting hold of two identical serial numbers, as well as noticing it, is practically zero. You ought to play the lottery, Jonas.'

Max clicked 'Play' with his mouse arrow and watched the interview again. When it got to 'In late summer these transports became more frequent' he paused the film and asked, 'Contini died in September, didn't he?'

'On the nineteenth.'

Max resumed the video.

For the last few minutes of the film, Max was so mesmerised by the interview that it was the only time he didn't have a glowing cigarette between his fingers.

At the end he said, 'Jonas, this is dynamite!'

*

Jonas had imagined Lili Eck to be younger. Jeff, his producer, had raved so much about her that it had never occurred to him to ask about her age.

Now a woman of at least fifty sat opposite him, her hair that bright red colour which is the result of dyeing snow-white to red. She was short and wiry, with adventurous black eyes. Her black, well-tailored suit gave her a ladylike appearance; perhaps she only wore it for interviews.

Lili's filmography was impressive. She'd been in the industry almost thirty years and she knew everything and everyone. He suspected that this was the reason Rebstyn was keen to hire her. If Jonas had been the producer, he too would have liked to have such an experienced production assistant at the side of a director making his first film.

Lili had another advantage: she'd been signed up for a project where the funding had just fallen through, and thus could start straightaway.

'Does "straightaway" mean tomorrow?' Jonas asked.

'Today,' she replied.

Jonas raised his eyebrows at Jeff. When the latter nodded he offered Lili his hand. 'Jonas. Welcome. Find yourself a desk; they're all free apart from mine.'

*

During their first chat that same afternoon Jonas got an idea just how valuable Lili was going to be for him. Together they went through the list of candidates for the team. In each case she knew whether and where they were working at that moment, and she also had firm opinions on who was right for the job, who would fit well into the team and who couldn't work with whom.

'May I?' she asked, before crossing out the first name. When Jonas nodded she didn't ask again. She cheerfully decimated the list, before adding new names.

When they showed Rebstyn the result of their first meeting, he frowned. 'But we've already decided on Kaspar Eilmann.'

Eilmann was the production manager Rebstyn had envisaged from the start. Lili had crossed him out with her red biro the first time she ran down the list.

Pointing at the place on the list, Jeff gave her a look of reproach.

'Eilmann and me doesn't work. I'd have to go.'

'So who does work with Lili Eck?' Rebstyn asked facetiously.

Without thinking about it Lili replied, 'Andy Fastner. The best.'

This took Rebstyn by surprise. 'Is he free?'

She nodded. 'He will be. In a month or so. Till then we can prepare the ground so that Andy can really get cracking.'

'But he's expensive.'

'He saves twice as much as the extra money he costs.'

The producer pretended to mull over the idea. Then he nodded. 'Have a word with him.'

'I already have.'

*

Lili's greatest coup, however, was to win over Tom Wipf – Tommy, as everybody called him. His name had been missing from all the lists of candidates drawn up by the assistant directors. Not because he was a nobody – in the business he was definitely a name – but because for years he'd been working in California and so wasn't in the running for Swiss productions.

But Lili had inside information. His girlfriend, a Swiss actress who'd tried her luck in Hollywood, had surprisingly been chosen for a television series in Switzerland and Tommy didn't want to let her go on her own. She was almost fifteen years younger and Tommy was a jealous man.

He agreed on the spot and brought to his first meeting with Jonas the draft of a production schedule he'd already put together on the flight to Zürich.

Jonas hit it off with him immediately. They were roughly the same age, found the same things funny, and liked the same films and stars. And they had the same ideas about *Montecristo*.

*

Dillier was really nervous now. Although Brand had rattled him when he'd produced the duplicate notes out of the blue, Just had soon brought the matter under control.

This time it was more serious. He was particularly worried by the man behind it all, a big shot in business journalism: Max Gantmann. A familiar face in living rooms throughout the country until a few years ago.

Right after Gantmann had called him he'd rung Just and pushed for a speedy meeting. He didn't want to say anything on the phone. Just had hesitated until Dillier used the international distress signal: Mayday, Mayday, Mayday.

They'd arranged to meet at the Dragon House again, the most discreet rendezvous in such situations. Dillier pressed the unlabelled top bell at the side entrance and was let in straightaway. 'Fourth floor,' Herr Schwarz's voice said. Dillier hadn't yet worked out where the camera was that identified him.

Just was not waiting for him in the Gentlemen's Room as usual. Herr Schwarz led Dillier instead to a minimalist office with designer furniture. The stock prices flashed up on a flat screen, two bottles each of still and sparkling water stood on a round conference table, together with two bottle openers, two crystal tumblers and two blotters with paper and biro.

Herr Schwarz invited him to take the seat facing the window. Dillier knew full well that this was on the instruction of Just, who wanted to have his back to the light.

Having let him wait for ten minutes, Just entered the room, snappily, as if he were between two important meetings. He came up to Dillier, his hand outstretched, reaching him before the latter could get to his feet. 'Please excuse me. Four o'clock – that's when their working day begins over there.' By 'over there' he meant New York.

They sat down, Just opened a bottle of water and helped himself. 'What's up?'

'Does the name Max Gantmann mean anything to you?'

'The former TV business expert? Is he still alive?'

'You bet. I got a call from him.' Dillier waited for Just to ask why. When the question failed to materialise, he continued. 'Because of the duplicate serial numbers.'

'Oh, I thought that had been dealt with. Didn't one of the notes turn out to be counterfeit?'

'It wasn't about that banknote.' Again he waited for Just to press him.

And this time he did: 'So what was it about?'

After a dramatic pause, Dillier said solemnly, 'Gantmann wanted to know if it was true that late last summer we printed large numbers of banknotes with duplicate serial numbers.' Pause. 'And delivered them to GCBS.'

What to Dillier seemed like a mini-eternity of silence was probably no longer than a few seconds.

Finally Just said, 'How does he know that?'

*

Frau Gabler didn't get out of the house much any more. She was eighty-four and not particularly mobile. Years ago she'd undergone hip replacement surgery and since then everything had got worse. First the wound refused to heal. The doctor said this was linked to her diabetes and her smoking, about both of which he'd had detailed information. She had to have a second and third operation – six weeks in hospital.

Further complications followed. She developed ossification around the muscles in the hip region and nobody knew why. Her movement was actually worse than before the surgery and she couldn't live without painkillers.

This is why she spent most of her time in front of the television or by the window – open in summer, closed in winter. There wasn't much to see, but the street offered greater variety than daytime TV. She was soon up to speed on all the comings and goings in the neighbourhood; she knew who burned the candle at both ends, which couples were rowing, and which latchkey children were bunking off school. She lived on the first floor and in summer could chat to the neighbours from her window. Not all of them, only those who said hello to her.

Max Gantmann had been one of those she used to exchange a few words with. Despite being a celebrity who was on television almost twice daily, he was never above having a brief chat with a disabled old lady. Until his wife died. Since then she'd be lucky even to get a response to her greeting. She could see him going to pot in front of her own eyes. If he carried on like this he'd soon be less mobile than her. When the lift was out of order, which was a regular occurrence, she could hear him wheezing up the stairs like a steam engine. And if she opened the door to her flat shortly afterwards the stairwell would smell like a pub.

On this cold February day she was standing with her Zimmer frame behind the curtain at the closed window, peering down at the dreary street, when Gantmann came waddling along the pavement. As always, he was wearing a black three-piece suit beneath his overcoat, which he hadn't been able to button up for ages. And, as always, a cigarette was clamped between his lips. He was still some way from the house when he began fumbling around in his trouser pocket for his bunch of keys, but he failed to locate it before he got there. He had to perform further contortions by the closed door until he finally found the keys. Looking up at her briefly, he nodded, although she knew he could only presume she was there rather than actually see her.

Shortly after the lift had gone silent, she saw a man approach the entrance to the house. He studied the names beside the door and pressed a bell. It rang in her flat.

With her Zimmer frame Frau Gabler shuffled over to the entry button and buzzed the man in. She heard the door slam below and then nothing more.

'Hello?' she called out.

No reply.

'Is someone there?'

Now a voice called out in English, 'Sorry, wrong address!'

Going out onto the landing she just caught a glimpse of a man vanishing below. Which was followed soon after by the sound of the front door closing again.

She went as fast as she could to the window, but the man was nowhere to be seen,

A few moments later she heard the lift motor rasp into action once more.

When, a few hours later, she told all this to an arson expert from the cantonal police, she couldn't even provide a description of the man. Apart from his red hair.

*

The *Montecristo* production office had become a hive of activity. Lili, Tommy and Jonas were working ten, sometimes twelve-hour days, interrupted only by breaks for sandwiches and pizza.

Camera and lighting teams, set-designers and prop people introduced themselves, while the walls were plastered with photographs of actors and filming locations.

Extra tables were set up for models of the studio sets, such as the prison cell and the visitors' room at Bang Kwang.

The nervousness of the first few days had dissipated; Lili and Tommy gave Jonas the security he needed to radiate the authority required of a director.

He felt happier and more fulfilled than at any other time in his life. The only cloud on the horizon was that he saw Marina too seldom. Either together with his team or at night.

But those nights were wonderful. Marina said, 'Happy men make the best lovers.'

In this period his dealings with Max's research had been limited to one brief phone call. Barbara Contini, the trader's widow, had said she was now ready to talk about the new findings relating to the death of her husband. He told her he was no longer involved with the matter and gave her Max's number.

Then Max, Contini and the duplicate banknotes disappeared into the background.

Until, at a stroke, they seized his attention again.

*

As with most things these days, Jonas learned about this from the internet. He was at his computer in the production office, getting distracted from work by his online newspaper. Right at the top, above the international stories, he saw the headline 'Fire in District 4'. The report read: 'A block of flats in District 4 is ablaze. Two fire-engines are at the scene. Updates follow.' The picture showed a cloud of smoke above the roofs.

Jeff Rebstyn's assistant summoned him to a set-design meeting and he didn't get back to his desk until an hour later. The report had been fleshed out. The fire was now under control. The inhabitants of the building had been successfully evacuated. One person was still missing. A photo gallery accompanied the report. Inhabitants with woollen blankets around their shoulders, aerial ladders by the burning building.

Jonas recognised the place: the house where Max lived. One person was still missing.

It took him almost half an hour to get to the scene of the blaze. He'd taken a taxi which had soon become stuck in the evening rush-hour traffic. After too long getting nowhere he'd paid and continued on foot.

Max's street was closed off. He showed his press pass to the police officer who stopped him, and was allowed through. Smoke was still rising from the building, but one of the fire engines had already left.

Two police cars were in front of the house, as well as a fire service car and a black car. An ambulance was just leaving.

Jonas looked up to the fourth floor. The windows of Max's flat were black holes, the façade above them darkened with soot all the way up to the flat roof.

Commotion broke out amongst the group of reporters and bystanders. Some firemen came out of the entrance with a stretcher on wheels bearing a black body bag. Two men in dark overalls arrived with a coffin and transferred the body. It was so heavy they needed the help of both firemen.

*

He called Marina from the scene. She said, 'Take a taxi home and I'll come over.' Half an hour later she got to his flat and took him in her arms like a child in need of comfort.

She helped him into the sitting room, brought him a beer and asked, 'Do you want to talk about it?'

He shook his head.

'Would you rather be alone?'

'Maybe, for a bit.'

She kissed him on the cheek. 'I'll come and check on you in ten minutes. If you need me before then just shout.'

He heard her pottering in the kitchen and thought how lonely Max must have been in that rubbish-strewn flat, where the only noises were the ones he made himself.

Maybe he ought to have looked after him more. He knew that Max's gruff manner was merely his attempt to give people an excuse to distance themselves from him, because he regarded himself as an imposition – Jonas was practically certain of this. And he, Jonas, had taken advantage of this excuse far too often.

Marina brought him another beer and stood beside him, uncertain of what to do.

He took her hand and pulled her towards him. 'Please stay.'

She fetched herself a beer and sat down beside him. 'How did it happen?'

'If you'd seen his flat you wouldn't be surprised. Max was a hoarder; he couldn't throw anything away. Not a single book, newspaper, scrap of paper, worn sock, nothing. Then there was all his wife's stuff. Pills, ointments, women's magazines. Plus the fact he was drunk half the time and chain smoked. Max's flat would have been ideal for a fire-safety campaign.'

*

It had been a bad night for Jonas. Time and again he'd been jolted out of sleep by haunting images: Max's litter-strewn flat, the windows gaping in the façade like black holes, the cloud of smoke visible from far away, Max stamping out the cigarette butt that had burned his fingers, the body bag that needed four men to lift it.

The following day only a few reports on the fire appeared in the media. Most simply reproduced the official press release almost verbatim: Fire claimed one victim. All other inhabitants evacuated. Damage estimated at several hundred thousand francs. Road will reopen to traffic at seven pm. Fire started in victim's flat. Cause of fire still under investigation.

The following day there was a short obituary in the largest daily paper. It carried a picture of Max when he was still slim; the accompanying text consisted of a potted biography and, as far as Jonas was concerned, a much too short appraisal of his merits as a television business analyst. 'He'd made something of a name for himself as a TV business pundit.' The piece ended with the sentence: 'Two days ago Max Gantmann died in the fire in his flat.'

'Arseholes,' Jonas hissed, tossing the paper into the bin.

In the main edition of the television news there was a short item about him towards the end of the programme, using a still from the old news studio.

'They're acting as if he hadn't worked for them for years, and yet every day he sat just a few floors above them, doing the research and analysis that they themselves were too stupid to attempt,' he moaned.

Marina didn't say anything.

The following day a tabloid took up the story.

'Hoarder TV Star Burns to Death!' ran the headline. Two pictures of Max were inset into a picture of Max's chaotic office with the legend 'If this was his office, what must his flat have been like?' The first was an earlier photo, Max the television expert as the viewers knew him. And then a later one, Max obese and unkempt, as he'd been towards the end. It looked like a passport photo. Jonas wondered how it had fallen in to the hands of the reporters.

The short text recalled Gantmann's almost permanent presence on television during his best days, then mentioned the death of his wife and his subsequent self-neglect, which had led to the ex-star being banished from the screen.

In a text box with the picture of an old woman, the following was printed in bold: 'His flat looked like a tip. You could hardly get the door open.' Below this readers could learn that his neighbour, Frau G, had once brought Gantmann up a packet which had been left with her, affording her a peek into his flat.

Poor Max. He, the scourge of the popular media, had received his biggest obituary from a tabloid.

*

The funeral took place in a small cemetery chapel. Jonas saw a few faces he recognised from the television, a few he'd come into contact with in TV editorial departments and a few friendly faces from the canteen.

The service was conducted by a vicar, a slim version of Max, who turned out to be his brother. He spoke a few awkward words and a jazz guitarist played something totally improvised. It was the saddest funeral Jonas had ever been to. He was pleased that Marina had come with him and held his hand during the service.

Outside the chapel a video journalist he knew was waiting. Stepping in front of him she offered Jonas her hand.

'I know this is a bit weird, but would you mind giving a short statement for... well. I'll give you three guesses.'

Jonas paused. Although he knew what Max thought of Highlife, this was perhaps his last opportunity to bestow at least a little honour on his friend.

So Jonas nodded, Marina moved out of shot, the journalist said, 'Camera running,' and asked her question: 'Herr Brand, you were one of Max Gantmann's last friends. Can you tell us something about his problem?'

'Which problem?'

'Max Gantmann was a hoarder.'

'And you're a stupid cow!' Jonas said it so loudly that some of the funeral guests swivelled around.

Taking Marina's hand, he swiftly led her away.

On the narrow path to the cemetery exit they were held up by a middle-aged woman pushing an elderly lady in a wheelchair. Jonas had noticed her in the chapel; he thought he recognised her.

At a crossroads the younger woman pushed the wheelchair to one side, Jonas and Marina thanked her and walked past.

'Herr Brand!' the woman in the wheelchair called out.

Jonas turned round.

'I know you.'

Jonas nodded. 'I used to be on television occasionally.'

'But you also visited Herr Gantmann. I saw you. I'm his neighbour. Frau Gabler.'

Now Jonas remembered. This was the elderly lady who had told the tabloid about the mess in Max's flat. He came closer and, still smouldering from the argument with Highlife, snapped at her: 'It was very indiscreet of you to tell that paper about

Max's untidiness. He was a lonely widower and housework just became too much for him. Now people will remember him as a hoarder. Instead of the great business journalist he was.'

The woman pushing the wheelchair now got at Jonas: 'What are you thinking of, talking to my mother like that? She's not used to dealing with journalists. They put one over on her.'

Frau Gabler nodded. 'They didn't tell me they were from the paper. I thought they were from the police. I wanted to tell them that just before the fire started a man went up to his flat. But they weren't interested.'

'What sort of man?'

'He rang my bell, and when I buzzed him in he pretended he'd come into the house by mistake and was leaving again. But then I heard the lift go up to the fourth floor.'

'Were you able to describe him to the police?'

'Only that he spoke English and had a modern hairstyle. But they weren't interested.'

*

The moment he entered the police station he knew he was simply wasting his time. A few people were waiting in the corridor, and behind the reception desk three uniformed officers were chatting in that tongue-in-cheek jargon common to long-standing work colleagues. They ignored Jonas. He waited, trying not to think about all those things that weren't getting done in the production office.

Eventually one of the officers deigned to check his ID, take down his personal details and note his reason for coming.

Then he was made to wait for half an hour, just to be told that the investigation of fires fell under the competence of the cantonal police.

Unable to restrain himself, Jonas asked, 'You mean to say you've only just found this out now?'

The cantonal police had obviously been warned he was coming. They let him wait even longer, finally taking him somewhere that looked like an interrogation room in a TV crime drama.

Half an hour later a police officer entered the room, shook his hand and sat down opposite him. He'd brought a thin blue folder with him, which he now placed neatly in line with the edge of the table.

Jonas told him about the man who spoke English and who'd managed to gain access to the house just a few minutes before the fire. 'Frau Gabler, the neighbour on the first floor, mentioned this to your colleague, but he didn't seem to be interested, she said.'

The office looked him in the eye as if trying to examine Jonas's conscience. He was a bull-necked man of around forty with blond, close-cropped hair, and he smelled of stale cigarette smoke and old frying oil. Jonas held his gaze.

'So now you've come here, Herr Brand, to tell us how to do our job?' He picked up the blue folder from the desk and opened it. Jonas could see a file number on the cover.

'No, I'm not trying to tell you how to do your job; I've great faith in our police force. I just wanted to say that arson can't be ruled out here. Max Gantmann was working on a potentially explosive case.'

'Such as?'

'A bank scandal.'

'Really? Tell me more.' The officer gave him another searching stare. He had short blond eyelashes, like tiny yellow brushes.

'I fear that the evidence has perished with the fire. He kept it in his flat, for safety.'

The officer leafed through the folder. He sighed. 'Herr Brand. On 3 December you reported a break-in to our colleagues without any signs of a break-in. On the following day, a mugging without any witnesses or descriptions of the perpetrators. On 19 December you tried to persuade the Basel district police that a clear case of suicide was in fact murder. And now you're coming to us and saying that the fire which destroyed the flat of a chain-smoking hoarder was also murder, this time as a result of arson.'

'But they're all connected,' Jonas protested.

'Oh yes, Herr Brand, everything's connected. It's all one big conspiracy.' The officer spoke to him like a psychiatric nurse to a patient. 'If you like I'll make a written record of this and you can also press charges against an unknown person or persons.'

He held up the folder with two fingers. 'But if I were you, I shouldn't like the police to have a file like this on me. And I'd also be pretty uncomfortable if it kept getting fatter. Know what happens then? If, one day, you've got a real problem, an emergency and you need us? Nobody takes you seriously. Okay?'

He gave Jonas another hard stare.

'Right then, Herr Brand. Are we going to put this on the record or not?'

*

She stood in front of the full-length mirror in the bedroom – where shortly before she'd been standing with Jonas in a very different position – and checked her figure. She turned a little to the left, then to the right, faced back to the front and bent forwards slightly.

No, the cut of her neckline might be misconstrued.

She took off the dress again and laid it on the bed beside the other rejects: a trouser suit – too businesslike; a lady's suit – too ladylike; a cocktail dress – too festive.

The little black number was her next option. Having swapped the push-up bra which went with the low-cut dress for a normal one, she pulled it carefully over her hairdo and performed contortions to fasten the zip at the back.

It looked good. Black chiffon, round neckline, hem just above the knees. Plus the pearl necklace her mother had given her for passing her school-leaver's exams.

There was still some champagne left in the small bottle in the fridge. She refreshed her glass, took it into the bathroom and set about her make-up.

She didn't need much. A touch of foundation in those places which had a tendency to shine, a tiny amount of eyeliner and a bit of mascara. She'd do her lips when she'd finished her glass and the driver rang.

She daubed a little Chanel N° 19 behind the ears and on her wrists, because it went perfectly with the little black number, and now she was ready.

Was she nervous? No. A little excited, perhaps. But nervous?

When the bell rang, however, she gave a start, tipping her glass with such a jerk that some champagne missed her mouth. She dabbed her face with a tissue and said into the intercom, 'I'll be right down.' She went back into the bathroom, put on lipstick and then fetched her coat from the wardrobe. Marina tucked it over her arm with her handbag, took a final look in the mirror, locked the door and called the lift.

The black Audi was parked half on the pavement, its hazard lights flashing. A man in a black suit held open the rear door. Climbing in, she enjoyed the new car smell that immediately enveloped her.

They'd barely gone a hundred metres when her mobile rang. It read 'Jonas' on the illuminated display. She pressed 'Decline call', put the phone in flight mode and dropped it back into her bag.

Less than ten minutes later the driver climbed the pavement again and put on his hazards. He opened the door, took Marina to the entrance, and pressed the unlabelled top bell at the side entrance. 'Yes?' the voice of Herr Schwarz said.

'Lily Room,' Marina replied.

The door buzzed.

*

It was way past midnight, but the lights were still burning in the production office at 122 Blauwiesenstrasse. Marina had cancelled; she was busy preparing for an event in Bern. He'd forgotten what kind. She was spending the night there and they wouldn't see each other until the following evening.

This was perfectly fine by Jonas. He was worried about the production schedule. It was going over budget, and if they wanted to bring it back into line they'd have to rework the screenplay. Change locations and shorten scenes or cut them altogether.

It was a job you had to stick at and for which he needed Tommy's help. Tommy was free that evening because his girlfriend was on a night shoot.

They were both in the sort of mood you enter after going beyond a particular stage of tiredness and everything seems simple and logical. They thought the trimmed-down screenplay was more compact and gripping, making them wonder why they hadn't resorted to the red pen earlier. They were looking forward to the reaction of Jeff and Lili the following morning.

Rather than heading straight home, they went for a nightcap to Cesare's to celebrate their breakthrough. It was within walking distance from Nembus.

There was little activity in Cesare's at this time of night. The slow tracks they played at closing time were on, and it was clear from the body language of the staff that new customers were not especially welcome.

They sat in the quietest corner and Jonas felt it was time to tell Tommy about his Bangkok experience.

'Do you want to hear why I almost dropped out before things really got going?'

Tommy did.

'And if you'd been right,' he asked when Jonas had finished, 'would you have really dropped out?'

'Of course.'

'The bank would have been able to keep the money and you wouldn't have been able to do your film. Nor any in the future, I imagine.'

Jonas nodded animatedly. Yes, that's how high the price was for keeping your conscience clean.

'I don't know,' Tommy said. 'If I'd been given an opportunity like that I wouldn't care less about the reasons behind it. But maybe I've been living in California for too long.'

'And maybe I've spent too long in Switzerland.'

*

Jonas strolled home through the night-time streets in a peculiar mixture of euphoria and thoughtfulness. The apartment blocks lining the streets were dark; only occasionally did he glimpse a chink of light between the curtains or the blue flickering of a television on a ceiling.

By the kerbs were the remains of dirty snow and grit, while patches of snow lay in front gardens like tiny continents.

It struck him that he hadn't thought about Marina all evening, ever since she'd declined his call. He took out his mobile. On the display it said, 'putting into sleep mode. goodnight xxx m.' The message bore yesterday's date and a time of 23:12. Now it was almost two in the morning.

Frau Knezevic had again left the exercise book on top of the espresso machine where he couldn't overlook it. Jonas checked how much he was in arrears and put the difference plus some more housekeeping money between the pages of the book. Unusually for him he simply ticked the bill without going through the calculations.

Whenever he was alone in his flat he was still gripped by the anxiety which had plagued him since the break-in. Jonas turned on the light in his bedroom, went into the bathroom and squeezed a little toothpaste from the tube onto his brush. But he left it on the side of the washbasin. He was too unsettled to go to bed.

He turned on the light in his studio and booted up the computer.

Ever since Jonas had been working at Nembus, he'd been using the email on their server. Here in his studio he only got post from those people who still used his private address.

There were a few new messages. When he saw one of them a shiver ran down his spine. It was from Dropbox and read: 'Hello Jonas. Max Gantmann invited you to a shared Dropbox folder called "Dynamite" with the following message: "Dear Jonas, download this immediately onto an external hard drive, make two copies and store them in two different secure places. Not in your safety deposit box! Max.'

Below was a link saying: View 'Dynamite'. Jonas could feel

his heart pounding wildly. He fetched a beer from the fridge, sat down at the computer, clicked the link and entered his access details.

A folder called Dynamite appeared. He opened it. It contained a number of small Word documents and a large video, which was the first thing Jonas opened.

The screen was filled with Max's head and shoulders – clearly filmed by the camera on his monitor. He was sitting at a cluttered desk with overflowing bookshelves in the background. The light, which cast harsh shadows, must be coming from his desk lamp, which Max had angled towards himself.

In the corner of his mouth was a freshly lit cigarette and his reading glasses were perched a long way down his nose.

'Jonas,' he began, 'perhaps you're right. Perhaps I'm suffering from a persecution complex and I'm a conspiracy theorist. In that case you can simply delete all of this and we'll meet for a few beers at the Schönacker.' He paused to take a drag on his cigarette.

'But perhaps *I'm* right. And in that case I'm afraid I have to involve you. You're the only person I can trust over this.' Taking the cigarette out of his mouth, he flicked away the ash before putting it back between his lips.

'And this brings us to the first problem: trust. Trust nobody. This affair is so huge that you're the only person it's safe with. If I publish it, I'll do it with at least three different media and make sure that each one knows the other two have got a copy. Don't discuss it with anyone before it's made public. And when I say *any*one, that includes your new girlfriend, what's her name? Ina?' He winked at the camera without forming his mouth into a smile. 'Not Ina either.'

'Right, let's deal with these things one by one. Your first suspicion was correct; Contini did lose money through speculation, with Russian securities, property and energy. Apparently he squandered somewhere between ten and twenty billion. He offset these losses with fictitious profits from fictitious derivatives. I know, no one understands derivatives, not even the bankers who sell them. But if you want to have a go anyway, you'll find all you need to know in "Doc1". If it ever got out that the profits offsetting the losses didn't exist, that would be curtains.'

Max lit another cigarette off the stub of the one he'd almost finished and continued: 'One day Contini admitted everything to the Chief Risk Officer. But instead of reporting the matter to the risk committee, as was his duty, he went to the CEO, William Just. This gargantuan loss would have brought the chronically undercapitalised GCBS to the brink of disaster. You see, if it had become known it could have led to a run on the bank.

'After all the experiences of the last financial crisis, for the state to intervene to save a bank would have been a political no-no, even if the bank was "too big to fail". That's why the two of them decided to keep a lid on it.' Max paused, as if to give Jonas time to take this all in.

'Contini – now listen to this – was plagued by his conscience, and he decided to speak directly to the Swiss Banking Supervisory Authority, in fact to its president, Konrad Stimmler.'

Jonas remembered the man in the lobby of the Palace Hotel in Gstaad having a tête-à-tête with William Just, the CEO of GCBS.

'Whether he did so, I don't yet know. In any event, this phase of the story coincides with Contini's change of mood as described by his wife and his colleague, Jack Heinzmann.'

Max paused for effect. 'And it also coincides... with his death.'

Jonas paused the recording. Until that point pretty much everything Max had said he knew already. But this was new. Paolo's announcement that he was going to report the matter to the supervisory authority would have been a strong reason to have him killed. He resumed the video.

'Now I bet you want to know how I know all of this. It's down to you, old chap. Down to the fact that you gave Contini's widow my telephone number. She called me and I went to Basel. Just imagine! Me taking the train to Basel! You'll find out all about it in "Doc2". Most importantly the draft of a letter Contini intended to write to Stimmler. If he did actually send it, Jonas, and the president of the SBSA has hushed the matter up, then here we have an affair which could blow up at any moment, bringing the entire financial centre to its kn...'

Jonas paused the video again. Max's face froze with his mouth half open and one eye screwed up because of the cigarette smoke.

Raising the can of beer to his lips, Jonas noticed that his hand was shaking. 'Max, Max!' he said to the image from the hereafter. 'I don't want to know any of this. Why didn't you keep it to yourself? I'm a director, not an investigative journalist! Just let me make my film!'

He clicked 'Play' and Max started moving again.

'...ees. If the supervisory authority was in the know, then it probably knew about the banknotes too. And then...' Max took a sharp intake of breath.

Max needed another cigarette before he could go on. 'Listen Jonas, I'm not trying to be melodramatic here, nor do I want to burden you unnecessarily with this affair. You should concentrate on your film and I sincerely wish you the greatest success with it. All I ask of you is to keep this material in a safe place. You don't have to do anything more with it.'

Max made another dramatic pause.

'Unless something happens to me.'

Jonas watched Max take hold of his mouse and his eyes search for the 'Off' icon. Then he thought of something else.

'And if it does,' he said, 'try to find out what "Lily Room" means. I haven't managed to yet.'

His eyes scanned the screen again and all of a sudden the image was gone.

*

In the 'Dynamite' folder was a document with the name 'JB', Jonas's initials. In it were links to the Vimeo video site and the access codes to two films. This was the footage he'd taken relating to the banknotes and the customer incident, and which to his great relief he'd handed over to Max.

Jonas opened the file with the name 'Doc1'. Entitled 'Fictional Derivatives', it was riddled with specialist terms Jonas didn't understand.

He was more interested in the folder entitled 'Doc2'. It contained an mp3 file entitled 'Conv.BC'.

Jonas started it.

Max Gantmann's deep smoker's voice asked, 'Do you mind if I smoke?'

A soft woman's voice replied. 'Yes, I mean, it doesn't bother me personally that much, but the children. You can't get rid of the smell. In the garden though…'

Max interrupted her: 'No, don't worry, I'm not that addicted.' Jonas couldn't help chuckle. Max – not addicted!

His voice said, 'Conversation with Frau Barbara Contini,' and he stated the date and time.

Then Max began: 'Frau Contini, allow me to briefly

summarise our last conversation, but please interrupt me if you'd like to correct anything.

He cleared his throat. 'You told me you still believe your husband did *not* commit suicide, but was the victim of a crime. You said as much back in…' he paused, and there followed the sound of paper rustling, '… December to my colleague, Jonas Brand. In the meantime, has any more evidence emerged to support your theory?'

'This letter.'

Max expanded on her answer for anyone who might be listening to their conversation: 'Frau Contini has shown me the draft of a letter which, in her opinion, could be related to the crisis her husband faced during the last few months of his life. The letter is addressed to Konrad Stimmler, President of the Swiss Banking Supervisory Authority, SBSA. It talks of a large trading loss for which he, Paolo Contini, was responsible and which he offset with fictitious derivatives. It also says that he informed the Chief Risk Officer of the matter but, to the best of his knowledge, this information was not relayed any further.'

Barbara Contini's soft voice said, 'If you want to smoke, please go into the garden.'

'Oh, I'm terribly sorry, that was just pure habit. No, no, I don't want to smoke. Sorry. Back to the letter. Did you ever speak to your husband about this matter?'

'We never spoke about his work. I don't understand anything about it.'

'So you don't know whether he ever sent a final version of this letter either?'

'No idea. But it does talk about a massive loss. Perhaps that's why he was so stressed and gloomy.'

'But you don't believe that the situation he was in could have made him kill himself?'

There was a pause.

'You're shaking your head. How can you be so sure?'

'I already told your colleague. Paolo was happy and relaxed during those last few days. As if a huge burden had been taken away from him.'

'That could have also been because he'd decided to commit suicide.'

Slightly louder than before, she said, 'Or because he'd decided to write this letter.'

'Or,' Max added, 'because he'd decided to send it.'

The other document in the folder was a pdf of the draft letter. Contini had crossed things out and made corrections by hand. At one point there was a red semi-circle, as if the writer of the letter had been drinking a glass of wine.

*

Jonas remembered a time at primary school when he occasionally had to bring home letters from his teacher to his parents. He didn't know what the content of these was, but he had a pretty good idea.

Each time he brought home a letter he would put it on top of the shoe cabinet with the rest of the post. But he would push the pile so far back that all it took was a slight nudge for some of the pile to fall between the cabinet and the wall. Jonas always made sure that other post disappeared along with the ominous letter; it made his exploits less suspicious.

Although the letters to his parents would turn up eventually, this might not be until the following spring, by which time they were out of date and so their effect was not quite as devastating.

Jonas intended to do exactly the same with the explosive material Max had sent him. Which is why he found the request to copy everything and store it in several different places very convenient.

He saved the Dynamite folder and the Vimeo films onto a USB stick and made two copies. One of them he rolled up in a plastic bag and buried in a box of farfalle. He put the other in his key pouch in order to hide it somewhere in the production office. The third copy went into his safe, the Vietnamese mother goddess, where the two one-hundred franc notes were still stashed, the genuine one and the counterfeit one.

When Jonas was finished and about to go to bed he heard a slurping noise in the street. He went to the window and peered out.

The orange light of a snowplough was flickering outside. It had been snowing the whole time that Jonas had been busy with the perilous material Max had bequeathed him.

*

There was no point going to bed now. In a couple of hours was the meeting at which Tommy and he were going to present the revised screenplay to Rebsytn and Lili. He wanted to get to the office early enough so he could photocopy the revised pages.

Jonas took a long shower, allowing the jet setting to massage his head and shoulders. Then he got dressed, went into the kitchen and made himself some coffee and fried eggs.

Just before he was about to leave the house Marina called. It was twenty past seven and practically still dark.

When he saw her name on the display he remembered Max's instruction regarding secrecy. *Not even Ina.*

'Did you miss me as much as I missed you?' was her first question.

'More, I expect,' he replied. 'I wasn't on sleep mode like you.'

She laughed. 'If I have to get up at six I need my sleep. Have you got a lot of snow too?'

'A winter's tale.'

'What have you been doing?'

'Working. You?'

'Working.'

'When are you coming back?'

'On the next train.'

'When can we get together?'

'This evening. Your place.'

Jonas looked at the dark screen where Max's face had spoken to him. Overnight his flat had become even creepier. 'No, I'd rather we were at yours.'

* * *

He was the first person to leave his block. His winter boots left deep prints in the new snow on the way to the garden gate. It was still snowing.

The new flakes had given the dirty heaps of snow left behind by the plough a white blanket. The few cars that were on the roads were driving slowly and with windscreen wipers working away at full pelt. His head bowed, Jonas walked through the silent streets. His black woollen hat was covered in snow.

He tried to focus on *Montecristo*, but in his mind the bloated face with its harsh shadows kept popping up, as well as the mouth talking to him with a cigarette in one corner.

'You don't have to do anything more with it,' the mouth said. 'Unless something happens to me.'

And now something had happened to him. As it had to Paolo Contini. And almost to Jonas himself. All for the same reason.

This realisation made him shudder. Thrusting his hands

deeper into his coat pockets, he quickened his pace.

The brick building was dark, with only the lamp above the entrance casting a circle of light into the swirling mass of snowflakes. Here, too, the short path from the pavement to the door was covered in virgin snow.

Jonas unlocked the front door and the door to Nimbus productions, and switched on the light in the hall. He went into the production office, turned on his computer, put the stick into the USB slot and copied its contents onto Nembus Productions' hard drive.

While this was happening he went and photocopied the revised pages of the screenplay and production schedule.

When he came back the files were still copying and Tommy was standing in front of the monitor.

'Dynamite?' he asked.

'An old project I stumbled upon while clearing up. I wanted to have another look at it when I get the chance.'

When he was alone again in the office he printed out a still of the red-haired railway passenger. This man had been on the train when Contini died. And when Jonas met him for the second time he felt as if the man was shadowing him. And he also had 'a modern hairstyle' as the old woman, Frau Gabler, had called it. Jonas encrypted the Dynamite folder and stuck the USB stick beneath the middle drawer of his desk.

*

On the way to Marina's he passed by to see Frau Gabler, Max's disabled neighbour. He'd found out that she'd been put in an old people's home and he arrived at the reception carrying a bunch of tulips.

Frau Gabler was sitting watching television in a small room.

She was wearing a quilted dressing gown and a headscarf. Her wig was sitting on a polystyrene bust that stood on a sideboard.

She'd responded to his knocking with a surly 'Come in!', but then gave her unexpected visitor a look of surprise. 'How nice!' she said when she recognised him.

Jonas gave her the flowers.

'Tulips in February! It's a crazy world! Press the bell by the bed and someone will come to put them in a vase. Or maybe not. Sit down, look, there's a chair. You can just put your things on the bed.'

Jonas obeyed and sat opposite her.

'The others are eating now, but I don't eat with all those old people. I'm just here temporarily. Until my flat's habitable again. I'm afraid I can't offer you anything; I don't have anything.'

She stared at him and smiled. 'How nice.'

Frau Gabler's delight at his visit forced Jonas to wait before embarking on the real reason why he'd come. He let her ask him about Max, how they'd met, whether he'd known his wife; then had to listen to how devotedly Max had looked after her and how much he'd changed since her death. Leaving the subject of Max, she moved onto the other neighbours.

It was almost an hour before Jonas got the opportunity to leave and then, Columbo-like, said at the door, 'Oh yes, that visitor you told me about who rang your bell and then probably went up to see Max…' He took out the picture from his coat pocket and unfolded it. 'Could it have been this man?'

He went back to his chair and handed her the photograph. She asked him to pass her the pair of glasses that was on the bed and examined the picture carefully. Then she shook her head. 'I only saw him from above. But that could be the hairstyle. And the colour too.'

Marina had cooked adobo again, the second time since they'd met. 'For one thing this is the national dish of the Philippines, and secondly, it's pretty much the only dish I know how to make,' she'd explained.

'And thirdly, as we know, it only gets better the longer it stays on the stove,' he'd added, dragging her into the bedroom.

Now they were lying side by side on the bed in quiet satisfaction.

'Can you live with that?' he asked, motioning with his chin at the bunch of white lilies in a floor vase by the window.

'The smell? Barely.'

'Why do you buy lilies then?'

'I got them as a present.'

'From who?'

Marina laughed. 'Is that any business of yours?'

'Isn't it?'

She gave him a kiss. 'From a client.'

'Why?'

'He thought I'd done a good job. But chuck them away if they bother you.'

'You can also remove the stamens.'

'Or hold your nose.'

They fell silent.

'How was Bern?' Jonas asked.

'Exhausting. What about Zürich?'

'Tiring.'

'But successful?'

'We cut, streamlined and saved. But yes, I think it was successful. How about you? What did you do in Bern?'

'Oh, you don't want to know. Nothing special. So what did you cut?'

Jonas talked late into the night about the changes they'd made, and about the euphoria he and Tommy had felt. He also mentioned their nightcap at Cesare's. He kept quiet about the ghost of Max Gantmann.

'What else?'

'Nothing.'

'Are you sure?'

'Yes, why?'

She shrugged. 'Oh, you know. You just seem a bit strange. As if something's weighing down on you.'

'I'm still upset by all that Max stuff.'

'I can understand that. Try to forget it. Concentrate on your film.'

'That's what I *am* trying to do.'

'That scoop about the bank, too – forget it. Let it rest with Max's ashes and his rubbish.'

Jonas leaned on his elbows and looked at her. Marina's eyes were closed, her face shone like polished ivory in the weak light seeping through the half-open door. 'What makes you think I might waste another second of my time on the matter?'

She kept her eyes closed. 'Won't you?'

'No.'

She opened her eyes, sat straddling his chest, pushed his wrists down onto the mattress and said, 'Promise me. Let me see you take an oath!'

'But I don't have a free hand.'

*

He got the call the following morning via the Nembus Productions landline.

'There's a Frau Kleinert who wants to speak to you,' Rebstyn's assistant said.

'Don't recognise the name. Did she say what it was about?'

'It's private.' She put the woman through.

The woman had a deep voice. She said, 'You don't know me, but I'm passing on regards from a mutual friend of ours. Max Gantmann.'

Jonas was silent for a moment. Then he said, 'Max is dead.'

'I know. I wouldn't be ringing you otherwise.'

'I don't understand.'

The woman sounded like somebody forced to perform an unpleasant duty: truculent and in a hurry. 'Max wrote to request that I should get in touch with you if anything happened to him.'

'And you're only doing that now?'

'It was a normal letter. I'm not on email. And I only got back from holiday today. Where can we meet?'

'Can't we discuss it over the phone?'

'No. How about the Rabeneck? Three o'clock. It's nice and quiet at that time.'

The Rabeneck was a sort of alternative restaurant run by a cooperative. Sandra Kleinert fitted in perfectly there. She must have been just over fifty and everything about her was round. She wore her grey hair short, no make-up, and her grey eyes gazed serenely into Jonas's.

Apart from two mothers, whose children were sleeping beside the table in thickly padded buggies, they were the only customers in the restaurant. It smelled of the lunch menu, the most prominent note being cabbage. Sandra Kleinert was already sitting down when Jonas arrived. It looked as if she'd eaten. On the table was a half-litre jug with the remains of some red wine.

No sooner had Jonas sat down than she handed him a letter. It was short and in Max's unmistakable handwriting:

Dear Sandi,

In case anything happens to me (and let's hope it doesn't, as the insurance broker always says) then please tell Jonas Brand about what we discussed. You'll reach him at Nembus Productions.

In the hope that this will never be necessary, with my very best regards,

Mäge.

'Mage'

'That's what we used to call him. I knew him through Effie. We were friends, but since her death I'd had no contact with him.'

'What did he mean by "what we discussed"?'

The waiter came to the table and asked him, 'What can I get you? We only have cold food.'

Jonas ordered a sparkling water. The waiter poured the rest of the wine into Sandra's glass and took the jug away with him.

'He rang me out of the blue between Christmas and New Year, saying he wanted to see me. We arranged to meet in the Schönacker. My God, Max had put on weight! He wanted me to leak some information about the committee.'

'Which committee?'

'Moviefonds. I'm on the committee there. Didn't you know?'

'I had no idea.'

'Well now you do. He wanted to know how you'd suddenly been awarded one and a half million francs of funding.'

'So that was you?'

'I told him that the decision was taken over our heads. I mean, we rejected the proposal years ago. As I'm sure you know.'

'I do. Why, actually?'

'We thought the screenplay was a pile of crap.'

Jonas was shocked into silence.

'Including Serge Cress, by the way.'

The waiter brought Jonas his water. By the time he'd left Jonas had regained his composure and asked, 'So where did the money come from?'

'From the fund. And this is mainly provided for by GCBS's arts budget.'

'But Cress says they have no influence over the allocation of money.'

Sandra smiled. 'In theory they don't.'

'But in practice?'

'He who pays the piper calls the tune. It's also true in arts funding.'

Jonas pointed at Sandra's glass. 'Will you have some more wine?'

'Just a glass.'

He beckoned the waiter over and ordered.

Sandra continued: 'Just before he died Max called me again. About the same matter. He wanted to know if it was correct that the funding decision was taken on 10 December. I couldn't remember off-hand and had to check.'

'And?'

'It was later, of course. Just before Christmas.'

*

'Are you not feeling well?'

Lili Eck was sitting at her computer and turned towards the

door when Jonas entered the production office.

'I'm OK, why?'

'You're as white as a sheet.'

'I haven't slept much in the past few days.'

'Then go home and come back properly rested tomorrow. You're fit for nothing in this state.'

Jonas would have loved to follow her advice, but he was spooked by the thought of his empty flat. He'd planned to go home after his meeting with Sandra Kleinert, but had turned back half way there and gone to Cesare's. He needed some time on his own to collect his thoughts.

Cesare's was almost as empty as the Rabeneck had been. Having opted for a table in the darkest corner, Jonas had ordered a small carafe of Barolo and put his notepad and biro in front of him. Not because he intended to jot anything down, but he simply didn't want to be disturbed by the waiter, who had a habit of sitting down next to customers if he got bored.

It was perfectly clear: he had been bought. GCBS had paid out one and a half million francs to divert him from their scandal. It was almost certain that they'd had their trader killed. Likewise it was almost certain that they'd had Max killed. And it was equally probable that they'd tried to get rid of him in Bangkok. If they discovered how much he knew and that he was still pursuing the matter, they'd surely try to eliminate him a second time. The affair was too big; 'Dynamite' Max had called it. And the bank was as dangerous as a wounded grizzly bear.

What should he do now? Given that he couldn't play the innocent any longer? Tommy had said, 'If I'd been given an opportunity like that I wouldn't care less about the reasons behind it.' But that was Tommy. How corrupt was he, Jonas?

Could he possibly bail out now? What excuse could he come up with for chucking it all in?

He realised he hadn't touched his wine and was about to take a sip, but found the smell so abhorrent that he put his glass back down.

All of a sudden the equation became perfectly clear: if he dropped out of *Montecristo*, GCBS would know why. Which meant his life would be in danger. He had no option but to continue.

'Something wrong with the wine?' the waiter asked when Jonas paid.

'No, it's fine.'

'So why haven't you drunk it?'

'I don't fancy any wine.'

'Why did you order it, then?'

'Am I a psychiatrist?'

Jonas left the baffled waiter and went to Nembus Productions in Blauwiesenstrasse. It had started snowing again.

Lili's maternal fussing was getting on his nerves. He snapped at her: 'I can't lie in bed in the middle of the day; I've got a film to make, remember?'

'Precisely,' she said gently, going to the door.

'What do you mean?' he shouted after her.

*

But the following day he couldn't stick it out. He'd spent the night at Marina's and hadn't slept much. During the day he nodded off several times in front of the computer. On the first two occasions, Lili noticed but didn't do anything. The third time he said petulatnly, 'OK, OK, I'm going.'

She refrained from passing comment, just saying, 'I'll only

call you if something urgent crops up. Otherwise, see you tomorrow.'

Tommy entered. 'What do you mean see you tomorrow?' he asked in surprise. 'I thought we were going to have a look at the casting.'

'Let's do it tomorrow; I've had it for today.'

'Just an hour, an hour and a half. It won't take any longer.'

'Let him go to bed, Tommy; he'll collapse otherwise.'

Jonas went back home through the snowy streets. With a bad conscience but a light heart, as he felt when he used to skip school.

It was only three o'clock by the time he got back to Rofflerstrasse. The door to his flat was open and he could hear Frau Knezevic singing to herself.

'Don't get a fright, it's only me, Jonas!' he called out.

She came out of the bathroom. 'So early? You've just missed him.'

'Who?'

'The computer man.'

'I wasn't expecting any computer man. What did he want?'

'But you gave him key. He was already here when I arrived. He was mending something on computer. I don't know, I speak no English.'

Jonas felt his knees giving way. He went into his studio and Frau Knezevic followed him.

'You not feeling well?'

'What did he look like?'

'Elegant. Shorter than you. Had short red hair. Left just before you arrived. Had phone call, had to go quickly.'

Jonas sat down at his computer, switched it on, went to the Vimeo web site and entered the code for the film. He received an error message saying that it didn't exist.

He went into Dropbox. Max's Dynamite folder had been deleted.

Now he started panicking. He ran into the kitchen, followed close behind by Frau Knezevic. He shook the farfalle onto the kitchen table. No USB stick.

He hurried into the bedroom. At the door he turned around to his housekeeper. 'Do you mind waiting a minute? Shutting the door in her face, he opened the secret compartment in the back of the Vietnamese statue.

The two banknotes were still there, plus some money and… the USB stick. He hadn't found it.

Jonas took it back to his computer and plugged it in. Frau Knezevic had followed him again.

'Was in woman, no?'

Jonas looked at her in surprise. 'Which woman?'

The data on the stick was all still intact. Jonas fast forwarded the 'Customer incident' film until he got to the sleeping passenger with red hair. Even before he could freeze the picture Frau Knezevic said, 'Computer man.'

*

Twenty minutes later he walked back into the *Montecristo* production office, surprising Tommy, who was at his desk and on his computer.

'Your large screen is clearer for working on the production plan,' he apologised. 'Do you need your computer?'

'Yes,' Jonas replied, 'I do.'

Tommy closed the programme and made way for him.

'That was a power nap at best,' he remarked.

'I'm too nervous to sleep. Has Lili gone yet?'

'No, she must be in the building somewhere.'

'Could you look for her please?'

Tommy was taken aback. He wasn't used to being given such tasks by Jonas. But he went without a grumble.

As soon as Tommy was out of the office, Jonas opened the middle drawer of his desk and felt underneath. The USB stick was gone.

He opened the Nembus hard disk and searched for the encrypted Dynamite folder. It wasn't there.

Once more a calmness set in, which was a new experience for Jonas. Just as when he'd happened upon the bag of cocaine in the Mandarin Oriental, he didn't panic and his thoughts became crystal clear.

There were accomplices at Nembus. Someone from here had called the red-haired man to warn him that Jonas was coming home earlier than planned. Lili perhaps? Or Tommy? The latter had watched him save the Dynamite folder onto the hard drive. And he was handy with computers.

In any event, now the others could be in no doubt as to how much he knew. That could cost him his life.

What should he do? Pretend nothing had happened. Focus squarely on *Montecristo*. But that wouldn't mean he was out of danger.

He'd only be safe when the scandal became public. Which meant he had to juggle both things: continue working on *Montecristo*, while secretly turning the bank scandal into a broadcastable form as quickly as possible.

When Tommy came back with Lili he had an idea.

'You don't look much more rested to me,' Lili said, by way of a greeting.

'I can sleep after the première,' Jonas replied. 'Can you book me a flight to Abu Dhabi? I want to do a recce of the scenes in the UAE.'

'Now?' she asked, surprised.

'No, tomorrow.'

'We've got art direction all day tomorrow,' Tommy protested.

'You can do that without me. I don't have any feeling for the Arabic section of the film. I've never been to that part of the world. In the screenplay it reads like a travel brochure.'

'How long?'

'Three, four days. Five at most. Just leave the return flight open.'

Lili went to her desk, shrugging like an employee resigned to the whims of her boss.

Tommy decided to be his usual practical self: 'Shall we look through the scenes in the UAE?'

*

This time the meeting was more formal and the group slightly larger. Herr Schwarz had chosen 'Chez Chez' for the catering, a gourmet firm experienced in discreet jobs. The dishes were delivered ready prepared – a sort of cold buffet in courses. The caterers saw nobody but Herr Schwarz, and all he had to do was to remove the cloches.

The table, a pretty Biedermeier piece large enough to seat eight people, had been set for four. After a brief reception around the fire in the small room – a glass of champagne and some puff pastries – Wilhelm Just, the host, had invited the guests to the table.

The seating plan was dictated by the company. Adam Dillier, CEO of the banknote printing firm, and Konrad Stimmler, President of the Swiss Banking Supervisory Authority, sat together on one side, because the CEOs of the two largest banks were present and had to sit beside each other for strategic reasons.

The second bank representative was Jean Seibler, Chief Executive Officer of Swiss International Bank, SIB.

Seibler was around sixty, about the same age as his counterpart, Just, but slightly chubby, with thinning hair and a bespoke suit to match his host's. His demeanour was different from the military deportment of the three other gentlemen; he spoke thoughtfully and his movements were leisurely. But anybody who knew him was well aware just how acerbic and sharp-tongued he could be.

Herr Schwarz pushed the serving trolley into the room and set out the four plates. He removed the cloches, starting with the bankers, followed by the bank overseer then the money printer.

Herr Schwarz uttered the words he'd learned by heart in the office: 'Rustic terrine of chicken liver and peppered pork belly with chicken aspic and toasted slices of farmhouse bread.' Then he poured everyone some white wine, a Thomas Marugg Riesling–Sylvaner, before retiring from the room.

'Gentlemen,' began Just, the host, 'I should not wish to call this a crisis, but we are facing a precursor of one. I shan't bore you with the details – I'm not even familiar with them myself – but I cannot spare you the general picture. First of all, however, *A votre santé et bon appetit!*' He raised his glass and the diners toasted each other.

Putting his glass back down, Just continued: 'I'm afraid to say that the fire has not yet been fully extinguished. Our experts have evidence that it's still smouldering. It's possible that copies of said material still exist, and thus there is a danger that sooner or later it might become public. I do not have to remind you of the consequences should this occur.'

They embarked on their terrines wearing troubled faces.

Dillier from the printing firm asked, 'Is my information

correct that the material is still in the possession of the said journalist?'

'*Was*, as far as I know. And he is currently out of the country, busy elsewhere. My experts say he wouldn't use the material if he happened to have any further copies.'

Jean Seibler opened his mouth for the first time: 'That's a little too conditional for my liking.'

'The matter is and remains a time bomb,' Konrad Stimmler added.

Dillier nodded. 'I hope your experts will be able to defuse it.'

'That is what I'm assuming,' Just said as Herr Schwarz entered the small room with another course.

He cleared away the starter and lifted the cloches. 'Chilled Breton lobster in aspic with fresh almonds,' he announced.

The four waited until they were alone again. 'Hanspeter sends his regards to you all,' Stimmler said. 'He would have loved to have joined us, but he's over there at the moment. I'm sure you can imagine why.'

The other three nodded meaningfully.

Seibler's thoughtful voice rang out once more: 'Until the Contini position recovers, we are all staring into the abyss. And with the current situation in Russia there is little possibility of it recovering, or do you see things differently, William?'

Just agreed with him: 'The money is down the drain. But gentlemen, as we all know, that is not the issue here. We've ensured,' he said, looked Stimmler in the eye, '… we've been able to ensure that the loss doesn't appear in the books. The matter would be closed if the said journalist… I fear that we've had a lot of bad luck.'

'And not enough risk management,' Seibler retorted. 'Is your Chief Risk Officer still in a job?'

'I can hardly get rid of him. I might as well go public straightaway.'

The CEO of SIB had now dropped any joviality: 'That's what you should have done in the first place; we're agreed on that, aren't we, Konrad?'

'Of course,' the President of the Swiss Banking Supervisory Authority concurred. 'In any case, by the time I'd heard about it, it was all over. What was I supposed to do?'

They all knew what he should have done. And they all knew that GCBS would not have survived as a result. There was no point in bringing the matter up again.

Just cut to the chase: 'We're dealing with a situation where plan B is identical with the worst case scenario. Which is why we have to stick to plan A by all means available.'

'So long as it's in our power to do so,' Stimmler qualified.

'It *is* in our power,' Just insisted. 'We're combating the crisis with a dual strategy, as if it were an epidemic. We're destroying the virus and strengthening immunity. We've got everything under control. Which is why I invited you to this... I almost said report. To get you to assure me of your support. I promise I will continue to use any means necessary to prevent the affair from getting out of hand. I shan't burden you with details, but I want your full backing. Nothing more, but nothing less.'

After this rather dramatic pledge he pressed the small transmitter in his outside pocket and Herr Schwarz wheeled in the new course and cleared away the plates.

*

Jonas held the narrow end of the mustard-yellow sheet tightly by the corners and stretched it over the bottom end of the mattress. Frau Gerweiler did the same at the head.

'Normally the bed's made when guests arrive, but you didn't give me any time, Herr Hofer.'

Frau Gerweiler was a sturdy, blonde farmer around forty, with calloused hands and a hearty laugh. She rented out the Bütsch holiday apartment in Feldwil, which was in the Zürich Oberland, an hour's drive from the city. The apartment consisted of two rooms in a small old house with a shingle roof, about a kilometre away from the farmhouse where Frau Gerweiler lived with her husband and three adolescent children.

Jonas had found the apartment on the internet. It fulfilled all his criteria: it was secluded, with a garage and internet access. The small house had two floors. Jonas had opted for the ground floor; the upstairs was not being rented.

'The house was built in 1920. My husband and I renovated it ourselves two years ago.'

'Congratulations, great job!' Jonas forced himself to mutter. You could see the apartment had been a DIY job. The sitting room was kitted out with prefabricated panels; all inaccuracies in the corners and by the door and window frames were covered up with mouldings. The floors were laid with fake plastic parquet.

On the walls were framed photographs of landscapes, all hung too high. The dominant colours of the fabrics – sofa cushions, tablecloths, towels – were orange, ochre and yellow.

'So, what are you writing then?' Frau Gerwiler asked as they shook out the duvet and laid it on the bed. 'Anything we can read?'

'Oh, mostly technical stuff, really,' Jonas replied. 'Communications, publicity, that sort of stuff. Not terribly exciting, I fear.'

'Nothing we might know? Somehow you look familiar.'

Jonas had hoped that Highlife would not be a programme

watched regularly in farming families, and that he could rely on his assumed name, Hans Hofer, and three-day beard. 'A lot of people say that,' he replied. 'I've just got a very ordinary face.'

Frau Gerweiler seemed to be content with his answer. She said goodbye and told Jonas she hoped he would come up with plenty of good ideas. 'You won't be disturbed here,' she added.

He paid her the 530 francs for the week, plus the 200 francs deposit, then accompanied her to the garden gate and watched her old Mitsubishi rapidly getting smaller on the narrow road.

In front of the house was a small veranda, on the railings of which hung empty geranium-box holders made from old cartwheels. Beside the house's steep gable, a pole bearing a limp Swiss flag rose into the sky, which had turned black again in preparation for the next snowfall.

He walked slowly back to the entrance of the house which he would not be able to leave until the bomb had exploded.

*

He'd found it terribly difficult not to let Marina in on what he was doing. And now, not even five hours since his flight had supposedly taken off, he was sorry he hadn't. If he couldn't trust *her*, then who?

'Are you moving in with me, then?' she'd asked in amusement, when she came home and saw his bags beside her front door.

'I'd love to. But I've got to go to Abu Dhabi first.'

'When?'

'Tomorrow. 11.05.'

'So sudden?'

'It's a bit spontaneous, I know. But I'm groping in the dark as far as all the Arabic scenes are concerned.'

'Just cut them out, then.'

'Maybe I will in the end. But at least I'll know what I'm cutting.'

It had been a strange last evening. Jonas was in low spirits, as if saying goodbye for an eternity. And Marina was sprightly, as if she were delighted he was going away.

She wanted to go out to eat, but Jonas didn't. He'd be eating out in enough restaurants was the argument which finally convinced her. That, and a little erotic play.

When, later on, they attacked the fridge – yoghurt, gherkins, mozzarella, a dried end of salami – and she was still cheerful, he felt compelled to ask, 'Are you actually pleased I'm going away?'

'I'm pleased that you're keeping your promise and ignoring the stuff Max left behind.'

Fortunately she had an early appointment the following morning, and so wasn't tempted to drive him to the airport. Jonas had put his travel bag full of summer gear in his Passat, bought a cheap mobile with a prepaid card, and gone on his way.

In the small living room was a table with two chairs, which Jonas made his desk. He placed his laptop on it and plugged his power lead into the only socket in the room, taking out the standard lamp.

The internet connection was slow; Jonas braced himself for long transmission times

The first thing he copied was his final USB stick. While the time bar crawled almost imperceptibly along, he opened the window.

It was dark outside, and in the light pouring from his room the snowflakes fell thickly like a net curtain. The wheelbarrows, cartwheels, wrought-iron lamps and the rest of the kitsch outside the house had all been given a pretty dusting already.

It seemed as if the constant snowfall made the silence even quieter, and the house even more solitary. No noise apart from the ones he made.

Jonas closed the window. The bar on the screen hadn't even got halfway.

Suddenly he no longer saw the section that was getting bigger, only the one getting smaller.

Like, he thought, the time I've got left in order to survive.

*

He couldn't find any other background apart from the mustard-yellow sheet. Jonas took it off the bed and hung it on the landscape photos on the wall. In front of the sheet he put the second chair and created some light with his two LED lamps.

Then he mounted his camera on the tripod and pointed it at the man who was going to be sitting there: Jonas Brand.

He only had to say five lines on film, but he wasn't good in front of the camera, and had to keep going back and forth between the chair and the camera to cut and delete. It was almost midnight by the time he was halfway happy with the results.

Jonas made himself a coffee and ate some bread and cheese. Then he started working on the material that he'd filmed himself or got from Max.

He spent the rest of the night recording the voiceovers. Sometimes the length wouldn't be right, then the text; and when both fitted, he'd fluff the lines.

It was light by the time he'd finally finished his piece. He stretched and went outside.

The house with the shingle roof was snowed in, and the flakes were still falling thickly.

Jonas went back to his computer and looked at his ammunition again.

It was entitled 'Customer Incident'

CUSTOMER INCIDENT
INT. INTERCITY RESTAURANT CAR — EVENING

A man in a business suit approaches the camera, filling the screen, then walks past.

                    MAN (O.S.)
  Have you seen Paolo?

            FAT MAN AT TABLE WITH LAPTOP
  Wasn't he sitting with you?

                    MAN
  His phone rang and he went out to take the
  call. But he never came back.

                    FAT MAN
  Maybe he's the customer incident.

CUT TO: EXT. TUNNEL — NIGHT
IN THE DISTANCE A BUNDLE BESIDE THE TRAIN

COMMENTARY: On 19 September last year, the emergency
brake was pulled on the intercity 584. The train
came to a stop in a tunnel. The corpse of one of
the passengers was lying beside the tracks.

CUT TO: INSERT FACEBOOK PHOTO OF PAOLO CONTINI

COMMENTARY: The body was that of Paolo Contini, thirty-nine years old, married with two small children. He lived in Basel and worked in Zürich as a stock market trader for GCBS.

CUT TO: INT. INTERCITY BUFFET CAR — EVENING
Panning shot through the full buffet car.

COMMENTARY: Contini was one of the many commuters in the buffet car on the intercity 584. The police assumed it was suicide. But nobody could explain why he'd killed himself. He didn't leave a suicide note.

CUT TO: INT. JACK HEINZMANN'S LIVING ROOM — EVENING

JACK HEINZMANN
(Caption: Jack Heinzmann, work colleague)
Nothing. And there's no reason why he should have taken his own life. In fact there were heaps of reasons not to. Paolo was the star of the trading floor. He was happily married and had two children he was besotted with, five and seven. No one in his situation kills themselves.

JONAS BRAND (O.S.)
Could it have been an accident?

JACK HEINZMANN
What sort of accident? That he mistakenly fell out of the door? When the train's moving you have to pull the emergency bolt to open it.

JONAS BRAND (O.S.)

A crime, then?

                        JACK HEINZMANN
Paolo was very popular; he didn't have any
enemies.

                        JONAS BRAND (O.S.)
So you're saying it *was* suicide?

                        JACK HEINZMANN
It seems as if we're going to have to come to
terms with the idea.

                        JONAS BRAND (O.S.)
What does his widow say?

CUT TO: INT. BARBARA CONTINI'S LIVING ROOM — EVENING

                        JONAS BRAND (O.S.)
Frau Contini, do you believe that your husband
committed suicide?

                        BARBARA CONTINI
No.

                        JONAS BRAND (O.S.)
Why not?

                        BARBARA CONTINI
Because he was happy.

                    JONAS BRAND (O.S.)
So how did he fall off the train?

                    BARBARA CONTINI
Someone pushed him.

                    JONAS BRAND (O.S.)
Why?

                    BARBARA CONTINI
I don't know.

CUT TO: EXT. OFFICE CORRIDOR AT COROMAG — DAY
Slow pan across the interior of Coromag, zoom into
the office corridor.

                    JONAS BRAND (O.S.)
What at first appears to be a completely
different story brings us closer to answering
this question. We are at Coromag, the security
printer's where Swiss banknotes are made. At the
end of last year the following scene took place
in the office of Adam Dillier, Coromag's CEO.

CUT TO: INT. DILLIER'S OFFICE AT COROMAG — DAY
Dillier is sitting in an armchair, talking about a
one-hundred franc note.

                    JONAS BRAND (O.S.)
Is it possible for two notes to have the same
number?

                    DILLIER
Absolutely out of the question.

Dillier is handed another hundred note by the interviewer out of shot.

JONAS BRAND (O.S.)
So how do you explain this to our viewers then?

Dillier compares the serial numbers. Becomes nervous. Smiles into the camera.

DILLIER
Just give me a moment, would you? I need to take a closer look.

Dillier gets up, goes to his desk, returns with a magnifying glass, compares the features of the first note with the second, then vice-versa. Suddenly he looks up and thrusts his palm towards the lens.

DILLIER
Turn that off for a while.

CUT TO: INT. JONAS BRAND IN FRONT OF YELLOW BACKGROUND WITH TWO HUNDRED-FRANC NOTES

CUT TO: FINGER POINTING TO SERIAL NUMBERS

JONAS BRAND (O.S.)
It was no coincidence that both these hundred-franc notes, judged by the boss of the security printing firm, Coromag, to be genuine, bore the same serial number. One comes from a series manufactured unofficially for GCBS bank and delivered to their money depository in Nuppingen.

CUT TO: INT. GABOR TAKACS'S SICK ROOM — DAY
Gabor Takacs is talking from a hospital bed in his
sitting room.

GABOR TAKACS
Nuppingen! GCBS's cash depot! With eighteen
palettes of banknotes! Do you know how many
notes there are to a palette? Forty-eight boxes
each with ten thousand shrink-wrapped notes. If
we're talking about hundreds, that's one million
francs per box, 48 million per palette. If we're
talking about thousands then it's 480 million.
Per palette!

JONAS BRAND (O.S.)
And you're saying the money was taken directly
to GCBS. Is that unusual?

GABOR TAKACS
Unusual? You bet! It never happened before in
my nineteen years. I asked a friend of mine in
production — I'm not going to say his name — what
sort of delivery it was, and he said duplicate
numbers. He said the National Bank had recently
been printing notes with duplicate numbers. For
some sort of tests. I didn't tell him that the
consignments were going to Nuppingen.

CUT TO: INT. JONAS BRAND IN FRONT OF YELLOW
BACKGROUND

JONAS BRAND
And so we've come full circle again. Why were
pallets of unregistered banknotes delivered to
GCBS? Let's listen to the well-known business

journalist, Max Gantmann, who recently died in a fire in his flat, the circumstances of which remain unexplained.

CUT TO: INT. GANTMANN'S FLAT — DAY

MAX GANTMANN

Contini did lose money through speculation, with Russian securities, property and energy. Apparently he squandered somewhere between ten and twenty billion. He offset these losses with fictitious profits from fictitious derivatives.
(Cut)
One day Contini admitted everything to the Chief Risk Officer. But instead of reporting the matter to the Risk Committee, as was his duty, he went to the CEO, William Just. This gargantuan loss would have brought the chronically undercapitalised GCBS to the brink of disaster. You see, if it had become known it could have led to a run on the bank.

CUT TO: INT. JONAS BRAND IN FRONT OF YELLOW BACKGROUND

JONAS BRAND

The bank took other precautions, too. One such was the printing of these banknotes. They had to increase their strategic cash reserves so that if the matter did leak out, they'd be able to cope with a run on the bank. That's when customers rush to the counters to withdraw their savings.
(Pause)
And so we're back to Paolo Contini.

Martin Suter

CUT TO: INT. GANTMANN'S FLAT — DAY

MAX GANTMANN

Contini — now listen to this — was plagued
by his conscience, and he decided to speak
directly to the Swiss Banking Supervisory
Authority, in fact its president, Konrad
Stimmler. Whether he did so, I don't yet know.

CUT TO: INT. JONAS BRAND IN FRONT OF YELLOW
BACKGROUND

Jonas Brand is holding a sheet of paper towards
the camera.

JONAS BRAND

This is the draft of a letter to the president
of the Swiss Banking Supervisory Authority.
(reads from sheet)
Dear Herr Stimmler, I'm writing to you today
about a matter which has been weighing on my
conscience for some time.

CUT TO: CLOSE-UP OF LETTER

JONAS BRAND (O.S.)

I work as a trader at GCBS and in this role
I made and then concealed a trading loss
of tens of billions of francs. I offset this
position with fictitious profits from fictitious
derivatives. I have informed my superiors, but
it seems they have not reported the matter as
they ought to have. I am aware of the enormity
of what I have done and am ready to accept the
consequences.

Please don't hesitate to contact me for any
further information.
Best regards
Paolo Contini

CUT TO: INT. JONAS BRAND IN FRONT OF YELLOW BACKGROUND

JONAS BRAND
Did GCBS manage to prevent Contini from
sending this letter? And if so, how? And if
not, why does the public know nothing about
this scandal? Is the Swiss Banking Supervisory
Authority aware of it?

CUT TO: INT. LOBBY OF GSTAAD PALACE HOTEL — DAY
William Just, CEO of GCBS, is sitting at a small table
with Konrad Stimmler, Swiss Banking Supervisory
Authority, SBA. They toast the camera.
(Caption: William Just, CEO GCBS, with Konrad
Stimmler, president of the Swiss Banking Supervisory
Authority, SBA)

JONAS BRAND (O.S.)
Who else is up to their neck in this?

*

The contents of Max Gantmann's office had been bundled into
a container and taken away, the stained carpet replaced and the
walls freshly painted.

The door to the office was open when Heiner Stepler, the
television editor-in-chief, came past. Even through the odour
of fresh paint he fancied he could still smell Max's fug of stale
air and cigarette smoke.

He was on his way to see the director general, for the circumstances had arisen in which he was obliged to consult with the boss immediately, irrespective of how busy the latter was.

The PA was expecting Stepler and took him through the anteroom into the corner office. The director general was standing by the window, hands behind his back, staring at the snow-laden roofs of the suburbs.

Without turning round he asked, 'Has he been in touch?'

'Yes. From Abu Dhabi.'

'And? Is it so explosive?'

'I haven't seen the footage. He sent it via Filemail, more than a gigabyte, and he's only going to give me the access code on certain conditions.'

'Such as?'

'He wants a firm promise that we'll broadcast it on the six o'clock news this evening.'

'A pig in a poke?'

'Not exactly. If we're interested he'll give us the code for the same file, but in a low resolution format that we can't broadcast. Then we'll have to decide.'

Now the director general turned round. Stepler could see that he found the situation abhorrent. He found it difficult to reconcile what he was being forced to do with his political outlook and the image he had of himself.

'We can do that, can't we?'

'We don't have much choice. He's made TVch the same offer.'

Mention of the other broadcaster made the vertical lines either side of the director general's nose sink deeper into his face. TVch was their biggest private competitor. 'So if we don't show it, they will?'

'No, they're going to show it anyway. Whether we go ahead or not.'

'OK, agree to it and show me the report the moment you've got it.'

Heiner Stepler returned to his office. Yet again as he passed Max's office he thought he could still smell the fug through the paint.

He wrote a few words to the address dynamite@hotmail. com: 'Please send small file then we'll decide.'

A couple of minutes later he got a message from Filemail with the subject 'Dynamite'. It contained a link to a file and the relevant password. Stepler saved it onto a USB stick and went back to the director general.

They watched the video in silence. When it was finished the director general said, 'Dynamite. The title is spot on. We'll accept his conditions.'

'So we're going to broadcast it on the six o'clock news? Just as it is?' the editor-in-chief asked in disbelief.

'Bring me the material as soon as you've got it. And don't show it to a soul.'

Half an hour later the two men reviewed the report a second time, this time in broadcast quality. Stepler jotted down some notes about the commentary they would use to accompany the piece.

When he got up at the end of the video, the director general barked, 'Wait!' and had his assistant put him through to the CEO of their competitor, TVch.

They had a short conversation, the upshot of which went against all that the journalist in Heiner Stepler stood for.

*

It said 'Caller Unknown' on the display of Marina's mobile. She answered with a cool 'Hello?'

'It's me, Jonas.'

'Jonas! I've been trying to call you the whole time. What's happened?'

'Nothing. My mobile fell into the pool. It's drying out in a kilo of rice.'

'I thought anything could have happened. Are you OK?'

'I'm fine. How about you?'

'I'm missing you.'

'Me too. Not long now, though.'

'When are you coming back?'

'Maybe tomorrow. Depends.'

'On what?'

'Watch the news. Six o'clock tonight.'

'Why?'

'You'll see. Where are you?'

'At home.'

'What are you doing?'

'The sort of stuff one gets up to on a Sunday at home. Getting bored. How can I get hold of you?'

'On this number.'

'It's withheld.'

'Wait a sec, I'll give it to you.'

She could hear him pressing buttons. The line went silent and then she heard the engaged tone.

'He says I should watch the news,' she said.

'We will,' replied Tommy, Jonas's assistant director, who was standing at the counter that divided the kitchen from the sitting–dining room.

*

Sacha Duval, the first secretary of the Swiss embassy, was standing at the window of his office on the seventeenth floor of the Centro Capital Center in Abu Dhabi. From here he could see the American embassy which was less than a kilometre directly to the north west.

This was where Donald Tryst worked, head of the US Liaison Office, who he'd just been talking to on the phone. They'd met a few times at social events and were on first-name terms: Sacha and Donald.

Their conversation was brief, informal and it never took place.

Donald said, 'Immigration has confirmed that the subject never entered the country.'

Sacha replied, 'Thanks. Hope to see you soon.' He hung up and called Bern.

*

The stove was out of oil. Jonas fetched the canister from the shed, which also served as a garage, and filled the tank. Folding up one of the pieces of paper for starting the fire, as his landlady had shown him, he lit it, tossed it into the stove and watched it drown in the oil that was flowing in.

For half an hour he tried to get the stove going before giving up. Jonas took down the sheet that was still hanging as a backdrop on the wall, made the bed, set the alarm on his mobile and slipped under the duvet. He felt shattered and hollowed out, but all the same it took him quite a while to fall asleep.

Jonas was woken by a loud rattling and the engine noise of a heavy vehicle. He sprang out of bed and went to the window.

Outside a tractor with a plough attached to the front was

turning. It had pushed the snow into a wall which towered above the fence.

The driver, wrapped up warmly, spotted him at the window and gave him a wave. Jonas waved back, then watched the vehicle drive back down the freshly ploughed country lane.

Large snowflakes were still falling. The garden decorations could only be made out as gentle undulations in the thick layer of snow. It was getting dark.

The apartment was cold and reeked of heating oil. It was only a quarter to four – a good two hours still until the evening news.

Having found some kitchen roll, Jonas began twisting sheets into fat wicks to soak up the deluge of oil in the stove. When he'd used up the entire roll he continued with loo paper. It was almost five o'clock by the time he'd finally managed to get the stove working again. Everything stank of heating oil.

He spent the following half hour putting on his snow chains. They were unused, still in their original packaging together with plastic gloves and unintelligible instructions. It didn't take Jonas long to turn the first chain into a tangled knot of metal. He put on the second chain without any problems and decided to leave it at that.

The apartment had warmed up in the meantime. He washed his hands, made himself some instant soup and sat in front of the television.

The fact that the story didn't feature in the opening summary ought to have been a warning. But he watched the entire programme until he realised. Nothing.

The main topic of the news was the heavy snowfall of the past few hours and the chaos it had caused. No mention of Jonas's report.

Throughout the programme he kept switching to TVch.

Not a hint of the GCBS scandal there, either.

Right at the end the newsreader said, 'And now a report from the police of a missing person...'

The screen was filled with the photograph of him that Nembus Productions had taken as the official press photo for *Montecristo*. In it Jonas looked exactly as he did now: head and face covered in three-day stubble. The newsreader gave a description of Jonas, as well as the colour and registration number of his VW Passat. The police were calling for any relevant information.

Switching over to TVch, Jonas glimpsed the fading image of the missing Jonas Brand.

He began packing in a hurry.

He had to stamp twice through the deep snow covering the path between the front door and the shed to load his luggage, computer and camera equipment into the car. And then a third time to leave Frau Gerwiler a note beside the key and to turn off all the lights.

The snowbound house stood there in the dark as he drove past it slowly. He was grateful for the one chain, the loose end of which knocked rhythmically against the mudguard.

He drove cautiously through the tunnel of glowing snowflakes, which his headlights opened up before him. When he approached the Gerwiler family's farmhouse he switched on his parking lights and slowed to walking pace.

A yellow light shone dimly in the stable windows, but the kitchen was so brightly lit that he could see the family gathered around the dining table. A television was on and the farmer was standing by the door, talking on a phone that was fixed to the wall.

One of the children ran to the window. They must have heard the chain knocking.

He didn't know how long he'd been driving when he got to the main road. It had recently been cleared. He stopped and fixed the loose chain. Then he drove a little faster in the fresh tracks of the snowplough. He was heading westwards, back to the city.

Only now did he manage to muster a logical thought. The two television channels must have come to an agreement and made the joint decision not to show his piece. But under pressure from whom? Who wielded so much power that they could force two editorial offices to suppress a story of such magnitude? The bank? Or the other parties Jonas had mentioned at the end of his report?

He was even more troubled by the missing person item on the news. It meant not only that his opponents knew he wasn't in Abu Dhabi; it also turned him into a hunted man.

Half of German-speaking Switzerland now knew his face and registration number, and they wouldn't hesitate for one second to pass on relevant information to the police.

If his report had been broadcast everybody would have still known his face, but the bomb would have exploded and thus he'd have been safe.

Ahead in the distance was a flicker of orange in the snow flurry. It looked as if he'd soon catch up with the snowplough.

His last resort was his plan B. He had to put the report on the internet. In as many different video portals as possible. No matter how powerful his opponents were, they couldn't control the internet.

But for this he needed time and somewhere with a decent internet connection.

This meant he needed the help of someone he could trust.

And only one person still fitted that bill.

*

The flashing of a blue light now mixed with the orange flicker of the snowplough.

Luck was with Jonas. On the right-hand side of the road was the entrance to Müller Argo, a workshop for agricultural vehicles. The drive had been ploughed.

Jonas switched off his lights and followed the tracks of the plough. They led behind the garage, ending up in a covered car park full of farm vehicles and second-hand cars. Maybe this is where the snowplough came from, which he'd been tailing the whole time.

Jonas saw the blue light flash past, vanishing into the direction he'd come from. He parked his Passat amongst the cars, took out the mobile phone that had supposedly fallen in the pool and switched it on.

The signal was very weak and it took ages for the GPS app to locate his position. He made a note of it and turned the phone back off.

Taking the prepaid mobile from his pocket, he dialled the number.

'Marina, I need your help,' he said as an opening gambit.

'Where are you?'

'Have you got a pen to hand?'

'Do you know that they've released a missing person's announcement for you?'

'That's why I need your help. You've got to come and pick me up. Do you have a pen?'

After a moment she said, 'Go on.'

He gave her the coordinates. 'Do you know how to put them into the GPS?'

'Of course. You never went to Abu Dhabi, did you?'

'No. Listen, I'll tell you everything. But you've got to pick me up before the others do. I'm at a workshop for agricultural vehicles. It's called Müller Agro. I've parked at the back. I've got to leave the Passat here; they gave out the registration in the missing person's report.'

'It would be more sensible if you went to the nearest police station.'

'I will. But there's something I've got to do first. Something important. It's absolutely essential. And I need your help. Please, Marina!'

'OK, Jonas. I'm on my way.'

*

Half an hour later he saw headlights approaching.

Jonas ducked behind the dashboard. Marina couldn't have driven here that quickly.

The loud engine noise came closer. The lights turned around the corner of the garage and made straight for Jonas.

It was the snowplough returning. It turned and reversed into the shelter, ready for its next outing.

The lights went out, the engine died. The driver in his orange protective clothing climbed down, gave a stretch and approached the Passat.

Jonas crouched down further.

He heard the driver's footsteps and his voice uttering incomprehensible swear words. Then the door of the car next to Jonas was opened and shut. The engine burst into life and the car drove off.

It took Jonas a few minutes to summon the courage to sit back up.

He was trembling, and not just because of the cold. He started the engine to heat up the car again, as he'd done several times since his call, and waited.

When all this was behind him, what then? He'd presumably have to forget the idea of a film career. And he'd finally draw a line under his job as a lifestyle video journalist. Maybe uncovering the GCBS scandal would open a few doors and he'd be employed somewhere as a serious video journalist.

What about his private life? Maybe it was time to get serious about that too. To have another stab at what had failed in the past. A committed relationship. Perhaps even get married. He wondered what Marina would think about that. He'd be forty in two years' time. It might be too late already. On the other hand, ten years' difference, maybe that was still alright.

The sound of an engine came closer, but he couldn't see any headlights.

Jonas ducked down again behind the dashboard.

Nothing happened.

Probably Marina, who hadn't spotted his car immediately and was too cautious to switch on the lights.

He slowly raised his head. He thought he could see the outline of a car beside the snowplough. Opening the door, he crept out. The snow was still falling.

'Marina?' he called out quietly.

Suddenly he was standing in the glare of headlights. Figures ran towards him, men's voices all shouting at the same time.

Seconds later he was lying on the ground, an arm twisted behind his back and a hard knee pressing on his spine.

Someone grabbed both his hands roughly, and he could hear the tag whizz over the serrated cable tie, binding his wrists tightly.

He was lifted back on his feet and half dragged, half shoved over to a dark-coloured delivery van.

The men were dressed all in black: cargo trousers, jump boots, bomber jackets and balaclavas revealing nothing but their eyes.

One of them pushed him onto the bench seat and did up his seat belt.

Then he sat opposite Jonas, did his own belt and removed his balaclava.

The delivery van set off. In the light from the car behind, which briefly shone through the small, grilled rear window, Jonas recognised the man with the spiky red hair.

*

Jonas was paralysed by the fear of what awaited him, and by despair at Marina's betrayal.

The delivery van had poor suspension and the driver took the winding route bumpily and at speed, despite the snow. Unable to support himself with his hands, Jonas kept being caught by the seatbelt just as he was about to tip over.

His wrists, which hurt badly to begin with because of the tight cable ties, had become numb. It was as if he didn't have hands any more.

'Marina's betrayed me!' was the only thought in his mind. 'Marina's betrayed me!'

The red-haired man didn't say a word. Nor did he intervene when Jonas almost slipped from the bench seat. The man just sat there, puffing on an electronic cigarette that emitted a strange scent.

All of a sudden the drive became smoother and the engine louder. They must be on the motorway.

What did his silent guard have in store for him? While they were still on the country road, Jonas was expecting them to stop somewhere, haul him out of the van and simply do away with him. But now he sensed they were heading to a particular destination. Jonas relaxed.

'Where are we going?' he asked. When he didn't get an answer he repeated the question in English.

All he could see were the weak outlines of the face and the glow of the ridiculous e-cigarette. A contract killer who looked after his health. Like other bank employees.

How did a large bank recruit such people? Were there headhunters for them? Did they have to undergo assessment too? He spoke English, Frau Grabler had said. Was he American or British? Or perhaps Australian or South African? Could he be an employee of a PMC, one of those private military companies that had become established in Switzerland? What did it cost to hire someone like that? And how were his wages accounted for?

The van slowed; they'd left the motorway and were on roads with traffic lights, crossroads and junctions. Jonas struggled once more to keep his balance.

All of a sudden they stopped for a moment, then slowly descended a steep slope, going down and down in a spiral. The vehicle stopped again and the sliding door was opened. He was blinded by harsh neon light.

His guard had put the balaclava back on. Undoing Jonas's belt, he dragged him out, where a second masked man was waiting.

They took him along a corridor full of air-raid shelter doors to a goods lift. As the lift went up to a higher floor, one of the masked men – judging by the smell it must be the redhead – cut the cable ties.

The door opened, they pushed him out and then it closed again on his two abductors.

*

Jonas was alone in the middle of a long corridor, on both sides of which were doors, most of them closed. He was aware of a familiar smell, but couldn't place it.

He started massaging his numb hands and heading slowly in the direction where he thought he could hear voices coming from.

The fifth door was open. Two men were sitting at desks; one of them was on the phone. Neither noticed Jonas.

He knocked on the doorframe with a numb knuckle. The man who wasn't on the phone looked up. 'Yes?' he said. Then, appearing to recognise Jonas, he stood and came up to him. He was wearing a shoulder holster with a pistol. Now Jonas could place the smell: police.

'My name is Jonas Brand. I was abducted.'

The man on the telephone interrupted his conversation and dialled a different number. 'He's here,' he said, then hung up.

*

Ten minutes later Jonas was back inside an almost windowless van. This time he wasn't restrained and his two companions wore dark-blue police uniforms with the Bern coat-of-arms. They were as taciturn as his abductors, but more polite. They said 'please' when they prompted him to sit down. And when they'd reached their destination and it was time for him to get out, they gestured courteously.

Their destination was the underground car park of a modern building. And again he was taken to a lift.

They accompanied him to a small room. The walls were hung

with some engravings of the city of Bern and there was a suite of period furniture.

When the policemen invited him to take a seat, he sat on a Biedermeier armchair. The officers remained standing and waited.

Jonas glanced at his watch. He felt as if he'd been on the road for an eternity, but it was only just after half-past nine.

His anger at Marina and fear at what awaited him had given way to a gaping emptiness. He didn't care what happened from here.

*

There was a second door in the room. This now opened and an elderly gentleman came in. He was wearing a grey suit, which looked a little like a uniform, and he had a slight limp in his right leg.

'Herr Brand, would you mind coming with me?'

Jonas stood up. His hands were still practically numb and he was a little unsteady on his feet. Nodding to the police officers, he followed the man, who led Jonas along a corridor and stopped by a door.

'Would you like to freshen up?'

Jonas entered a bathroom with a toilet. He used it, went to the washbasin and was horrified when he saw himself in the mirror. Pale and bleary-eyed, red eyes with dark bags beneath them and a stubbly head with more grey hair than he recalled.

He washed his hands and face, and cleaned his teeth with one of the disposable toothbrushes which had been laid out. He also used some of the eau de toilette that was on the shelf by the mirror.

The man took him on to a walnut door with brass hinges and knocked.

'Come in!' a man's voice called out.

Judging by the underground car park and the rooms at the back, they were in a modern building, but the room they now entered must have been removed in its entirety from a neo-classical country house and reinstalled here. It was panelled all over with walnut and laid out with furniture from the period, including a slate table with space for two dozen guests. At one end of the table was a large parquet floor, like a dance floor, informally set out with armchairs, also neoclassical.

Beyond the other end was a cosily furnished smoking lounge with a marble fireplace that must have come from the same large house. A fire was crackling away. This part of the room could be separated off with sliding doors. Its centrepiece was a huge desk, from which a short, chubby man stood up when they entered. He looked familiar to Jonas.

'Ah, here comes public enemy number one,' he smiled, offering him his hand. 'Gobler, Finance Administration. Please excuse the circumstances in which you were brought here. Can I offer you something? A beer? They tell me you're a beer drinker. First thing we have in common.'

While Jonas was being welcomed, the elderly man closed the sliding doors and now waited for further instructions. 'Two glasses of beer, please, Herr Rontaler,' Gobler said to him. The smoking lounge had its own door, through which Rontaler limped out slowly.

Gobler! That's why the man was familiar. He was Director of the Swiss Finance Administration. The top official under – or above, as many people said – the minister in charge of the finance department.

He invited Jonas to take a seat at the large desk, before

making his way round to the other side, where he sat in an armchair which looked to Jonas like a throne.

'Do take off your windcheater; you must be stiflingly hot!'

Jonas got up, hung his coat over the back of the chair and sat down again. Only now did he notice the laptop in front of him with a sticker saying 'Montecristo'. It was his laptop. Beside it a USB stick. The same type that Jonas used.

'Over there is what we call the Lily Room. It comes from the former country estate of Lilienrain, which had to be demolished in the 1980s to make room for the motorway. The department uses it for particularly important occasions.' Gobler paused. 'Occasions like this one.'

There was a knock and the department chief said 'Come in!'

The limping butler entered carrying a tray with two beautifully poured glasses of beer. It took a while for him to serve both the men and leave the room again.

'Thank you, Herr Rontaler,' Gobler called after him. Then he took the USB stick from the desk, held it up and said, 'First of all my warmest congratulations for this.' He gave it an approving shake. 'A mature piece of investigative journalism, Herr Brand.'

'Thanks,' Jonas said, only partly ironically.

'Just a shame it can never be broadcast.'

'At the particular request of GCBS, I assume?'

Gobler put the USB stick back on the desk and waved his hand dismissively. 'Oh, GCBS! They're the least of our worries. At the particular request of the country, Herr Brand. At the particular request of the industrialised nations. At the particular request of the developing nations. At the particular request of the world.'

Raising his beer glass, he toasted Jonas allusively and drank half. 'Do you know what would happen if that were made public?'

Jonas had taken a sip, too, and now wiped the foam from his lips. His hand smelled of the designer soap from the bathroom. 'I can more or less imagine.'

'You see, Herr Brand, I actually doubt that, I really do. Otherwise you would have left the matter alone long ago. You may well be able to guess the consequences if it got out that GCBS had printed money unofficially. And you can probably imagine what would happen to our biggest, most vital bank if the public found out that it was hushing up a loss running to tens of billions because it, like all our banks, is undercapitalised.'

He paused, as if waiting for acknowledgement, then continued: 'The state wouldn't even attempt to lend a hand. Any politician merely toying with the idea would go down with the bank. So far, so bad.'

Gobler took a breath and now started speaking a little louder. 'But do you have any idea what would happen if our largest bank collapsed because it was undercapitalised? People would ask how well capitalised the second largest bank was. And do you know what would happen then? Yes, precisely.'

Gobler drank the remaining half of his beer.

'Even if SIB, with its own means, could absorb the direct impact of the crisis triggered by its competitor, it would be dragged down – that's how closely interrelated our banks are.'

He put down the glass so noisily that Jonas flinched. 'But even that's nothing. Just try to picture the reaction if it became known that the supervisory authority which ought to be monitoring our financial centre knew all about it. And covered it up.'

He paused again and Jonas used the opportunity to speak himself: 'So you believe there's a critical point, beyond which a scandal should never be disclosed?'

Gobler nodded keenly. 'And this point is reached when disclosure would be more harmful than beneficial to the general public. In our case, we're well beyond that point. A long way. Have you never come across a situation, Herr Brand, in which the truth does more damage than a lie?'

Jonas didn't respond. Of course he'd been in such situations.

The department chief reached for the telephone. Someone answered straightaway.

'Herr Rontaler, bring us two more beers, please. And kindly ask Herr Anderfeld to join us. Oh, and ask him what he'd like to drink.'

He hung up and sneered to himself: 'Fizzy or still?' Then he turned back to Jonas, whose glass was still practically full. 'We have another guest who will explain the matter to you from his perspective.'

Herr Rontaler came in again soon after, bringing two more beers and a glass of water. He cleared away the empty glass and almost full one, and departed with the same infuriating slowness.

Gobler continued: 'And do you believe that the supervisory authority could keep such a bombshell secret without the connivance of the National Bank?'

Jonas shrugged.

'If not, what do you think would happen to our financial centre if it became known that the Swiss National Bank was implicated in the affair? It would spell the end. In the eyes of the world we'd be a banana republic!' Gobler shook all his fingers as if he'd burned himself.

The door opened and another familiar face appeared.

*

Gobler got to his feet and Jonas followed suit. 'Hanspeter,' Gobler said, 'allow me to introduce Jonas Brand.'

Jonas had recognised the man instantly. He was Hanspeter Anderfeld, President of the Swiss National Bank. An ascetic character with thick, snow-white hair and rimless spectacles with a golden bridge and frame. He offered Jonas his hard, dry hand. 'You're causing us no end of trouble, Herr Brand.'

'I could say the same,' Jonas replied.

'We can resolve the matter here and now, then all go home trouble-free.'

They sat back down, Anderfeld beside Gobler, Jonas opposite again.

'We were just discussing whether the National Bank knew about the affair, Hanspeter. And if so, what that might mean.'

Anderfeld took a sip of mineral water, leaned on his forearms, clasped his hands and looked Jonas in the eye. 'The National Bank, Herr Brand, knew nothing and will never have known anything about it. Do you know why? Because it never happened. There are things that don't happen, simply because they mustn't happen. But if,' he said, raising his bony index and middle fingers to gesture quotation marks, 'they *do* happen, people like us are duty bound to damned-well *un*do them. The two of us, as well as a whole host of other responsible individuals are involved in this task. More than you'd suspect, Herr Brand.'

Lukas Gobler, the department chief, drank his beer, nodding absentmindedly like an audience member at a dull lecture.

Anderfeld continued: 'Do you know who Rederick Corncrake is?'

'The president of the FED,' Jonas answered like a good pupil.

'Can you believe he calls me three or four times a week?'

'How did he find out?'

'The Americans,' Anderfeld said, making a vague hand

gesture, 'have their sources, as we well know.'

Jonas didn't respond.

'And do you know why Corncrake rings up? Because he's worried. About us. About you, Herr Brand.'

Jonas listened to this monologue as if it had nothing to do with him.

'It's not only the FED that's worried. Don't imagine for a moment I'm not getting calls from the Bank of England, the German Bundesbank, the International Monetary Fund, the European Central Bank. Although they don't know anything for certain, there *are* rumours. Rumour, Herr Brand, is the angel of death of finance. Do you know what set the last financial crisis in motion?'

'Lehman Brothers?'

'Correct: the collapse of Lehman Brothers. That's small beer in comparison to what we'd be facing. We're not talking here about the collapse of a big bank. We're looking at the collapse of one of the most important financial centres on earth. Maybe even the end of our financial system. The implosion of the economic system. You cannot begin to imagine what the broadcast of this here,' he said, searching for the USB stick, which Gobler handed to him and he held up in the air, '... what sort of crisis this would unleash. We'd be facing a global economic catasatrophe the like of which the planet has never seen. Unemployment, food crises, starvation, wars.'

There was silence to let the speech take effect.

Anderfeld's speech had made an impression on Jonas. But as ever when something made an impression, his contrariness was pricked too. He said, 'It sounds like a noble objective, but is it really the solution to everything? Your efforts and those of all the other "responsible individuals" as you call them, have cost human lives.'

Now Gobler stepped in again. 'I know nothing about that. And even if I did I wouldn't believe it. Do you have any idea how many human lives would be lost in the crisis our efforts may well be preventing?'

The two men looked at Jonas as if expecting an estimate that was even half close.

Jonas said nothing.

Gobler shoved the USB stick across the table; Jonas caught it.

'What am I going to do with this?'

'You decide.'

'What? Whether to destroy it?' He looked at the two men. Both of them shook their heads.

'How to destroy it?'

They both nodded.

Jonas twiddled the data stick back and forth in his fingers.

'Who is the one doing the good deed?' Gobler asked. 'The man who lights the match that sets the world on fire? Or the one who stamps it out?'

Jonas's contrariness was aroused once more: 'And if the world learns nothing about the affair, is it then saved? Even if I were to join your little conspiracy, at some point someone else would give us away, and then the system would explode with an even bigger bang.'

Gobler and Anderfeld exchanged glances, as if trying to agree silently which of them had the right answer.

It was Gobler who said, 'But until then we'll all keep floating in our bubble, moving as carefully as possible, because nobody wants it to burst.'

Hurling the stick on the floor, Jonas stood up and scrunched it with his heel. He picked up the broken pieces, went over to the fire and tossed them into the flames.

Gobler and Anderfeld had both risen from their chairs and were congratulating Jonas as if he had just won an important election.

'Herr Brand,' Gobler said in an emotional tone of voice, 'you don't know how delighted I am about your intelligent decision. Well done!'

Anderfeld's claws gripped Jonas's hand tightly. 'Herr Brand, welcome to our little secret society of… well, patriots doesn't go far enough… responsible citizens of the world. Yes, that's more accurate.'

Jonas let the congratulations pass over him, wondering what Max would say.

'Gentlemen, please sit back down,' Gobler said, gesturing to the two chairs.

In the brief embarrassing silence that ensued after they'd all retaken their seats, Jonas asked, 'What now?'

'Well, now,' Gobler explained, 'we're all going to have a little celebration. But first there's someone who'd very much like to meet you in person.' Picking up the telephone he said, 'Please let him know we're ready.'

Gobler hung up and turned back to Jonas. 'I… we have a request, Herr Brand. In a moment my boss, Minister August Schublinger, will join us. There's no need for you to go over the details with him; he's responsible for the big picture, if you see what I mean. He's going to welcome you as a new member of our circle. You'll have a brief chat and then there's a small reception with those other Lilies who we were able to summon at such short notice and at such a late hour. "Lilies" is what the members of this secret circle call themselves, after the Lily Room, where they meet for such occasions.'

In the ensuing silence, while they were waiting for the finance minister, Jonas became aware of sounds that for a while had been coming softly from the other side of the closed sliding doors: the clatter of crockery, clinking of glasses and murmuring.

The door opened and in walked Minister Schublinger in person. Jovial-looking, as Jonas knew him from the television. He was followed by Herr Rontaler, who Jonas now thought might be a ministerial attendant.

Schublinger was a stout man of medium height, around sixty years old and bald save for a white crown of longish hair, which made his short neck look even more diminutive. He came up to Jonas, offering his warm, soft hand. 'Herr Brand!' he called out, as if it were the opening of a long welcome speech, the rest of which he'd sadly forgotten.

His chief official leaped up. 'Herr Brand is the first film director amongst the Lilies, Minister.'

'Congratulations! I thought we already had representatives from the film business.'

'We do, but no directors yet.'

'Oh yes, you're right.' The minister had run out of conversation and his thoughts seemed to be drifting elsewhere. But then, out of the blue, he said, 'Marvellous thing this Lily Group. Marvellous. Terribly happy to lend my support.'

The two men nodded. Jonas nodded too, hoping that his cluelessness wasn't noticeable.

Opening his arms wide, as if addressing a large audience, the minister exclaimed, 'Right then, Toreador, on guard!'

The attendant moved over to the sliding door, Schublinger took Jonas's arm and ushered him forward, while Gobler and Anderfeld followed.

There was a slight delay while Herr Rontaler opened the sliding doors.

The hubbub got louder at first, then fell silent at a stroke.

*

Jonas was standing beside Minister Schublinger in the opening, flanked by the director of finance administration and the president of the National Bank.

A few dozen guests were in the room, all holding glasses which waiters in white jackets and black bow ties were topping up with red and white wines from a variety of state vineyards. Waitresses in black with white collars and aprons were circulating with finger food on silver trays.

All heads had turned to face them; it was like a paused film.

There didn't appear to be any particular dress code, presumably because the invitations had been at such short notice. A few guests were wearing cocktail dresses or dark suits, others were in casual gear, and a third lot looked as if they'd come straight from work.

Some of the faces were familiar to Jonas. Maybe they were media people, maybe he'd met them through work. Some were politicians and prominent figures from business and public life; he'd come across them before.

Minister Schublinger addressed the gathering with the volume and assurance of a man used to speaking in public. 'Ladies and Gentlemen! I'm delighted that you've come at such short notice, at such a late hour and in such numbers. It is a particularly great honour for me to be able to introduce the first film director in our circle: Herr...' he said, having to pause for a second, 'Jonas... Brand.'

The frozen image came back to life. The guests laughed and clapped as best they could while holding their glasses and finger food.

Then they resumed their small talk.

Barbara Contini, the widow of the trader, was hanging on every word of Jack Heinzmann, her husband's former colleague.

Hans Bühler, the handball player and boss of the trading floor, turned back to Adam Dillier, the CEO of the money-printing firm.

William Just, CEO of the General Confederate Bank of Switzerland, GCBS, elegant as ever, was laughing again with Heiner Stepler, the television editor-in-chief, and Lili Eck, Jonas's production assistant.

Konrad Stimmler, President of the Swiss Banking Supervisory Authority returned to his conversation with Jean Seibler, CEO of Swiss International Bank, SIB.

The editor of Highlife was talking animatedly to Karin Hofstettler, the press secretary of GCBS.

A woman moved away from a small group consisting of Jeff Rebstyn, his producer, Serge Cress, the chief executive of Moviefonds, and Tommy Wipf, his assistant director. She was tall, slim and oriental-looking.

Approaching him with a smile, she raised her shoulders.

*

By the door stood a man with shaved hair in a dark suit. He wore a headphone in his left ear.

'Where's the loo, please?' Jonas asked.

The man pointed him in the right direction.

Jonas headed down the long corridor. But he walked straight past the door of the loo where he'd freshened up earlier. The doorman started moving; Jonas heard the footsteps behind him.

Turning the corner of the corridor, he hurried to the small

room where the policemen had taken him. He went in and exited by the second door.

Jonas found the lift he'd been taken in earlier. Beside it was a door leading to a stairwell.

Three floors down he came to a glass door with the words 'EMERGENCY EXIT' written above in red. Jonas stepped outside.

He was at the rear of a featureless office building. Although it had stopped snowing, the snow hadn't yet been cleared.

Jonas crossed the street and trudged along the pavement opposite until he came to a crossroads. From there he could hear the noise of a heavy machine clearing one of the main roads.

Jonas was cold. He'd left his windcheater behind in Gobler's office. His hands were thrust deep in his trouser pockets, and he walked speedily through the wintry city, his chin tucked tightly to his chest.

He wasn't heading anywhere in particular; he just wanted to get away. Away from the humiliation. Away from the ridicule he'd exposed himself to. Away from Marina.

Marina, who couldn't stop making fun of Max the conspiracy theorist, had been part of the conspiracy herself! She, the only person he'd trusted in the end, had callously betrayed him.

All of a sudden he found himself in the old town of Bern. He could keep his feet dry walking through the almost empty arcades, while on the streets the snow ploughs were going about their work.

A police car drove past slowly. Jonas hid behind a pillar. The car stopped.

Were they coming after him? He didn't know this secret society's rules. Did members have to swear an oath or undertake an initiation pledge before they could move about freely?

The police car was still stationary. Jonas went back in the

direction he'd come from. He heard the car turning around and soon they were side by side again.

Jonas gave up. He stood in the next arch of the arcade and waited. The police car drove up to the kerb. The back door opened and out stepped – Marina.

'Thanks,' she said back into the car, before shutting the door and coming up to him.

Jonas turned his back to her and went quickly on his way. He could hear her high heels clicking behind him, and after a while her voice: 'Jonas! Wait! Let me explain!'

He quickened his pace.

'Jonas! Stop being so childish!' she called out. Then he heard her run. The clicking of her heels got closer. He started by breaking out into a run, but then felt foolish. He stopped and waited for her to catch up.

She was slightly out of breath when she said, 'Please let me explain, that's the least you owe me!'

'*Owe!*' he shouted. 'You think I owe *you* something? What for? You betrayed me. I've never been betrayed like that before!'

An elderly man with a dog came towards them in the arcade. 'Be nice to each other,' he said as he passed.

Only now did Jonas see in the dim light of a shop window that Marina had tears in her eyes.

He repeated, more calmly, 'Why do I owe *you* anything?'

'For having saved you from Max's or Contini's fate.'

'Oh, I see,' he retorted sarcastically, 'so that was you.' He set off again, and she stayed right beside him, without making any physical contact.

They walked side by side in silence for a while until the arcade came to an end in a large open space. On one side of this snow-covered square stood the broad, sedate parliament building.

'That's a little too symbolic for me,' Marina commented. Jonas didn't smile.

They went towards and then past Parliament, coming to a large park-like terrace, where the snow had been disturbed by only a single set of footprints leading to and back from a park bench, where some snow had been wiped from the seat.

It was Jonas who spoke first. 'Have you been with them long?'

'Since I was in Bern for work that time. In fact I stayed in Zürich and met Just.'

'How on earth did you meet *him*?' Jonas felt jealousy surging inside him.

'Oh, at some launch party. Then I realised that this was just an excuse. He was actually there to invite me to a secret meeting.'

'You let old men come on to you?'

'If they tell me it's about you and you're in big danger, then yes.'

They'd reached the wall of the terrace. Beneath them the River Aare was dark; above it glistened the lights of the Kirchenfeld district.

'And so you met him?'

'In the Dragon House. In a luxurious apartment bang in the middle of the old town. But not just him. Lili was there too. And Tommy, and a few others I didn't know. There was champagne and canapés, Just gave a brief introduction, then Gobler, Director of the Swiss Finance Administration, came and swore us in.'

'He's good at that,' Jonas conceded. 'But why didn't you lot let me in on it? As you've seen, I can be convinced.'

'That's what I said, too.' But Just thought you were as dangerous as an unguided missile – no one ever knows when they'll explode or where they'll strike.'

'And so it was your mission to steer this unguided missile.'

Shaking his head, Jonas took some snow from the parapet and rolled it into ball.

Marina pulled her coat more tightly around her shoulders. 'I know it all sounds silly now, but the way they explained it to me, there was a huge amount at stake.'

Jonas hurled the snowball. They watched the night swallow it up. 'Us,' he said. 'That's what was at stake.'

'Precisely. That is a huge amount.'

'Was.'

They fell silent. On Kirchenfeld Bridge the lights of a snow plough flashed eerily.

'Did you seriously believe I would have dropped the bombshell if I'd known what was at stake?'

Marina shrugged. 'Not really. But I couldn't exclude the possibility altogether, could I?'

He'd started making another snowball. 'Then you don't know me terribly well.'

After a pause she said, 'My mum says a whole lifetime isn't enough even to get to know oneself.'

Jonas threw the snowball. 'Why didn't they just eliminate me like the others?'

'Maybe you had too much up your sleeve. And they didn't know where you'd buried all your mines.'

'Mines, missiles – it's like a war.'

'For them it *is* a war.'

'They're turning it into a war because in wartime all means are permissible. Including high treason.'

Marina didn't respond. Behind them a weight of snow fell from the branch of a tree with a dull thud. They both jumped.

She put her hand on his shoulder. Jonas shook it off.

'We didn't betray you, Jonas; we protected you.'

'We, we – I don't give a fuck what the others did. But you!

You were the only person in the world I trusted.'

Marina tried to warm her upper arms by rubbing them. 'Sometimes,' she said, 'sometimes you have to betray someone to protect them.'

'Just's words again?'

'Gobler's.'

'I'd like to hear that in Marina Ruiz's words, please.'

'I knew I might lose you if I did it. But if I hadn't, I'd have lost you for certain.'

More snow fell from a tree.

'Let's go before we freeze,' Jonas said.

They walked back in their own footprints. After a few metres she took his arm; he didn't resist.

'Do you think,' Marina asked, 'you'll ever be able to trust me again?'

'I don't know.'

*

Almost a year had passed and the bubble was still intact. Like a monumental airship it hovered just above reality, never more than a whisker from its prongs.

Almost as much snow was on the ground as had been on that memorable February day, when the Lilies gathered late in the evening and at such short notice. And the snow continued to fall just as heavily.

Thick flakes swirled in the lights of the Kronos cinema, outside which a throng of première guests and media people had crowded. 'Montecristo' stood in large letters above the entrance.

Inside, helpers were waiting with the coats and furs of guests who were being filmed, photographed and interviewed on the red carpet.

Besides the celebrities there was an unusually large gathering of prominent people from politics, business and the arts. For example, Minister Schublinger, the most important politician there; his chief officer, Lukas Gobler; and the President of the National Bank, Hanspeter Anderfeld – all accompanied by their wives.

Or William Just, CEO of the General Confederate Bank of Switzerland, together with his competitor, Jean Seibler, CEO of Swiss International Bank, SIB, likewise with their wives.

The director general of state television had come, too, as had the CEO of TVch – two rivals who usually took care to avoid each other.

They all stood smiling in front of the photo wall with the Montecristo logo, answering the journalists' tame questions.

The only searching one was aimed at William Just, and came from someone working for the review section of one of the main daily papers: '*Montecristo* received 1.6 million francs of funding from Moviefonds. Can you confirm that the lion's share of this came from your bank's art budget?'

'The statutes of Moviefonds prevent me from confirming or denying this.'

'Do you think it's a sensible funding policy to support inexperienced directors with generous grants while projects by established people come to nothing because they can't get backing?'

'No offence, but I'm going to pass on this question. Finance should keep itself out of arts policy. I'm just looking forward to the film.'

The director and writer of the screenplay, Jonas Brand, appeared with his partner, Marina Ruiz, who was also responsible for organising the première. She was wearing a high-necked sequin dress that was low cut at the back, beside which Brand looked rather underdressed in his dark suit and open white shirt.

The video journalist from Highlife asked him, 'Herr Brand, as a director you are an unknown quantity and this is your first feature film. And yet the world and his wife seem to have gathered here for your première. Doesn't that make you nervous?'

'I've felt worse,' Jonas replied.

For his advice, careful reading of the text and constructive criticism, I should like to thank Peter Siegenthaler who, as director of the Swiss Finance Administration, managed the Swissair and UBS crises and chaired the specialist commission 'Too big to fail.'

Thanks are also due to Urs Rohner for his expert eye in looking through the manuscript and making an important dramatic suggestion. Thanks to the former Federal Councillor D Moritz Leuenberger for his suggestions and for providing me with valuable contacts. Thanks to Bertrand Dayer for his quick response in helping to clarify the premise and plausibility of the story. Thanks to the film producer Marcel Höhn for his advice on matters relating to film production. Thanks to my editor, Ursula Baumhauer, not just for the professionalism of her comments, but for the speed with which she worked. Thanks to Ruth Geiger, head of Diogenes Verlag's publicity department, for everything she has done for this novel and all the others before it, in this instance making a contribution to the book's content too. Thanks to my wife, Margrith Nay Suter, for once again taking on the thorny task of being an incorruptible first reader.

And thanks to those experts, who didn't want to be named here, for their time as well as creative and practical assistance.

Martin Suter

About Us

In addition to No Exit Press, Oldcastle Books has a number
of other imprints, including Kamera Books, Creative Essentials,
Pulp! The Classics, Pocket Essentials and High Stakes Publishing
> oldcastlebooks.co.uk

For more information about Crime Books go to > crimetime.co.uk

Check out the kamera film salon for independent, arthouse and
world cinema > kamera.co.uk

For more information, media enquiries and review copies please
contact marketing@oldcastlebooks.com